ALSO BY DAVID GATES

Jernigan

Preston Falls

The Wonders of the Invisible World

The Wonders
of the
Invisible World

Stories by
DAVID GATES

ALFRED A. KNOPF   NEW YORK
1999

THIS IS A BORZOI BOOK
PUBLISHED BY ALFRED A. KNOPF, INC.

Some of these stories first appeared, in slightly different form,
in the following publications: "The Bad Thing" in *Esquire*;
"Beating" and "The Wonders of the Invisible World" in *GQ*;
"The Mail Lady" in *Grand Street*; "A Wronged Husband"
in *Ploughshares*; "The Intruder" in *TriQuarterly*.
A portion of the story "Vigil" first appeared
in the on-line magazine *Atlantic Unbound*.

Knopf, Borzoi Books, and the colophon are registered
trademarks of Random House, Inc.

Library of Congress Cataloging-in-Publication Data
Gates, David, [date]
The wonders of the invisible world : stories / by David Gates.—
1st. ed.
p.   cm.
ISBN 0-679-43668-5 (alk. paper)
1. United States—Social life and customs—20th century—Fiction.
I. Title.
PS3557.A87W6   1999
813'.54—dc21   99-18497
CIP

Manufactured in the United States of America
First Edition

My thanks to Gary Fisketjon, for his care, energy,
taste and judgment.

Also to Will Blythe, Candy Gianetti, Reg Gibbons,
Rob Grover, Sloan Harris, Jeff Jackson,
Elizabeth Kaye, Tom Mallon, Helen Rogan,
Michele Scarff and Denise Shannon.

To Amanda Urban.

To Cathleen McGuigan and my other editors at *Newsweek*.

To the John Simon Guggenheim Foundation for
its generous support.

And to Susan and Kate.

For he said unto him,
Come out of the man, thou unclean spirit.
And he asked him, What is thy name?
And he answered, saying,
My name is Legion: for we are many.

—Mark 5:8–9

Contents

The Wonders of the Invisible World

The Bad Thing

He has never hit me, and only once or twice in our two years has he raised his voice in anger. Even in bed Steven is gentle. To a fault. Why, then, am I wary of him? Obvious. Well, so if you're wary of him, what are you doing here? Also obvious. For one thing, I have his baby inside me.

Ye gods, *his* baby. I think of it that way because he and Marilyn never had children, and what other chance is he going to get? But it's not his baby, of course, nor mine. The baby is its own baby. I think of it as a girl, because the idea of a tiny man inside me is, is, is what? Repulsive, I was going to say, though sometimes I think, *A little man, yes, squeezed out into the world to do my will.* But at other times I pray, *Dear God, if You've made it a boy, go back, in Your time-scrunching omnipotence, and re-do the instant of its conception.* Not forgetting to add, *If it be Thy will.* You know, the kind of thing God does all the time, going back and changing what His will is.

So I'm trying to take it as it comes; even that seems wildly ambitious. Two days ago, after Steven had finished working and I'd come to a stopping place, we climbed the hill up behind Carl's house until we reached the power line. Steven put on his skis, I put on the snowshoes he bought me. I'm not to ski anymore, until after. Another thing I'm not to do is address Carl Porter as Carl; Steven sees it as a class thing. Slipping along by

3

my side, he praised my walking in the snowshoes. "Big deal," I said. "You put one foot in front of the other." "Ah, but that," he said, raising his index finger, "is ofttimes the hardest lesson of all." Big joke with Steven is to intone fake profundities, raising his index finger to make sure you see he's kidding. I thought, *Right, I'm learning that. Being married to you.*

Oh, I know, bad. You should be reaching out to him.

Been tried, honey.

Like our first night in this house. We'd both learned—not from each other; we've both been around the block—that the big moments you plan never work, so we decided against the French restaurant two towns over with the forty-dollar prix fixe dinner, and went to the diner on 28. We took a booth, ordered pancakes and sausage and sat waiting for the modest magic by which the everyday becomes precious. Steven flipped page after page of jukebox selections, fingering the little metal tabs at the bottom. The country songs in green. Then he flipped back through in the other direction.

"Nothing," he said. "Zip. Unless you want to hear fucking Randy Travis."

By this I understood that I was not to want to hear Randy Travis.

I put a hand on his. "Something's worrying you," I said.

"Don't," he said, pulling his hand out from under. I saw tears come up and fill his eyes.

"What?" I said. "Talk to me."

He shook his head. "You've heard the same shit forty-eight times," he said. "Maybe the pills will help."

Forty-eight was one of his numbers I hadn't heard before. Usually they were round and overwhelming, like fifty thousand (*I've done fifty thousand of these fucking children's books*) or ten million *(Ten million fucking fax machines at fucking J&R, and I get the one that craps out)*. Afterward I thought about it. Forty-eight was how old he'd be in June. When his first child would be born. Oh, but Steven was such a *complex* man; could it possibly be that simple? One thing that might help: to get my contempt under control. Since he doesn't seem to be doing much about his. Now *that* would be a mood drug I could get behind.

We moved up here for the beauty and the quiet, and so we'd each have a workroom. It's all so postindustrial: no need anymore to be bodily on Lexington Avenue from ten to six. Up here I'd be able to take my job lightly and my work seriously—as seriously as Steven takes his. But needless to say.

Yesterday we had to go to Oneonta for groceries. It had started snowing in the morning; when we got back, it was still coming down and we couldn't get up the driveway. He insisted on trying to shovel—after making three trips all the way up to the house with the stuff, which he wouldn't let me help with. I told him forget it, come inside, we'll drink tea and get snowed in. Thinking, actually, of some Rémy in the tea—what he's taking is one of the new anything-goes antidepressants—and stretching out by the pellet stove, our feet together under the shiny maroon comforter. And so on. We'll get Carl to plow us out in the morning, I said. He said I treated the locals like old family retainers. Which was so uncalled-for when for once I was trying to take some care of him. He was already pale and sweating, and his chest was heaving. I went into the bathroom and cried, then washed my face. When he came in, looking even worse, he found me sipping tea (with Rémy) and reading *Mirabella*. Or, rather, staring at the pages and feeling put-upon because now that I'd cut myself out of the loop, I would never design anything but monthly newsletters and annual reports. *Bitch*, I'm sure he thought, and clomped upstairs.

The Bad Thing

When it got dark, I opened a can of soup. Then I stopped bothering with the tea and drank myself pretty nearly to sleep. Just managed to get up the stairs. Then woke up, of course, at two in the morning, mouth dry, head killing me. I went to the bathroom to pee and get a drink of water and some aspirin, and heard the music still going in Steven's workroom—his damn Louis Armstrong—and saw a line of golden light along the bottom of his door. Inside was the Kingdom of Art, from which I'd been exiled. I crept back to bed like a dirty animal.

Sneaking around a dark house at night: just like old times.

When I was twenty-two, my boyfriend and I shared a big old farmhouse in Rhode Island with his best friend and the best friend's girlfriend, and once a week or so I would leave Dalton in bed and make my way down the creaky stairs to find Tod waiting on the sofa. He would be drunk, having got Kathleen drunk enough to put her to sleep, and not gentle with me; I would have put Dalton to sleep by fucking him as sweetly as I knew how. More sweetly than I know how anymore. But saving my orgasm for Tod. Knowing it was of no value to him, except as proof that he could make me do it when Dalton couldn't. Though of course Dalton could. And I didn't always save it.

It started in the summer, one morning when Tod and I were alone in the house. He asked if I wanted coffee, then ran his index finger down my bare arm (me in that blue sundress with the yellow flowers, him in blue jeans and a T-shirt I couldn't imagine how he kept so white) and said, "Wouldn't it be funny if we put the horns on Dalton?" *The horns.* What more did I need to know? And yet. I heard two voices in my head, talking at me as I stood there in the doorway between the kitchen and the living room: my own voice saying *This is bad for you* and a man's voice saying *Do what I say.* I narrowed my eyes, trying to hear which was right, and I could picture myself as Tod saw me, looking intense and tempted. *This is a beautiful boy,* said another voice, a voice that wished me ill, *who knows how to touch you.*

Did I simply have bad character, or was I a strong young woman going after what she wanted and willing to pay the price? Though how strong were you really if you couldn't, finally, get it? One thing I promised myself, I would never again let myself in for this kind of humiliation. When Tod finally dumped me, I did the one bit of bitchy damage I could: I said I'd always known the real romance was between him and Dalton. I hope he still hears me saying that in his head.

It was a mistake to have shown Tod's picture to Steven. At the time, I thought I was doing it to leave nothing unshared. But actually it must've been to put him on notice: that once I had been desired by a beautiful blond boy. Tod's beauty was a means of convincing Steven that *I* was beautiful. (How fucked up is *that?*) I'm sure Steven thought it was more evidence of my bad taste, to have been attracted to the merely beautiful. As if it had never happened to him. Now, there's another thing we were never going to do: marry a man who wasn't on speaking terms with his own desires.

I woke up again at seven and came down and fixed myself a tray with coffee and a bowl of Count Chocula. Steven loves the Grand Union in Oneonta—when we lived in the city he refused to shop in supermarkets—and every week he selects another brand of sugared-out kiddie cereal. "I was raised on fucking puffed rice," he said the first time he placed a box of Cap'n Crunch in the cart. "This is a quiet man's rebellion." I don't generally eat this stuff, but I had to get something in my stomach immediately. I brought the tray up to my workroom and turned on the computer. Out the window, I saw a white cloud issuing from the tailpipe of Carl Porter's empty truck, so I picked up the phone. "You didn't need to ask, Mrs. Sturdivant," he said. "I meant to do you first thing." Lovely man.

Listening to his truck humming and rumbling as he plowed the driveway, I ate the cereal and looked over the pages I'd laid out yesterday, telling myself that one bowl of Count Chocula wasn't so irresponsible; they probably spray the stuff with vitamins. And only then did it hit me what I'd done last night: got stinking drunk while four months pregnant. Four months: what did that mean in terms of how major a birth defect might be? Wouldn't it be more major the earlier you did the bad thing? I pictured a bullet, fired at conception: deflect that bullet almost at the target and it would miss by only a little, but deflect it early on and it would veer off wide. Four months. That was less than halfway there. I slid from my chair to my knees and prayed, *Dear God, since I did it without thinking, please don't let it count.* Just the kind of prayer God likes to hear. Oh, right, *If it be Thy will.* I listened down into my body to try to discern any damage, any change from yesterday. Nothing. Oh, God. Well, we just wouldn't think about this. But what if Steven looked at the bottle? I remembered him saying, *I want to make a baby with you. I know you must think I've said everything before to somebody else, but this is a first.* A first. He actually said that.

The thing to do was to hop in the car and go buy a pint of Rémy to get the level back up—put anything else in there and Steven would instantly taste something wrong—then hide the empty. But it was twenty miles to Oneonta, the nearest liquor store classy enough to stock the stuff. And it was seven-thirty in the morning.

At nine-thirty I started down to make more coffee. Still another thing I wasn't to do, drink more than a half cup a day, but I absolutely had to finish the last six pages this afternoon without fail, and I had nodded out staring at the screen. I was looking at this one page, trying to care whether or not the vertical picture should be moved to the right and the pullquote brought down to compensate, and then I seemed to be at a performance of *Hamlet*, I think it was—and I suppose it's a rule with dreams that if you think it was, it *was*—and my dress was too tight on me and I wanted to go to the ladies' room and let out the waist. All pretty obvious. But before going down the stairs I stopped and eased open the bedroom door with my fingertips. Steven, in pajamas, was clutching my pillow, his mouth gaping. His hair looked damp; he must've taken a shower before coming to bed. It made me sad that I'd never known him when his hair was all black. I tried to think what *his* life must be like—a first?—but I really couldn't see that anything was so terrible. I'd never been able to take seriously enough the Central Tragedy, which was that he'd never become, I don't know, Jackson Pollock or whoever he'd wanted to be when he was eighteen.

Back in my workroom, I drank the fresh coffee and stared at that page. This was a simple decision. Which I still couldn't make. I got up again and went down the hall to Steven's workroom. So cold when I opened the door: the window wide open. He'd finished another illustration. How could I have thought one of my little moods would slow the march of his work? Last night's production was a peasant family standing by a cottage. The cover from *The Forest Is Crying* was sandwiched in my cookbook stand, and he'd spattered paint on the Plexiglas. So that was where he'd gotten the woman peasant's colorful costume; the man peasant and the little boy he'd put in brown shirts and trousers and clumpy boots. There was something familiar about the landscape, too. Then I spotted the Edward Hopper book on the floor. Aha: the thatched-roof cottage was that Mobil station, and the peasant family stood in place of the round-headed gas pumps. He'd done it well, what else was new.

The Bad Thing

I'd said my piece about this new phase when he showed me the first one, for which he'd used a Currier & Ives print of a man knife-fighting a rearing grizzly. "Oh, please," he said. "This is an *hommage*." Learn a new word, Paula. Then, probably because he realized he was being a pompous ass, he went into one of his pompous-ass parodies. "Think of this bear," he said, "not as a bear, but as Old Man Depression. The gallant mountain man? Yours truly." He inclined his head. "And behind the tree here"—he pointed to a second man, who was aiming a gun at the bear—"Dr. Seibert and his magic bullet." He'd only been taking the pills for a couple of days at this point. He gave his snorting laugh, the one that means *I hate myself.*

Even with this fresh cold air, I smelled cigarette smoke. In the wastebasket, under a crumpled page of a sketch pad, I found butts, ashes and burned-out matches. I counted the butts. Sixteen. So he was back at it with a vengeance. How had I not picked up the smell off him? Ah: wet hair.

Paula Wilson-Sturdivant, girl detective.

It's one of my amusements up here. The other morning I was unpacking a box of PAPERS & MISC when I looked out the window and saw him in the backyard by the old oil drum where the people who'd lived here had burned their trash. Steven, who puts the caps from toothpaste tubes in with the number-two plastics to be recycled—I swear—was touching a match to a big sheet of paper and thrusting it from him as flames leaped up. "Just a particularly lousy piece of work," he said when he came in. I said the obvious: if it had bothered him enough to burn it, it must've had something he could use. He asked if I was reverting to hippiedom, saying it in a way I was supposed to think was only kidding.

So when he left to go get the mail, I went out to the barrel. But he'd even smashed up the ashes.

.

Around one this afternoon, I heard Steven go downstairs. The upstairs bathroom is right over the kitchen, and there's a grate in the floor for heat to come up. I tiptoed into the bathroom and knelt to watch. I could see a corner of the stove and most of the sink, where I'd put the filter basket with soiled filter and spent coffee grounds still in it. I saw him pick it up; his shoulders rose and fell, a martyr's sigh.

I printed out my pages and went downstairs. He was lying on the sofa reading *The Pickwick Papers.* The last time he went on one of his reading binges, it lasted for over a month. This was back in the city. He got through seven Dickens novels and blew off an album cover that would have paid him three thousand dollars. He told them he'd been mugged and his arm was in a cast. "But what if you run into one of them?" I'd said. He'd said, "I don't plan to be going out."

"Good morning," I said. I didn't mean it as a bitchy way of saying it was already afternoon; it just came out. "Listen, I have to run over to Oneonta to the stationery store. You need anything from the outside world?"

"Am I not invited?" he said.

"Of course," I said. "Sure. You just looked so comfortable." How could I do what I needed to do at the liquor store with him along?

"The master of illusion," he said.

"How's the book?"

He shrugged. "Reads about the same as last time."

"No, I mean the wolf book." The children's book he's working on is about a lost wolf cub, which is adopted by a peasant family but finally returns to the forest to be with its own kind. The crap he's handed is not his fault.

"Oh, the *book*," he said. "Why didn't you say so?" This, I

guessed, was meant as a lighthearted peace overture. "Good," he said. "Rockin' right along."

I tried to think of a delicate way to find out if he was on the verge of another Dickens thing. Finally I said, "When do they want them by?"

"What's today?"

"Thursday."

"Thursday," he said. "So, a week from tomorrow. Not a problem. Barring a sudden coffee shortage."

What about a cigarette shortage? I thought. He'd gone through nearly a pack last night. How could he be lying there not jumping out of his skin? Why would he want to come with me to Oneonta instead of trying to hustle me out of here so he could smoke? Then I got it. He must have run out, and at some point he would excuse himself to do an "errand." With any luck, he'd take long enough for me to get to the liquor store. But wait: if he hustled me out of here, he could just walk down to Webster's. I didn't get it.

"I was looking through this," he said, "to see if there was anything in the Seymour stuff I could use. I always thought Phiz was way overrated, and I sort of wanted to give old Seymour a tip of the Hatlo hat. You know the story, right?"

"What story?" I said, obediently.

"Okay, Seymour was the first illustrator on the book—see, Dickens was just this young guy they hired to crank out text. But in the middle of the thing Seymour kills himself, and they got some bozo to fill in for a couple of weeks or whatever and then they found Phiz. Look at this, this is the last thing Seymour did."

It was an ugly picture of a dying man on a bed.

"Why did he kill himself?" I said.

"Got *me*," he said. "I know Dickens sort of ran roughshod over him, which I guess didn't help matters. But I think it was just, you know, his life."

He got up and located his boots, his checkbook, the car keys, his red plaid hat. "Carl plow the driveway?" he said, peering out the kitchen window as he zipped up his red plaid jacket over his down vest. "Did a great job." As we walked out the door, he handed me the keys.

In Oneonta, he came into the stationery store with me; while I bought a ream of paper I didn't need, he picked out a half-dozen pen tips. Then he wanted to go have rice pudding at the luncheonette, where he got quarters for the jukebox and played Randy Travis singing the forever-and-ever song. How could he bear the irony? How could he put *me* through it? I watched his hand, the one with the ring, beat time on the Formica. He never announced he had an errand; I tried to think how to manage a run to the liquor store, but it couldn't be done. On the way back out of town we hit the Grand Union, where I bought stuff for Chicken in a Bread Loaf, and craftily omitted the dried mint.

When we got home, he kissed me—on the lips, warm—and went up to work. He hadn't had a cigarette, apparently, since sometime last night. If he was a man who could pick up a thing and then just drop it, where did that leave me? Thinking about Marilyn, I suppppose. He was married to her for fifteen years, then dumped her because she got old. (He says that's not what happened.) She was only forty-two. I took the pad from next to the phone and figured it out. Forty-two minus twenty-nine: I would be forty-two in thirteen years. In the same thirteen years, he would be—forty-seven plus thirteen—he would be sixty. Past the point where he could get another twenty-nine-year-old, unless she was supremely stupid, and probably fat as well. Not the kind of security one might desire, but neverthe-less. I put the pad back, leaving the sheet with my calculations. On the off chance he might ask what they were.

I waited half an hour (did dishes, cleaned the top of the stove, scrubbed the downstairs toilet, put the dishes away, scoured pot marks out of the kitchen sink), then went up and knocked on his door. Loud saxophone jazz. He called, "Yo."

"Sorry to interrupt," I said to his door. "I have to go back to Grand Union. I forgot the stupid mint for the chicken."

He opened the door. No smell of smoke. "You forgot *what?*"

"Mint," I said. "They call for mint."

"Oh, for Christ's sake. Don't they carry mint at Webster's?"

"I doubt it," I said. I'd forgotten about goddamn Webster's. Actually they were pretty well stocked if you didn't mind paying their prices.

"Well, hell," he said, "just leave it out. You don't want to go all the way back to Oneonta. How much do they call for?"

"Tablespoon," I said. It was a teaspoon.

"Bag it," he said. "It'll be fine."

"It really won't," I said. "It's going to taste blah."

He sighed. "Christ. Well, look. Why don't you just fix something else? Roast the chicken like you would anyway, and we'll eat the bread as *bread*, you know?"

"But you like the other so much," I said, feeling vile.

"Paula," he said. "It's truly decadent to drive forty miles round trip for a tablespoon of mint, for Christ's sake. You're putting wear and tear on the car, you're burning up fossil fuels . . ."

I tried to think: if my motives had been pure, would I be justified in thinking he was being a prick? And: would it seem more suspicious to fight him on this or to acquiesce? More suspicious to fight, I decided.

"I don't know," I said, "I guess you're right. Look, what I'll do is, I'll run down to Webster's and if they *don't* have mint I'll figure out something else for dinner, okay? You sure you won't be disappointed?"

"*Au contraire.* I will admire your resourcefulness in the face of domestic crisis." He reached around and patted my ass.

I threw my sketchbook in the backseat—that would be my alibi—and drove to Webster's, where I bought a jar of dried mint and a pack of Care Free peppermint gum. I'd chewed all five sticks by the time I got to the liquor store in Oneonta. They didn't have pints of Rémy, so I had to buy the next size up, which I really couldn't afford. Then on the way back I remembered: fossil fuels. Steven wasn't so anal that he'd know the odometer reading, but he might know how much gas there was. I calculated forty miles at, say, twenty-five miles per gallon. I stopped at Cumberland Farms and put in two dollars' worth. Back at the house, just in case, I pushed the little button on the trip odometer to make all zeroes come up. Let him wonder.

I was smart to leave the bottle in the car: Steven stood there in the kitchen, the orange juice carton (no glass) in his hand. "Where the hell have you been?" he said, putting the carton back in the refrigerator. "Alice Porter called and I got stuck on the phone for an hour." An hour meant five minutes.

"So you shouldn't have picked it up," I said. "Why the good Lord made answering machines."

"I was expecting it to be Martin," he said. "Our auteur has made still more changes in her text, and he had to be sure they didn't affect the pictures. This woman thinks she's Flaubert. I mean, this has been going on and on and on. I told Martin, this is the end of it. *Fini.*"

"Are they going to make you change anything?" I said.

"No, it's just stuff like where she had the wolf with his tail 'held high,' it's now 'at a jaunty angle.' *Jaunty,* for Christ's sake. I mean, this is what my life has come down to, 'a jaunty angle.' I told him, I said, 'Look, the picture's done, he's got his tail in the fucking air, and if the goddamn angle isn't *jaunty* enough, they can shove it.'"

"Good for you," I said.

"So where've you been?" he said. "You didn't go all the way back there, did you?"

"No, you were right, they had it at Webster's. I went up to Randolph Pond and tried to do some sketching." I held up my sketch pad as evidence.

"Good for *you*," he said. "You haven't sketched for a long time. Let's see."

I shook my head. "They suck," I said. I got a book of matches out of the drawer. "I'm going to use the Steven Sturdivant method. Burn it before it gets out of hand."

"You're kidding, I hope. You know, you were absolutely on the money with what you said the other day. How does that thing go? 'The man of genius makes no errors'?"

"I'm not a man," I said, "and I'm not of genius. Be back in a second."

"Come on, now," he said, grabbing for the pad. "Let the old doctor have a gander."

"No, Steven." I twisted away. "I'm serious." If he'd gotten the pad away from me, he would've seen that the last sketch in the book was of a little girl at Jones Beach, with pail and shovel. But the word *serious* seemed to back him off. I slammed the door behind me, to lend myself still more power.

Standing over the rusty oil drum, I ripped out two blank pages and set fire to them. Then I ripped out the little girl and burned her up, too. When I came back into the kitchen, I heard the toilet flush upstairs. I listened to Steven's footsteps going back to his workroom, then went out and brought the new bottle in. I brought the level in the old bottle up to something like what I guessed it had been—apparently I'd hit it much harder last night than I remembered—took a slug of what was left for old times' sake and poured the rest into the sink, running hot water to chase it down. I put the empty bottle back in the paper bag, stuffed it into a milk carton and tucked it away in the bottom of the garbage. Okay: crisis averted. I lit the oven, unwrapped the chicken, sawed the top off the bread loaf with the good knife from Broadway Panhandler, and began clawing out the soft inside.

"I have a confession to make," he said as I lit the candles. "I smoked most of a pack of cigarettes last night."

"Steven," I said. "You *didn't.*"

"I decided I'm not going to do it anymore," he said.

"How come you did it at all?"

"Well, we had that—and believe me, I'm not blaming you—but we had that unpleasantness yesterday that never really got resolved, and I felt like I was under the gun with those pictures, which it turns out I'm not, I mean I'm actually in very good shape with them. I think all it really was, I was just looking for an excuse to do it. So I did it."

"I don't know what to say. I'm sorry if I contributed." I began cutting the stuffed bread loaf into inch-thick slices.

He shook his head. "Not your responsibility. It was my choice."

"And you had them around," I said.

"Yeah. I had them around." He did his snorting laugh. "But I think this has taught me something. I mean, if *you* weren't reason enough, there's Trigger Junior to think of." Trigger Junior was his provisional name for the baby.

"What about you?" I said. "Aren't you reason enough?"

"Well, I never *have* been," he said. "Maybe that's changing. Did I tell you? I think these pills might be starting to do something. This morning I woke up and I felt just sort of—I don't know. Not heavy of heart for a change. I can't really describe it. But I definitely didn't want a cigarette, despite putting all that nicotine into my system last night. Which I find almost scary."

"But that's wonderful," I said. I laid a slice on his plate and a slice on mine.

"God, that looks splendid," he said. "At any rate. Full disclosure." He cut off a corner and speared it with his fork. "I'm assuming we still care about that."

"I think we do." What else was I to say?

"Good." He put the corner in his mouth. "Mmm. Surpassed yourself."

"I'm glad you like it," I said, not meaning it to sound that dismal.

"In the interest of even fuller disclosure," he said, "I must further confess to you that I nipped a bit at the cognac while you were out this afternoon. I don't actually know why. Except that it was like, I really wasn't craving a cigarette and *that* freaked me out. It was like nothing was wrong, you know? And that made me suspicious that something was *really* wrong that I didn't even dare bring to consciousness, so I thought I'd better drink to sort of preempt it. Does that make any sense at all?"

"Absolutely," I said. I wasn't paying attention. How could he not have noticed that so much was gone out of that goddamn bottle? And now what? Try to keep him out of the kitchen and pour out some of what you just poured in?

We ate.

He took a second slice.

Half of a third.

Now he was talking about names for the baby. Lately he'd been liking Margaret. Did I know that was the same as Pearl?

"The same in what sense?" I said, getting up to clear the table.

"You know, etymologically," he said. He stood up too, and reached for the platter with the remains of the stuffed bread loaf.

"Sit," I said. "I'll take care of it. I think you've had a hard day."

"Only in my head." He carried the platter and the salad bowl out to the kitchen; I set the plates and glasses on the counter next to the sink. "Tinfoil be the best thing?" he said, pulling open the drawer.

"Why don't you just let me take *care* of it?" I said. I snatched the foil out of his hands. "Just go and sit and relax. Actually, you know what would be lovely? If you would put on some music, I'll take care of this stuff and then bring our desserts out to the living room. How would that be?"

"Now you're talkin'," he said. He took down a brandy snifter.

"What are you doing?" I said. "I'll get that for you. Go and sit *down*."

"I can get it." He opened the cupboard door, took out the bottle of Rémy, looked at it and said, "What the *hell*?"

He looked at me. Then I saw his eyes go down to my hands and get big. I looked down, too. I was sawing the saw thing on the aluminum-foil box across the thumbprint part of my thumb. There was blood on the front of me.

"You've been drinking," he said.

"Obviously," I said. I couldn't feel the pain yet. I had a picture in my head of a bad person in shame.

"You're pregnant and you're drunk?" he said. "Don't you know what that can do? Do you *care*? How could you *do* it? What the hell is going on in your mind?"

"I'm *not* drunk," I said.

"You're a whore," he said. "Where did you go this afternoon?"

I wasn't angry. Or frightened, really, even though I cringed to appease him. He would never be a hitter. That fist he was raising at me would wham into the cupboard door, hurting

The Bad Thing

only himself. I saw it all happening, then it really *did* happen. But I didn't understand the whore thing. Why was he confusing the drinking with the other? Then I got it. Obvious. It was all mixed up for him, all the same thing: the drinking, the other, anything that could make a woman free.

Star Baby

When Billy gets home, his nephew's playing with that thing where marbles roll down slanting wooden rails and drop through holes onto the rail below. It takes a supposedly entertainingly long time for a marble to make it all the way down. This was Billy's toy when he was a kid; Deke found it in a box in the basement.

"Hey, tiger. How was *your* day?" He sets the *Times* on the dusty Baldwin spinet and nods at Mrs. Bishop.

Deke says, "Watch this." He lets a marble go.

Billy waits until it's halfway down to say "Cool."

"Yeah," Deke says, "but *watch*."

Billy watches the marble roll and drop, roll and drop, then turns to Mrs. Bishop. "How was it today?"

She looks over at Deke. "He's a good boy."

So nobody's giving him a straight answer. But at any rate the TV's not on. Unless she just now snapped it off, having heard his car. He could touch a wrist to it and check, but that would be a bit much. Cassie had let Deke have a TV in his room, which he'd watch for hours while she did what she did. Seven years old.

"I guess Uncle can take it from here," Billy says. He opens the hall closet, hangs up his jacket and gets out Mrs. Bishop's coat. Here's your hat, what's your hurry? But Mrs. Bishop used to baby-sit Billy and Cassie when they were little—she seemed old then, *is* old now—and this arrangement would be even more bizarre if the boundaries got blurred. Mrs. Bishop's all right, just boring and religious. As far as Billy can tell, she simply regards him as a "bachelor," maybe not even "confirmed": she's been keeping him up to date on her semi-bohemian granddaughter, now divorced and living in Saratoga. "Thanks again," he says, and holds up her coat as she backs into it. "Oh. By the way. Your honorarium." He hands her an envelope with a hundred and fifty dollars in cash. "So we'll see you Monday?"

"Lord willing," she says. It sounds to Billy like some old ballad. *Lord Willing rode home on his snow-white steed/And spake to his servants three/O something something something something/And all for the love of thee.* Billy's a tad overeducated for all this—and of course fatherhood had *not* been in the cards—but he's doing it.

He listens for Mrs. Bishop's car to start up, then says, "So it's you and me, partner. Got a whole big weekend ahead of us. And tonight's a bath night." Billy's funning: every night's a bath night. Cassie had him using the shower—when she thought of it—but Billy's theory is that a bath is not just relaxing but primal, a ritual no kid should be done out of. So it's play a quick game of something, put together a dinner while Billy's in the bath, then right into p.j.'s, eat dinner, brush teeth, read and safe in bed by eight o'clock.

Since Deke's already into the marble game, that'll be tonight's amusement. Billy chooses a clear marble with red boomerang shapes inside—God, he remembers this very marble—and sets it at the topmost point, then lets it go. *Zoop plop, zoop plop, zoop plop.* "Kewel," he says in his mindless-hippie voice.

"Kewel," says Deke. He's good at mindless hippie. "Can Caleb come over for a playdate?"

"This is somebody in your class?"

"Kind of. He's in my reading group."

"Does he *want* to come over?"

"I don't know."

"Oh. So I guess step one is for you to ask him, and then I can call his parents. What's his last name?"

"Jacobson."

"Really. I wonder if—I think I might know his dad. So what do you want for dinner tonight? We've got pasta or spaghetti. Which would you rather?"

Deke gives Billy his faux-disgusted look.

"Okay, pasta it is. To tell you the truth, I hate spaghetti."

"It's the *same thing*."

"Oh," Billy says. "Well, in that case." He goes into the kitchen and runs water into the big Revereware saucepan. They've had pasta the last three nights. Deke would eat it indefinitely, and Billy doesn't care. If they want variety, they can always get a different Paul Newman sauce. Deke has come in to watch. "Today the marinara, tomorrow the world," Billy tells him. Deke laughs; he seems to like stuff that's over his head. If he's going to be with Billy, he might just as well.

This is supposed to be a temporary arrangement, while Cassie—as Billy explains it to Deke—is "getting better." But he doesn't see why they can't just keep going. After her thirty days in the hospital, she moved into a halfway house and went back to work, but nobody involved with her treatment—Cassie included—seems in any hurry about reuniting her with her son. And Billy isn't pushing it.

After high school, Cassie had gone to Boston to study piano and composition at Berklee. Billy thought she had the true gift. How many eighteen-year-old girls—especially in Menands, New York—aspired to play like Red Garland? But she also had the other thing, which he guessed went with the gift, and she lasted less than a year. Selling her baby grand, she later told him, had bought only two months' worth of dope, but it was two months to die for. Then she'd done her scary turnaround: stopped using, cut off the down-to-her-ass hair, bullshitted her way into a job with Shawmut Bank, married Vic, got pregnant, divorced Vic, had the kid. By the time she crashed and burned this fall, she was making a hundred thousand dollars a year, living in a co-op apartment tower with a view of Boston Harbor—and, it turned out, using big-time and sleeping about one night in four. Ever since Berklee, she's refused to touch a piano, even last Christmas when their dying mother bullied them into singing carols. Billy finally had to back them up, picking out the chords with aching pauses in between as he tried to get his fingers on the right keys.

The place Cassie's in has a no-number pay phone in the front hall; they can make one call a day and are allowed no incoming calls at all. She phones every other night and talks first to Deke (whose end of the conversation is mostly *No* and *Yeah*), then to Billy. She often says she's glad Deke's "in good hands." Which always makes Billy think of that Sherwood Anderson story.

But he secretly thinks that Cassie secretly knows Deke is in *better* hands. Back when Deke was born, it was Billy who talked her out of naming him Duke, in honor of Duke Ellington; did she really want to give her kid a name like a German shepherd? Billy's enrolled Deke in school here, the school where he and Cassie used to go. He drops him in the morning on the way to work, Mrs. Bishop's there when he gets off the bus in the afternoon, Billy's back by six, then it's two hours to bedtime. All doable. Dinners had seemed daunting, but pasta's just a matter of putting on water and heating up sauce; in another pan he steams vegetables with his mother's vegetable steamer, a thing that looks like a Bucky Fuller dome on little legs. Once a week, he has Mrs. Bishop put a chicken in the oven. He's bought age-appropriate CD-ROMs: *The Magic School Bus Explores in the Age of Dinosaurs* and *The Magic School Bus Explores the Solar System*, each described as "A Fun-Filled, Fact-Packed Science Adventure." (He passed on *The Magic School Bus Explores the Human Body*.) He reads Deke bedtime stories, and he's gotten good at doing the characters' voices, even in crap like *Bugs Bunny and the Carrot Machine*, where he has to do the proto-faggot Elmer Fudd. He's made Deke a go-to-sleep tape of Horowitz playing a sequence of sweet, unjumpy pieces: the quieter sections of *Kinderszenen*, a couple of gentler Chopin waltzes. And he's considered teaching Deke the first couplet of "Now I Lay Me," without the die-before-I-wake part.

This playdate thing, though. He can see it all now: him with little boys in the house, villagers converging with pitchforks. This Caleb must be Andy Jacobson's son; Andy stayed here in town after graduation, married Angie somebody, two classes behind them, and went into his father's fuel-oil business. Definitely not one of the guys Billy came out to back in high school. Around here, Billy's thing has always been not to be *not* out but not to make an issue of it—when he was living in New York, it was a whole other story—and he's sometimes more cagey than the situation requires. He introduced Deke to Mrs. Krupa next door as "my sister's boy" rather than "my nephew" because it sounded more folksy, and because *nephew* seemed like a euphemism for *catamite*.

But a playdate crisis was bound to come sooner or later. You can't lock a kid up and never let him make any friends—which in fact would look more suspicious than anything. So maybe they could go to Caleb's house. *Or* come here, with Mrs. Bishop as duenna.

Billy thought at first that Deke might need psychiatric care and feeding. (Maybe Cassie's sticking him in his room in front of the TV hadn't been such a bad idea, considering what he

might otherwise have seen.) But he seems fine—if Billy's any
judge of what's fine—simply having a routine and getting some
attention. He doesn't even appear to suffer from TV with-
drawal, and asked only once if he could watch *The X-Files.* Billy
said it wasn't on until after his bedtime, so why didn't they play
Candyland instead. And Deke was fine with it. Billy's rule is, if
Deke brings something up, they talk. If and only if.

A couple of days after he got here, Deke asked when he was
going to see Mommy, and even Billy recognized this as a cue.
"You must miss her," he said. Hey, no shit.

"I don't know," Deke said. "Sometimes."

"Well, it's going to be a while longer," Billy said. "But I
called her at the hospital this morning, and she said be sure
and tell you she misses you, too."

Deke frowned. Billy could guess what he was thinking: if he
missed her and she missed him, then what the hell was going
on? But he didn't ask any more questions.

Billy *had* talked to Cassie that morning, that much was true.
She'd warned him not to trust Deke because he was a "star
baby." She meant a changeling left by aliens; the real Deke was
on some star being dissected alive.

"A star?" Billy had stupidly said. "Or a planet?"

"Oh," she'd said. "The stickler. You stick it in your
boyfriends' asses, and then they stick it in you. And you call it
the life of Riley."

When Billy left New York, his teaching job, his lover and the
cats, the forsythias were starting. Now the trees are bare again;
out in the country, orange pumpkins litter the brown fields.
This morning, while shaving, he noticed there's only a speck on
his earlobe where his earring used to be.

He sleeps in his parents' bedroom: bizarre, but less so than
it would've been to move back into his own little room across

the hall and leave the big bedroom empty. They probably conceived him in this bed, but it's like the time his father took the family to Gettysburg: long ago something happened on this spot, but now so what? He's put Deke in *his* old room, which his father cleaned out and repainted as soon as he went off to Brown. Cassie's room still has her single bed with the dust ruffle, her big old teddy bear Weezer, her books from *Pippi Longstocking* through *Lady Sings the Blues.* Deke will stay in there for hours, going through drawers, exploring the closetful of toys. Once, while outside raking leaves, Billy watched him through the window. He'd hauled out this old game of Cassie's called Operation, where you touch different body parts with this penlike thing and tiny bulbs light up. He'd knelt on the floor, touching this spot and that—Billy couldn't see what—and moving his lips: a healing ceremony for his mother? When Billy moved closer to the window, he could hear that Deke was singing "The Ants Go Marching One by One."

Last Christmas they were all in this house, in their former configurations. Mom was still alive, still well enough to get the stepladder out of the garage and string the colored lights on the twin spruces flanking the front walk. (She never took them down, and Billy's of two minds about whether to plug them in come December.) Cassie and Deke had driven out from Boston, and Billy and Mark had taken the train up from the city after throwing their own Christmas party, at which Mark—who called himself "a prolapsed Catholic"—had given everybody those WWJD bracelets, explaining that they stood for "Who Would Jesus Do?" What happens this Christmas, Billy can't imagine.

His mother died at the end of February. His father had died nine years before, the quintessential family man's death: heart attack after shoveling snow. That was in February, too; Billy flirted with seeing it as noncoincidental, but the dates (the seventh and the twenty-third) didn't resonate. Mark saw Billy through the vigil at the hospital and the funeral, then, two weeks later, made his announcement. Two weeks to the day. They could, and should, still share the apartment, but Mark had decided to make the thing he was having with Garrett— which he'd been calling a "friendship"—be his real thing. In fairness, Billy had to admit (to himself) that he had a "friendship," too. For the past few months he'd been thinking up nighttime errands—he'd turned super-responsible about the cats' litter—and calling Dennis, who always worked late, from pay phones. Dennis was living with Giuliano—who Dennis suspected was seeing somebody else. And they all more or less knew one another. It was like some daisy-chain soap opera out of the Age of Disco, with a certain "I Love Lucy" quality, if you stepped back far enough. Billy, finally, stepped way, way back.

During spring break he went to Key West: sat in the sun, drank gin and tonic. And after a couple of days, he called and added a connecting flight from LaGuardia to Albany to his return ticket. There was an empty, mortgage-free house where he could live for the cost of the property taxes and utility bills. He could take the train down twice a week to finish out the semester, and meanwhile look for a used car and a job. A job a regular person might have. The day he mailed in his students' grades, he bought a '95 Honda Civic with forty-three thousand miles on it; two weeks later he started work at a company that did tech support under contract to Microsoft. Billy liked computers, and he was a quick study; he had no experience, but neither did half the employees. He'd worked up a little song-and-dance for the interview to explain a career change at thirty-two: he grew up here, liked the area, was burned out on New York City. If that didn't play in Albany, he didn't know Albany. But he never got to say his piece. They were hiring: end of story. If he didn't work out, somebody else would.

Cassie had worked on him about moving to Boston, but that would've been settling for the merely second-rate. Choosing the suburbs of Albany and your own childhood home had a perverse grandeur, like an episode in the lives of the great Proustian-Jamesian queer recluses. (Mark's name for Albany was "Ulan Bator.") And taking a job in tech support seemed, to Billy, a little like Rimbaud giving up poetry for gunrunning or whatever it was. A very little.

He didn't bring much from 75th Street besides his clothes, his tapes and CDs, his books—most of them are still in boxes— and his computer. He spread his one decent kilim on the wall-to-wall carpeting in the living room, but the colors clashed; after a week he rolled it up and stuck it in the hall closet. He's learned to live with wallpaper, and while he took down the intolerable shorescape (lighthouse, dunes, gull on post of jetty) in the master bedroom, he left the snow scene (covered bridge, icy brook, hemlocks) as a tip of the hat to the old man. He also left the denim-and-gingham square dancers in the kitchen, painted on varnished plywood in a Chuck Jones–meets–Thomas Hart Benton manner.

Deke's been here since Labor Day weekend. That Sunday morning, Cassie's Porsche-driving druggie boyfriend called in a panic—looking for Mom, actually, forgetting she was dead. If he'd ever known. He said they'd gone to his beach house in Wellfleet, where Cassie, already up for three days on coke and crank, made the mistake of eating these 'shrooms they'd been saving for the right occasion. He'd taken her to the hospital— he was sure Billy would see he'd had no choice—but what was he supposed to do with her kid? The social worker at the hospital was going to put him in foster care, but—

"Where's Deke now?" Billy said. "Okay, listen, stay right there."

He woke up Labor Day morning, fried from driving to the Cape and back the day before, and with no more idea than the boyfriend of what to do with a seven-year-old kid. Deke was already up. Billy found him in Cassie's old room, playing with her Barbies, and decided to take him to a ball game. The Albany-Colonie Diamond Dogs were playing the Adirondack Lumberjacks for the Northeast League championship that afternoon. Billy's father used to take him to games back when Albany still had a Yankee farm team; Billy found it heartening that these upstarts should be named after a David Bowie song.

Deke was really too young to follow the game—the Diamond Dogs hit two home runs in the bottom of the first, and he missed them both—but he seemed to like the crowd, the bright green grass and the bursts of music and sound effects from the loudspeakers. The Dogs' cleanup hitter popped a foul ball into the aisle between the grandstand and the bleachers (sound effect of breaking glass), and a crowd of boys ran to chase it down. Deke leaped up, then looked at Billy. "Can I?"

"Just make sure I can see you," Billy said.

Deke was still scrambling down into the aisle when one of the kids held the ball up as little hands grabbed for it and the crowd applauded. Deke ran halfway over, then turned back to Billy with a stagy shrug and a genuine smile.

By the seventh inning, the Dogs were up eleven to nothing. Billy told Deke about the seventh-inning stretch, and Deke made him sing "Take Me Out to the Ballgame" in his ear to prep him; he claimed he'd never heard it. The Dogs went down one-two-three in the bottom of the eighth, and Billy, wanting to beat the crowd, asked Deke if he'd had enough. No: he wanted to chase more foul balls.

To get out of the parking lot took them all three movements of Shostakovich's First Violin Concerto, but Billy had no plan for what to do next anyway. Deke said he was hungry, so that settled that: they went to McDonald's. On the way home they listened to the Barney tape Deke had carried with him from Boston to Cape Cod and from Cape Cod to here. Predictably namby-pamby—amazing that Cassie, of all people, would give it houseroom—but not without its fascinations. Like that song "The Old Brass Wagon": was it really a wagon made of brass, like some warrior's brazen chariot, or just a wagon to haul scrap metal? It seemed folkloristic. The Golden Bough. The Old Brass Wagon. The dying god hauled to his funeral pyre. A harvest thing. The sun was going down on Labor Day. Summer was over.

Billy does the dishes while Deke takes his bath, but he keeps coming in to check, imagining the worst: Deke standing up, slipping, cracking his head, drowning. He's relieved that he hasn't found the boy's narrow nates and teensy penis at all arousing. At the same time, he's irked with himself for being relieved. Does he assume that straight men reflexively slaver over girl children in their care?

After he's dried Deke's soft hair with the hair dryer, they snuggle on the sofa and Billy reads him his nightly trilogy. Tonight Deke chose *The Tale of Peter Rabbit*, *The Runaway Bunny* and the loathly *Bugs Bunny and the Carrot Machine*. An all-rabbit program. Billy marvels at how Deke has devised it: a calming, ritualistic opener, then the emotionally heavy stuff—the mother who'll always come after you and take care of you—and then a farce as the end piece.

After Bugs Bunny overloads the carrot-making machine and blows it up—a not very subtle parable about overreaching—Billy takes Deke by the hand and leads him to bed. "Goodnight and sleep tight."

Deke lets his head sink into the pillow and looks up at the ceiling. "Good night and sleep tight. Did you know Mommy has Old Maid in her room?"

"No kidding. You know, I'd forgotten about Old Maid. We used to play all the time."

"Can we play?"

"Sure. How about tomorrow?"

"Tomorrow *morning*."

"Tomorrow morning. Surest thing you know. That's what my—what your grandfather used to say. 'Surest thing y'know.' He was an epistemologist."

Deke looks at him. "Mommy said he was a teacher."

"That was his day job, sure."

"But what's a pistemologist?"

"*You* know." Billy's sorry he started this. "Somebody that mows the lawn and stuff. Reads the paper. Shovels snow in the winter."

"Like you?" Deke's frowning. He clearly knows there's something he's not getting.

"*Exactement.*" Billy gives him his best imitation of a guileless smile. "Sweet dreams." Kisses his fingertips, presses them to Deke's forehead, then hits PLAY on the boom box.

He puts away the dishes, then goes down to the basement and sticks a load of clothes in the washer. He pours himself a finger of Macallan—*dernier cru* Scotch, Mark called it—and settles in with the *Times.* Down the hall, Horowitz tinkles away. Deke pipes up for a glass of water; Billy brings him half a glass, holding his breath when he bends close. As if a seven-year-old would detect the smell. Though this one might.

When he finishes what little he reads of the *Times* anymore, he gets up and vacuums the living room; to keep from feeling like a drudge, he does just one room a day. Then he goes back down and puts the clothes in the dryer, pours another finger of Macallan, brings it into the bedroom and shuts the door. After his father died, his mother had an extension phone put in. Billy's with his father on this: it's an indulgence, like a box of bonbons. But he's gotten to like it, and once in a while, usually after a drink, he'll lie back on the bed and call somebody he used to know. There's not much to say about his life anymore except for specialized anecdotes of tech support, so he draws out their stories with questions and quasi-alert reactions. *Really. Mm-hm.* A *No kidding* where it seems right.

He takes off his shoes, stacks the two pillows and stretches out on top of the covers with his chin jammed into his breast-bone. Solid comfort. He looks up Dennis's office number just to make sure, punches it in and gets the voicemail, then waits for the tone and tells Dennis he's probably surprised to hear from him but he just has a question. Then, thinking how *that* must sound, says, "Nothing heavy." If Dennis calls back, he'll think up a question. Mark's name for Dennis was "Miss Monica," because of his dark hair and smooth cheeks and what he pretended to imagine were Dennis's preferences. Mark's snottiness about him was part of the attraction. But so was Dennis's sheer good looks. Mark wasn't exactly the Adonis of the Western world. Neither is Billy.

He creeps in, in stocking feet, to check on Deke. Sound asleep. When he hits STOP in the middle of the Waltz in A minor, he can hear the dryer humming in the basement. He hits REWIND, to get set for tomorrow night. Back in his bedroom, he locks the door and pulls out the magazine he keeps under the mattress and resorts to a couple of nights a week. He finishes off, cleans up, knocks back the Macallan, then goes down and gets the clothes out of the dryer. He's folding Deke's narrow blue jeans when it strikes him that he's insane to run such a risk. *If I should die before I wake.* Well, not so much that. But if one of these days Deke, who's into everything, should be exploring around and find *Fuckbuddies*—or, worse yet, if Deke and his friend should find it on their playdate. No, thank you. He could sneak it out of the house in the morning, folded in the *Times.* But what if he *should* die before he wakes?

He carries the laundry upstairs and looks in again: Deke's on his side, mouth slack, his outbreaths roaring in the silent house. Then he creeps into his own room, slips *Fuckbuddies* into the sports section of the *Times*, carries it out to the breezeway, still in his stocking feet, and sticks it in with the garbage. He pours yet another finger of Macallan, gets into bed and opens *The Interpretation of Dreams*, his current go-to-sleep book: in *The Western Canon*, his previous go-to-sleep book, Harold Bloom did such a good job of selling Freud as imaginative literature that Billy's giving it another try. He begins "The Dream of the Botanical Monograph," which sounds like a Sherlock Holmes title, or Borges maybe, but quickly becomes impenetrable. *Behind "artichokes" lay, on the one hand, my thoughts about Italy and, on the other, a scene from my childhood which was the opening of what have since become my intimate relations with books.* Do tell. He pages around and stumbles across the part about staircase dreams, which he'd always heard were supposedly sexual. So *that* was why? Because you mount higher and higher and pant as you reach the top? What incredibly silly shit.

He realizes after a while that he's been cruising along with his eyes closed, following some parallel story about painting over wallpaper with a roller; this is not, technically, reading. He reaches over and puts out the light, then instantly comes wide awake, worrying what question he could ask if Dennis should call. The only question he can think of is *Did you ever fly when you were a little boy?* Because he's imagining Deke in a Diamond Dogs uniform, soaring around the bases six feet above the ground, making smart right-angle turns like Casper the Friendly Ghost. So maybe he's asleep and doesn't know it.

The light wakes Billy up too early Saturday morning: those flower-print curtains of his mother's just don't cut it. He reads until he hears Deke calling, then delivers a clean outfit, goes to the kitchen to start coffee and puts on the Shostakovich, skipping right to the zippy second movement. Before breakfast they play three games of Old Maid. Billy's caught with the Old Maid each time, in scary defiance of the law of averages; but even if this meant something, it would simply mean what he already knows. He gets out bowls, milk, spoons and Product 19. No TV, no sugared cereals, no throwaway pop music—someday Deke will hold all this against him. Assuming Deke just stays on and on, which Billy shouldn't be assuming.

"So I thought today we better make a pumpkin run," he says. Halloween's a week away. Make it through that and they've got Thanksgiving. And then Christmas.

"What's a pumpkin run?"

"Maybe five dollars. That was a joke."

"I don't get it." Deke's eating with his face down in the bowl, holding his spoon overhand. Must this be corrected, or do kids grow out of it automatically?

"Don't worry, it wasn't funny. What I meant was, we should go out and get a pumpkin. You ever make a jack-o-lantern?"

"I don't know. Can we read first?"

"Sure. We got the whole day." Though in fact Billy would like to get the hell out of here before Dennis calls back. "What did you have in mind?"

"I don't know." But of course it turns out to be *The Runaway Bunny.*

"Heck of a story," Billy says when he's finished reading the thing. "Now, would you go get your shoes, please?"

"Thank you," Deke says. A reflex triggered by the *please?* Or is Deke actually thanking him?

"You're welcome." Billy decides to break the rule. "Tell me something. Are you missing your mom today?"

"Not really. Can we call her?"

"We can't call *her,* but she'll probably call *us* later on."

"Can we wait?"

This requires a lie. "The last time I talked to her, she said she probably wouldn't be calling till tonight." Mistake: this invention is checkable. "Or that's what I thought she said. So we have lots of time. Shoes?"

They drive up to Troy, then cut east toward Bennington. It's a flawless autumn day, the blue of the sky either absolutely deep or absolutely without depth. Billy's put on *The Magnificent Gigli*, and at least Deke's not complaining. They take a side road north, past barns and tractors, through intermittent odors of manure. Billy passes on his tractor lore: red for Farmall, green for John Deere, gray for Ford, orange for Case, Allis-Chalmers and Massey-Harris. And they make up a tractor game: Deke gets a point for every red one, Billy for every green, and points for gray and orange go to whoever spots them first. Deke's ahead four to two when they stop at a field with a beach umbrella, an aluminum chair and a PUMKINS sign.

There's nobody here, just rows of pumpkins ranked by size and a tackle box with a three-by-five card reading HONOR SYSTEM: LG $5, MED $3, SM $1.

"Can we get a big one?"

"But of course," Billy says in his French accent.

"But I feel sorry for the little ones."

"So we'll get some little ones too, for decoration. The little ones are the ones they make pies out of."

"Can we make a pie?"

"We can think about it."

"But can we?"

"Yeah, why not? I guess we could figure it out." One of his mother's cookbooks must have a recipe, though they're probably all based on canned pumpkin. Which must be more condensed, so therefore . . . something. Whether Deke's budding housewifeliness ought to be encouraged is a whole other question. But here's Billy encouraging it.

When he opens his wallet, he finds only three singles and a couple of twenties. The tackle box has two singles and three quarters. Hmm. Deke's walking through the big pumpkins, crowing "Look at this one—no, look at *this* one!" Billy steps into the road. That must be the house, way up there on the opposite side. A tall, pointy-roofed farmhouse with two-over-two windows, weathered gray. Not a place where he'd ordinarily knock on the door. If he left a twenty and took the two singles, they could get three big pumpkins and three little ones. Except he doesn't *want* three big pumpkins. And he doubts you need three little ones for a pie, even if the stuff's not condensed.

"Come here quick!" Deke calls.

"You find one?"

"You have to *see* this."

Billy walks over. Deke's sitting beside a knee-high pumpkin, classic pumpkin-shape on one side, the other side flattened, with diseased-looking patches of brown.

"Aw*right*," he says. "Good choice."

"We can just turn the bad side away," Deke says.

"Absolutely."

"So we can get it, right?"

"If I can lift it."

"I'll help," Deke says.

They wrestle the monster into the backseat, then pick out three small pumpkins. Billy puts a twenty in the tackle box and takes out the two ones. Five for the big pumpkin, buck apiece for the three little ones, ten dollars for the entertainment. He backs around, noses onto the blacktop, looks both ways and decides to drive on past the farmhouse instead of turning around and appearing to hightail it out of there. He points at the chickens pecking in the front yard and a small black-nosed sheep chained to a car wheel lying in the grass, and misses a Farmall tractor out by the barn.

"Can we listen to Barney?"

"Sure," Billy says. "You like that song 'The Old Brass Wagon'?"

"I guess so."

"I'm really into it, for some reason."

Deke looks at him and narrows his eyes, as if he's suddenly been dealt one *more* crazy adult. "How come *you* like it?"

"Just something about it. I guess I like how you don't really know anything about the Old Brass Wagon. It's just, there it is. The Old Brass Wagon. Deal with it. You know what I mean?"

Deke looks out the window.

"What do *you* like about it?" Billy says.

"I don't know, it's good."

Billy says, "Tell me something. Are you actually a Salinger character?"

Deke looks back at him. "What's a sowinger character?"

It scares Billy that he's allowed himself to say such an out-there thing. "Nothing. It's just a—you know, I was thinking what you could be for Halloween. Why don't you look in the dash and see if the Barney tape's in there?"

Deke opens the glove compartment and reaches in. "Yay!" He hands the cassette to Billy.

"Do you want to be Barney for Halloween?" Billy says. "They have a Barney costume at CVS."

"Could I be what you said?"

"What I said? Oh. A Salinger character?" It's a pretty beguiling idea. "Tell you what. When we get home, I'll show you a picture of one, and you can decide if that's what you want to be. Basically you'd wear a backwards baseball cap and a long coat. And you'd be carrying a suitcase."

"Oh." Deke looks out the window again. Barney and the kids start singing. *"Everybody in the old brass wagon . . ."* Oh, well. It would've been lost on the good people of Menands anyway. A vista opens: Deke in doublet and hose with a skull in his hand; Deke with greatcoat, bowler hat secured by string, stones in his pockets; Deke in a black frock coat, with fake whiskers, a harpoon over his shoulder and some kind of fake pegleg. The vista closes. Billy would never take advantage. He makes another left turn, which should eventually get them over to Route 40 and then back down into Troy.

After supper they carve the pumpkin, Deke drawing the face on it in Magic Marker, Billy doing the actual cutting. He hasn't done this since he was a kid, when his mother did the actual cutting. They scoop out the seeds in slippery, sticky handfuls and spread them on his mother's cookie sheet to roast. Just as his mother used to do, probably on the same cookie sheet. (The pie project, thank God, has been forgotten.) Deke's rendering of the face isn't much use as a practical guide to cutting, so Billy tries to keep the positions and proportions of eyes, nose and mouth the same while improvising the details. His mother never aspired to more than upside-down triangles for eyes, a right-side-up triangle for the nose and a crescent mouth. Billy now finds he can cut out eyes, leaving half-round pupils in the lower-left corners for a furtive expression, and a snaggletoothed cartoon-hillbilly mouth with irregularly spaced square teeth. He considers a Picasso nose—in profile, to the right of both eyes—but Deke put a pig-style snout in the center, so he'd better play it straight: a pair of round nostrils punched into the space implied by a thin, semicircular incision.

As Billy's gouging out a hole in the bottom for a candle, the phone rings. This must be Dennis: crap, what to say? Deke runs to pick it up, then cries, "Mommy! We're making a pumpkin!"

Billy considers it indecent to listen outright; still, he can't help but hear the conversation dwindle to the usual *Yeah, No, I don't know* and *Okay.* Finally Deke says, "She wants to talk to you," and clunks the phone onto the table without even a *Love you too.*

"Billy?" Cassie says. "This is breaking my heart."

"I know."

"You *don't* know. Listen, we have to talk."

"Okay."

"Well, we can't talk now. He's right there, isn't he?"

"This is true," Billy says. "How about Monday? You've got my work number."

"God, imagine putting yourself in a position where you're allowed one phone call a day. I've fucked up so badly."

"Nothing irretrievable." One call a day: it's never before occurred to Billy to wonder whom she calls on alternate days. "Except what wasn't worth retrieving anyway. If you know who I mean. So, you have any idea yet when Betty Ford's going to get out of that house she's in?"

"Betty *Ford*? I thought she was dead, for Christ's—"

"No no no, I mean the Betty Ford *I* know."

"The Betty—oh. *That* Betty Ford. That's cute. I don't know, really, but just from little things they let drop, I'm thinking sooner rather than later. But there's something I need to talk to you about."

"Well, whenever. I'm not going anywhere. Always on the spot. Like Johnny." It also strikes him that she must be free to call him from work: how could her keepers monitor that? Or do they have her on the honor system?

"You really have been," Cassie says. "Don't think I don't know that I can never, ever repay you—that's a lot of negatives, isn't it? I mean, to say a positive thing."

When Billy finally gets the hole gouged out and a votive candle in it, he burns his goddamn fingers reaching into the pumpkin with a match. He guesses the technique is to light a dinner candle, stick it through the mouth and torch it off that way. But when they turn the lights out, Deke says "Yesss" and Billy has to agree. The thing looks both sly and mind-blown.

"We should have a picture of this," Billy says, then realizes he doesn't own a camera. His mother's Minolta must be some-where. Right: he packed it in one of the boxes in the basement. "Tell you what. You want to take a ride to CVS? We can buy one of those disposable cameras."

"Yay!"

Billy ends up buying two, twenty-four exposures each. Since Halloween's coming up. Cassie will surely want pictures: otherwise there'd be these undocumented months in her son's life—though he suspects that before the crash-and-burn Cassie had let the picture-taking slide. On the way out, he shows Deke the Barney costume. "Cool," Deke says, looking away.

When they get back home, Billy checks the answering ma-chine. No calls.

On Sunday morning, he takes Deke to the Methodist church he and Cassie used to go to with their mother—his craziest bit of behavior yet, though to Deke it must seem no crazier than any of the rest. Sure enough, the 9:30 service still has a children's choir, and Billy and Deke share a hymnal and try to sing along, Billy moving his finger underneath the words for him. "See?" he whispers. "When those notes go up and down, the tune goes up and down." Deke nods, either pretending he knows or just humoring him. Wouldn't Cassie have explained this much? They've got a new minister—old Dr. Griffin must be dead by now—about Billy's age, whose glasses make him look like Philip Larkin. One of those not-queer/not-*not*-queer types. Billy checks the left hand: a wedding ring, for whatever that's worth. The first word of his sermon is enough for Billy to cross him off: *Hopefully some of you watched last night's special on the Holocaust* . . . If news of this ever gets back to Cassie, look out. In fact, maybe he should tell Deke not to tell her—or would that just make it stick out more in the kid's mind? Plus the whole issue of keeping secrets. No, thank you. Too much like queer-uncle behavior.

"So how was that?" he says as they walk down the steps into the sunshine. They've gone out a side door to avoid shaking hands with the minister.

"I don't think kids should sing," Deke says.

"How come?"

"'Cause they stink."

"Really? I thought they did great."

"They shouldn't be allowed."

What's *this* about? Billy can't think what the right response might be; then inspiration kicks in. "Well, adults aren't always perfect singers either. People sing just because they enjoy it sometimes." And another inspiration. "What about the kids who sing with Barney? They're not perfect either, but it's fun to listen to them."

"I hate them."

"Why do you hate them?"

Shrug.

"But you like listening to them."

Not even a shrug.

They get back in the car and Billy heads for the Howard Johnson's just off the 787 ramp; he didn't have time to fix breakfast before they left the house. He stops and buys Sunday papers: the *Times* for himself and the *Times Union* because Deke likes the funnies. The greeter girl—pretty, seemingly too young—leads them to an empty booth. Billy guesses that with his Diamond Dogs cap and nylon bomber jacket he can pass for a divorced dad with weekend custody. If that's his beau ideal.

Mostly he avoids taking Deke to restaurants, not because of the catamite issue but because the two of them look so alone in the world. The only person either of them has left is Cassie. Well, Deke does have another grandmother: Vic's mother, who lives in Provo, Utah. But the extent of her involvement is a hundred-dollar check every Christmas and a card signed *Mammaw*, the alias she devised for herself since Cassie's mother already had *Grandma*. Billy should probably make overtures: call every week or two, put Deke on. If only for practical reasons. Suppose he had a head-on crash coming home from work: Mrs. Bishop would take Deke that night, but then what?

Deke orders oatmeal and bacon; Billy has oatmeal and a half grapefruit. He cuts a section free, spears it with his fork and holds it out to Deke.

"No way."

"No, *thank you.*" Because if he's doing this, he's damn well going to do it right.

"Oh, yeah," Deke says.

Billy's been sneaking looks at the entertainment listings in the *Times Union*. This is already shaping up as a long day, but the movies look either inappropriate or unbearable, and mostly both. "Aha," he says. "Looks like they're having a young people's concert."

"What's that?"

"You know, a big concert that's geared to kids? Somebody usually comes out and talks about the instruments and whatnot. They must have those in Boston, right?" Which Billy flatters himself is a neutral way of asking.

"I don't know." Deke clamps his teeth on a piece of bacon and tugs it back and forth.

"Sound like something you'd be up for? Oh. Cool. They're doing *The Planets* today. That's this piece of music where each part is about a different planet. You want to check it out?"

"No, thank you," Deke says, chewing.

"Hmm. Looks like pretty slim pickings otherwise. Our alternative would be just to go home and hang out."

Deke crams the rest of the bacon into his mouth and nods.

On the way home they stop at the video place and return *Top Hat*, whose plot Deke hadn't been able to follow, and take out *Star Trek IV*, the whale one. Billy steals a glance over the top of the louvered doors into the back room, where all the covers have bodies with the same shade of tan. He happens to know they stock a few gay videos, in a section called ALTERNATIVE LIFESTYLES. But this will have to be a distant good.

They spend most of the afternoon playing Candyland, during which Billy gets to listen to Tatiana Nikolayeva's Shostakovich preludes and fugues. God knows what this Shostakovich obsession is about; anyhow, it'll run its course. He hits the Cherry Pits again and again, and Deke wins three straight games. During the fourth game, Billy starts feeling cooped up—which *couldn't* have to do with losing at Candyland—and they go out in the yard and toss the little rubber football around. Most of his throws bounce off of Deke, and Deke's return throws either fall short or go wide. But Billy says "Good arm" and "*That's* the way" whenever it's remotely applicable. Then they go back in—Billy checks the answering machine: nothing—and watch *Star Trek IV*. Deke doesn't follow this one either, but at least it's in color and feels contemporary. The first week Deke was here, Billy rented a compilation of '30s farm-animal cartoons: pecking chickens making typewriter sounds, that sort of thing. When he was little he used to love this stuff. After a couple of minutes Deke said, "Do we have to watch this?" What was bizarre was that Billy instantly saw how crude and depressing it was.

Since they had a late breakfast instead of lunch, Billy calls Domino's and has them deliver a pizza around five. Afterward he gets Deke into the tub and starts straightening up. The actual vacuuming he puts off until Deke's in bed; it's the chore that seems the most housewifely, that he most dislikes being seen at. He still uses his mother's old Hamilton Beach, a low gray cigar-blimp on casters that whines like a jet engine.

Into p.j.'s, brush teeth. Dry his hair. While he's picking out his bedtime books, make sure all his stuff's in his backpack for school tomorrow. And that's the weekend.

On Monday morning, Billy's on the phone with some techno-phobe who's whining that Windows is defective because when he tries to drag and drop icons on his desktop they won't stay put. "Okay, go to your START button," he says, and his other line lights up. "Sorry, could you hold just a second?" Dennis, perhaps, at long last? He hits HOLD, then 4427.

"Billy?" Cassie. "Listen, I'm in Albany. Can you meet me for lunch?"

"You what? Look, can you hold? Let me get rid of this call." He hits HOLD, then the blinking 4426, and tells the techno-phobe "a small emergency" has come up and he'll transfer him to somebody who can help him out. He hits the blinking 4427. "Cassie?"

"None other."

"What's going on?" Crap: he forgot to transfer the guy. "Why aren't you—"

"They let me have a whaddya-call-it. I have to be back by six-thirty. Poor Billy—I scared the hell out of you, didn't I? So can we have lunch? There's something I really need to ask you and it's, sort of, not for the telephone. Shit, I'm making this sound heavy and it's really not."

"Jesus, I wish you'd—sure. Yeah. I mean I'd love to see you."

"I'll bet. But really, I'm a lot, lot better. I promise you, this is not going to be painful."

"I'm just surprised is all. If you'd—"

"I know, I know. Like, how can they let her out if she's going to go right back to her impulsive behavior?" Billy hears her sigh. "It's not like that, believe me."

"So where did you want to meet?"

"Doesn't matter. Actually, you know where I'd like to go? Now, this *is* crazy. That HoJo's where we used to go with Mom and Dad."

"That's bizarre," Billy says.

"How so?"

"Because I just—you know, took Deke there."

"Oh." Silence. "So. How is he?"

"He's good."

"Are you judging me for not asking about him first thing? I can tell you are. Shit. See, I knew that was a mistake. I didn't want to seem like I was pushing, but I can see how you might think, you know, that I was, like—"

"Don't tie yourself up in knots. I'm not judging you, and Deke's doing fine."

"I.e., better than with me."

"Well. Better than back *then*."

"Oh," she says. "Tough love."

"You asked. I mean, don't you think so?"

"No, you're right," she says. "See? I'm learning." She sighs again. "But you're not impressed."

"Can we save this?"

"That's the question, isn't it? But you mean for over lunch. Save the bullshit for over lunch. Because you're busy at work. Don't worry, Billy, I'll be good. Now, what time?"

"What's good for you?"

"And the hits just keep on coming. What's good for me. Twelve-thirty. Twelve-thirty is good for me. She says decisively. So I'll see you then, at HoJo's?"

"How are you getting there? I mean, how did you get *here*?"

"Rented a car. That's another thing, I have to return the

car by six o'clock. So you're covered six ways from Sunday, kiddo."

Billy has to ask. "Had you planned to try to see Deke?"

"Had I planned, to try, to see Deke. Whew. You put that so beautifully. You really are a word person, Billy. You're wasting yourself in computers. God, it's like . . . No. Short answer: no. That would just be too much. For *everybody* concerned. Don't you think?"

"I do, actually. But it's your decision."

"Damn right," she says. "Not to put you on notice or anything."

"So I'll see you at twelve-thirty." He looks at the corner of his screen: 10:38.

"Unless you get lucky," she says. "That would be a novelty. Believe me, Billy, if *I* could go in there and sit across from me and handle this whole thing for you, I'd gladly do it."

"What are you going to do between then and now?"

"Wow, I've really got you worried. That must be the way I like it. No, that must be the way *you* like it. Actually, there's a Big Book meeting at the Episcopal church in Colonie. At eleven, so I better hustle. And when that lets out I'm going to stop by the Barnes & Noble on Wolf Road. Is that really the only Starbucks? In the Barnes & Noble?"

"Hey, at least we've got one," Billy says. "We're getting there, slowly but surely."

"What's this *we*?"

"Oh, I don't know—the civic 'we.' We of Greater Albany often talk this way."

"Hey, Billy?" she says. "Don't think I don't worry about you, too."

When he pulls into the parking lot, he sees her just getting out of a no-color Dodge Stratus with a paper cup in her hand. She looks right, then left, then shrugs and tosses it back into the car. She's wearing sunglasses, a blue blazer and khaki pants, and she's had a recent hundred-dollar haircut, judging by how perfectly the ends curve under. Billy noses into a parking space and watches her stride, long-legged, to the door, a briefcase dangling from a shoulder strap, hairdo bouncing as if in slow motion. She looks like she's overplaying it, not that he's any judge of where the ideal midpoint would be.

When he comes in she's talking to the greeter girl. If this is the same one as yesterday (which Billy wouldn't swear to), now she'll have got the complete picture: the divorced father meeting with the estranged wife to see if there isn't a chance after all. *Can we save this?* The girl leads her to the same booth he and Deke had yesterday; Cassie sits and immediately picks up her menu.

"Hey," Billy says, walking over, smiling. "You look great."

She looks up, smiles. "Hey. Gee, you too. Fatherhood doesn't seem to be grinding *you* down." She frowns and goes back to the menu.

Billy sits down and examines her face. In one corner of her mouth, the lipstick looks like a kid has colored outside the line—the result, probably, of freshening up in the rearview mirror. Otherwise she looks perfectly plausible. And young. His beautiful sister, who always liked the same boys he did.

"Deke's easy," he says. "We're having a good time."

"Easy for you, you mean?" She closes her eyes, opens them, nods.

"Look, I'm just glad I was there to step in."

A waitress appears. "Do you need more time?"

Billy guesses Cassie will hear a double-entendre in that, too.

"No, we're ready—*I*'m ready," she says. "I'll have the hamburger platter. And coffee."

Billy looks at Cassie. She shrugs. "Hmm," he says. "Can I just get a BLT? Whole wheat, no mayo? Coffee also." The waitress scrawls and goes. "Red meat?" he says.

"It's my new thing," Cassie says. "I mean—not red meat. But just deciding something and sticking with it. That's a big part of my problem."

"Deciding things?" This doesn't seem quite dead-center.

"Well, not that per se. Are you going to start twisting everything?"

"I'm sorry," he says. "I didn't mean to sound—"

"I don't mean *twisting*, that sounds paranoid, but, you know, *reacting*. It's like you're still trying to find out what's wrong with me. Well, I guess that sounds paranoid, too. I'm not getting off to a very good start, am I?"

"Sssh." He holds up a hand. "I can tell you're doing better."

"Oh, I am. I really am. You can't shake my faith in *that*." She gives a smile to indicate this is a joke. Then she frowns. "I'm fucking up. I came to ask you a very big favor—two very big favors, actually—and now I'm acting hostile to you."

"No, you're not."

"Well, that's nice of you to say."

The waitress sets their coffees down.

"So what are these very big favors?" he says. He decides not to point out that on the phone she had said this was nothing heavy.

"Look, I know you're already doing me a huge favor by taking care of Deke, and I appreciate it that you're not, like, grinding *that* into my face. Now, I didn't want to ask you this on the phone because you don't know who might be listening—I said *might* be, Billy. But do you think you could possibly go and clean out my apartment? Before I have to go back there?"

"Well—I mean I *could*. But it's kind of a trek into Boston. I'd be more than glad to pay somebody to go in there. Didn't you use to have that woman from—"

"Billy. I don't mean like scrub-a-dub-dub."

"Oh."

"I can tell you exactly where everything is. And you should

just feel free to go ahead and use it if you want. I mean, it's all really good, and I hate to think of it just getting flushed. Or if you're not into it, you must still know people who like to party."

"Well . . ."

"Oh, you look so scandalized. For God's sake, I'm an addict, I recognize *that*, but I'm not a fucking puritan."

"I don't know. Maybe *I* am. Anyway, sure. I could go take care of it next weekend. Would that be soon enough?"

"Oh, that would be *great*. Thank you so, so much."

"I'll have to figure out something to do with Deke."

"Why don't you just take him along? At this point it would probably be a good idea to sort of reintroduce him to the apartment. He can watch TV or play in his room. I don't have anything in there."

"Thank heaven for little mercies."

"Yeah, okay, I don't need you to give me shit, Billy. I know exactly what I did. *And* didn't do. I just need your help."

"Sorry, I don't mean to be a prick. I just, I don't know, care about him, and I get sort of protective. My motherly instinct."

"You mean you need to protect him from me." She nods her head. "Okay. I had that coming. I mean, you're absolutely right. Which kind of brings me to my other favor."

"Which is?"

"Well . . . Just if you'd still stay involved."

"Involved?"

"I mean, he's never had a father, or really any kind of man around except for, like, people that . . . You know. And now that he has you, and if that's suddenly taken away . . ."

"You mean you're going to take him back."

Cassie cocks her head and stares at him. "Well, what did you think?"

"Oh. I don't mean, I mean I always assumed that you—"

"Did you think I was never coming out?"

"I actually didn't think at all, you know, in the long term. I've just sort of been going along day by day. How sure are you that you'll be able to handle it?"

"Billy," she says. "You didn't have it in mind to fight me on this?"

"You mean legally?" He shrugs. "You're his mother. I'm his faggot uncle."

"Oh. So you *have* been thinking about it. What are you, preparing your little court case? 'And then she asked me to take him along while I cleaned the drugs out of her apartment.' "

"Listen to yourself," he says.

"Why? So even *I* would have to agree that I'm an unfit mother?"

The waitress is standing over them. "The hamburg platter?"

Cassie points at the tabletop in front of her and the waitress sets down an oval platter. Only the top of a bun is visible among the heaping french fries.

"BLT?"

Billy nods. A round plate, with chips.

"Anything else I can get you?"

"We're fine," Billy says.

"Enjoy your meal." The waitress turns away so quickly Billy feels a breeze from her skirt.

"You didn't answer my question," Cassie says.

Billy lets the waitress get a couple of booths away. "Which one?"

"Any question, actually. 'How's Deke?' 'He's fine.' 'Will you stay involved in his life?' 'We'll have to see.' "

"That's not what I said. Of course I want to stay involved. So you're taking him back to Boston?"

"What have we just been talking about? Hello?" She drops her mouth open, idiot-style, and waves. "Yes. It's where I *live.*

When I'm among the living. So in other words, when I take him home, that's too much of a *trek*, so you'll never see him."

"I'm not saying that."

She takes a bite of her hamburger, chews. "Good burger," she says. "*Not.* I'll tell you one thing, though. This time I'm going to make it."

Billy eats a potato chip. "I don't suppose you'd consider moving back here," he says.

"Please."

"I know, but think about it. The house is paid for, you and Deke could each have a room, you wouldn't—"

"We've got rooms. At home. Besides, I've *had* that room."

"We could switch. I'll take your old room and you can have the big room."

"*Their* bedroom?"

"Or you can switch with Deke. Take my old room. The piano's still here, it needs—"

"That house is death."

"That house," he says, "is a three-bedroom house. For free. In a safe neighborhood. With decent schools. Also, Billy wouldn't have to suddenly—"

"Yeah, I know the decent schools, too. It's where I used to boot coke in the toilet stalls."

"You could've done that anywhere. It was your choice. *I* didn't get into drugs."

Cassie's mouth drops open.

"Well, not like you did. Anyway, that was in high school. Deke's only in second—"

"I'm not discussing this." She stuffs a french fry into her mouth. "Mmm. Fries are good."

"So Boston's better."

"Better than Greater Albany? Yeah, I'd say so. Listen, I changed my mind. I want to see my boy."

"School doesn't let out until three," Billy says. "I thought you had to be back by six."

"No, I don't want him to see *me*. Can't we just go over to the school and peek in the classroom?"

"Not a good idea."

She gives him a quick shark smile. "Do you understand that I could call the police *any time* and say you're molesting him?"

Billy looks at her and nods. "Nice." Keeps nodding. "A truly lovely way to repay me."

"Oh, I thought you were too much of a saint to worry about being paid back. It's not reward enough, just feeling superior?"

"Cassie, why are you being so ugly?"

"Because I want to see my *son*, Billy, and you're giving me all this shit. Why can't we just go over and watch them come out for afternoon recess?"

"Line up behind the fence with all the pedophiles?"

"And the dope pushers," Cassie says. "You know, I don't need your permission. I know the way over there. I could drive it blindfold."

"Look. If we do this, I want you to—"

"Yay!" Cassie puts a fist in the air.

On the other side of the fence, kids are running and yelling, swinging and seesawing, swarming over the old jungle gym, a skeleton dome of smooth, dull gray pipes. Far across the still-green playing field, a pickup truck's parked by where they're building a modern playground with rubber mats and pressure-treated timber—so far away that you see a workman's hammer fall, then hear the *clink* on the upswing.

Billy points. That's Deke: in the blue-jean jacket, seesawing with a little girl.

"He plays with girls?" Cassie says.

"Yeah," Billy says. "He must've caught it from the toilet seat."

"You laugh. But you shared a bathroom with me all those years, and you ended up fucking men."

"Okay, now I believe you're Cassie." He looks at his sister, her hair tucked up into his Diamond Dogs cap. "I was afraid an alien had taken over *your* body."

"God, don't even joke about it. Listen, what's he going to be for Halloween?"

"I thought I'd dress him up as Carol Channing. No, actually, how about a space alien?"

"*Billy.* Jesus."

"Sorry. I've kind of had my eye on this Barney costume, but he doesn't seem to be into it."

"Actually, a space alien would probably be great. He's big into *X-Files.*"

"Really." Billy means this as a shot of disapproval, quick enough to be undiscussable. "By the way, if it's any comfort, remember that I only played with boys when I was his age."

"Come on," she says. "I was only kidding. I'm not a total right-winger."

"No comment. But if you want to know, my special faggot radar hasn't picked up any queer vibes from him."

"Stop."

"So you've seen enough? I mean, there he is. So you know I wasn't bullshitting you about his being alive and well. Or do you want to take this to the next level?"

Cassie hasn't taken her eyes off of Deke. "No," she says. She closes her eyes. "I've got to get back. I've got to get the damn *car* back."

He walks her over and opens her door. She stands there, still looking at the playground. "It's weird being here," she says. "That has to be the same jungle gym. How can you stand it?"

He shrugs. "See, I'm so used to it now that it seems weird I ever thought it was weird."

"Then you *are* in deep shit."

A bell rings, and kids start racing for the door.

"You sure you don't want to stop by the house for a second?" he says. "See how it feels?"

"No. You're really creeping me out, Billy. I mean, I don't mean to judge you."

"Yeah, God forbid. So I'm still not clear on when exactly . . . you know."

"Me either. But I definitely plan to be home before Christmas."

"Okay, that gives me some idea. Speaking of which, I guess we should plan to do a celebration. It's kind of down to the three of us."

"Definitely. Well, we'll talk, okay? I really better hit it." She turns the key in the ignition, then stops. "Billy? Wouldn't you even *consider* moving to Boston?"

"I'm always up for considering. But you mean would I? I doubt it. I've *had* the urban experience." Diplomatic of him, not going into New York versus second-rate cities.

"I was just thinking, we could sort of be a family. I mean, not that we're not, but—"

"Until your next beau comes along."

"You might find a beau, too, you know. The odds are a lot better in a place like Boston."

"Do I *want* a beau?"

"Don't you?"

"I think I'm suffering from beau burnout."

"Then I guess you're in the right place." Cassie starts the engine.

"Gee, sounds like the last lifeboat's going over the side," Billy says.

"If you weren't so smart—"

"With Leonardo DiCaprio waving me a wistful goodbye."

"—you'd be a lot better off." She looks back at the now empty schoolyard. "At least in the short run."

"Is there any other run?" Billy says. "I mean in the long run?"

On Saturday morning they stop at the car wash as a way of making their trip to Boston an occasion; in Billy's real life, a clean car is just more middle-class crap-o-rama. Going through with Deke reminds him of how exciting he used to find it: the King Lear hurricanoes driving against the windshield, the giant whirling brushes at the front and sides, the mysterious rubber fringe as you enter the region of winds and bright lights, then sadly out into the world again. Billy drops quarters into the vacuum and lets Deke do his own side—and doesn't criticize when Deke only rubs the mouth back and forth across a single patch of floor.

Then they stop at CVS to pick up the pictures; if there's a decent one of Deke, he'll buy a Lucite frame and leave it on Cassie's night table. But when he opens the envelope, all twenty-four prints show nothing but brownish murk. Last stop is HoJo's: breakfast here eventually might've become a little tradition, and maybe to Deke it already is. But he has to say, the kid's being a pain in the ass this morning. Complains they never made the pumpkin pie like Billy *promised*. Wants the pancakes but wants the oatmeal too, and whines that it *isn't fair* to have to choose. Over the long haul, living at this level of detail—Hegelian agonies over every fucking choice of food or garment or activity—would wear down Mother Teresa. It almost makes him feel some belated sympathy for the old man.

Heading south to pick up the Mass Pike, Billy explains that when he was a kid, the Pilgrim hats on the Mass Pike signs used to have Indian arrows sticking through them. "Cool," Deke says. But it's only good for a second's interest. The fact is, the arrows aren't there. They play I Spy, then the game where you have to spot the letters of the alphabet in order on signs and license plates; Billy lets Deke win, averting his eyes from the X on an exit sign lest the kid throw another shit fit. But eventually the big breakfast, Biber's *Mystery Sonatas* and warm sunshine in his face put Deke back to sleep, and Billy's free to think.

But all he can think about is the next time they'll make this drive, a month from now maybe. One last HoJo's breakfast, one last Deke-and-Billy expedition. Billy will hang with them in Boston for a while, they'll all do something together—the Aquarium, a movie, an early dinner—and at some point he'll ease out of the picture. And after that? A gay man, about to turn thirty-three, alone in a suburb of Albany. In his parents' house. In his parents' bed. What you do about *that*, of course, is you find somebody quick. (Dennis, the little prick, never called back.) There's a couple of possibles. Older guy, status unknown, who works a couple of cubicles down. Chatty ponytailed waiter in a restaurant on Lark Street—or he *was* there, before Deke came along. What you don't do is get into porn on the Internet. You don't get a cat. You could possibly get a dog, but not a small dog.

You could move to Boston.

He thinks he'll try to do what he's attempted so often: actually listen to a piece of music all the way through, move by move by move, without his attention wandering. He bumps the Biber back to Track 1.

Deke wakes up cranky and thirsty, so they stop at a service area. In the Roy Rogers Billy buys him a carton of milk, which Deke always chooses over soda. Does he drink so much milk because he has a calcium deficiency? (Due to Cassie's neglect?) Did Billy drink this much milk as a kid? Can't remember, though he does recall his father's scolding him for bubbling it. He gets himself a coffee and finds them an empty table. He's in no hurry to get to Boston, and he's truly not looking forward to ferreting out and flushing his sister's drugs. And no matter what she said, he imagines he'll be doing some scrub-a-dub-dub. On the other hand, he can't wait to park the nephew in front of a TV. He's spent the last month making conversation with a seven-year-old.

"You know who Roy Rogers was?" he hears himself say.

Deke shakes his head. Bracing for more ancient history.

"He was the King of the Cowboys."

"Cool," Deke says, though the epithet must communicate even less to him than it does to Billy.

"His real name was Leonard Slye," Billy says.

Deke's making a snake by twisting up his straw wrapper. He touches a drop of milk from the end of his straw to the paper and it begins to writhe. *We don't do that,* Billy should say—except he taught him this trick. He could tell the story of Laocoön and his sons, except all he really knows is the image of the naked man and naked boys, struggling with the serpent. The hydra, whatever. When Billy was little, he found the picture arousing—he spent lots of time looking at Greek and Roman statuary in the encyclopedia—but he hopes Deke might be spared. Basically, it's a fucked way to live. No pun intended. Though he also hopes the Aphrodite of Cyrene and whatnot won't do it for Deke either. Imagine a lifetime of lusting after the likes of Pamela Anderson. Wouldn't everybody of every persuasion be less unhappy if they all simply got fixed, like house pets? Lately, every time he uses his mother's serrated bread knife, he pictures himself cutting off his own penis.

Back on the highway, Deke's wide awake and whiny. "How come we have to go to Mommy's?"

Had Billy been calling it *Mommy's*—as opposed to *home*—or was this Deke's own formulation? "We're just going to clean up a little bit," he says. "Make things nice for her when she gets back."

"Is she going to be there?"

"Didn't I just say *when* she gets back?" He almost adds *Hello?* Kid either doesn't listen or doesn't think.

"Sor-*ry*." Deke's never been insolent before. Billy looks over and sees he's staring at his lap.

"*I*'m sorry," he says. "I didn't mean to sound impatient. I thought you understood that she's still in the hospital." Billy decided when they moved Cassie that it was simpler not to get into the whole thing of what a halfway house was. "But I think you'll be back home together before Christmas."

No answer. Billy looks over again. Deke's still staring down. Then he twists in his seat, wrenches at his door handle and tries to force the door open with his shoulder, but at sixty-five miles an hour, the wind resistance is too strong—and he's forgotten he has his seat belt on. Billy cries "Hey!" and darts his arm across to grab at Deke's door handle. A roar and rumble and shaking as the front wheel hits the warning strip of roughened pavement. Billy brakes hard, pulls over onto the shoulder and comes to a stop. "What the hell do you think you're doing?"

Deke glares at him. "I don't *want* to."

Billy can't pretend not to understand. "You have to realize," he says. Only now is his heart racing: the delayed adrenaline reaction that proves wise old Mother Nature's looking out for us. "When Mommy comes out of the hospital, she's going to be a lot better. The reason you sometimes had a bad time is because she was having such a bad time herself because she was sick. But she loves you so much."

"But I want to be with *you*."

Billy's heart begins to slow down. He looks over at Deke. The pale skin, through which a blue vein shows at his temple. The soft hair that should've been trimmed weeks ago. The ragged, scuffed sneakers Billy's been meaning to replace. So much need, and nobody else to help. He takes a deep breath, lets it out. "Well?" he says. "I'm here, right? I'm not going anywhere." Kid doesn't get it. Billy didn't get it himself, until just now.

The Wonders of the Invisible World

When the subway door's about to close, you hear these two tones, like the phoebe's call: three one. I tried to find it once on the clarinet, out of curiosity, and all it is, it's just a third. D down to B-flat, say. Yes, well, obviously the phoebe's call is sweet and breathy and organic and all that good stuff; I'm talking about the interval. And yes, I know it's cheap irony, this thing of juxtaposing urban and pastoral. What am I supposed to do, not notice it? And, again yes, I know the Robert Frost thing about how the phoebes wept or didn't weep or whatever the fuck. You know, what don't I know?

I know, for example, that my daughter now has a piano, a Yamaha, but a good Yamaha supposedly, and has begun taking lessons. Sometimes when I call, I'll hear the piano going. Lately Carrie won't talk to me, and Laura covers for her as gracefully as can be expected. *Oh, she's so earnest about her practicing, it's so dear to see it,* this and that. So I'll be getting the latest from Laura but really listening to Carrie playing "Lightly Row" or "Swans on the Lake," and sometimes reverting to "Chopsticks." Lots of fun, easy for everyone. And I know her teacher still uses the John Thompson book; Greenfield, Massachusetts, is a fucking backwater. Which of course is why it's basically good that she's growing up there and not here. Among other things, she stands a better chance of not getting an X-Acto knife held to the side of her neck and being told *Give it up, bitch,* which happened the other day to the woman who answers the phone for me and the two other assistant deans. When Laura told me that she and Walt planned to move to Greenfield, what could I say? After all, she and I had had a backwater of our own, though ours wasn't quite so Bedford Falls. We'd agreed that it was essential (we meant desirable) to have someplace to bring a kid to. If only on weekends, assuming we couldn't get out of the city for real. If we ever had a kid.

Our backwater was in this depressed part of Pennsylvania. Hey, *that* narrows it down. Two hours and fifty minutes, we used to tell people, not adding that this was from the GW Bridge. A beat-to-shit farmhouse on the last five acres of the original hundred; with our two salaries we could just about swing it. Gray asphalt shingles we were going to replace with clapboards. Among all the other plans. What ended up getting done was having the kid and ripping up the wall-to-wall carpeting. Okay, I'll stop with the hard-boiled tone. But the house and Carrie did go together. Laura must've thought so, too, since she chose it as the setting for her announcement. This was on a Thursday, in July. She called me at my work from her work and asked if we couldn't both get off early, drive out to the farm (as we called it) that afternoon and call in sick the next day. I said, "Absolutely. Fuck this." It was like ninety-five degrees, and when you looked along the street you saw brown air all the way up the sky. Which gives you an idea of how young I was, thinking we deserved better air than other people.

So we drove out and I cut the grass while she made dinner. I was finishing the last little bit by the toolshed when she appeared holding a tall glass in each hand as if she were—forget it, no stupid similes. She was a vision. A vision of herself. She handed me mine, then went and sat in a lawn chair with her legs tucked under her, bare feet pasted with grass blades. The air smelled of new-mown lawn, and every once in a while a phoebe whistled those two soft notes: three one. So am I wringing your heart yet? I took a sip and said, "Holy shit. If yours is as strong as mine, I hope you've finished the chopping and slicing."

"Don't worry," she said. "Enjoy it. You're going to have to be drinking for two for a while."

"What are you talking about?" I said.

And enough of that story.

The big news these days is that I've started fooling around with the clarinet again. In high school, I played in a Dixieland band that did "At the Jazz Band Ball" and "Midnight in Moscow," but in my junior year I sold the clarinet to buy an electric guitar and like an idiot gave away all my jazz records that weren't post-Parker. Even *Ambassador Satch*, the first album I ever bought, with all this amazing work by Edmond Hall. These days I buy nothing but early-jazz CDs, and some of the restorations sound so clear they bother me: I'm used to a hiss between me and the music. And for the last year or so I've been getting together with these guys on Thursday nights. Andy, a doctor in real life, plays okay trumpet (Punch Miller is his man), and we've got a good trombone player named James. I forget what he does; real estate or something. A pothead who thinks he's discreet, going to the bathroom two or three times a practice.

I'm playing better, I think, although I'm still more comfortable on the slower stuff. Thank God we all agree that "High Society" has been done to death. I've never actually mastered the Alphonse Picou solo, which maybe I should call the George Baquet solo—didn't he invent it? (It's so *me* to know this yet not be able to play the thing.) I'm supposedly this big purist, but my man is actually Pee Wee Russell. A Chicago guy. And white. *And* zero technique, which is what I really like about him: just a bunch of bleating, supposedly denoting passion and pathos.

We use the piano player's loft on Grand Street. He has a Steinway grand there, and his neighbors bang only if we go past eleven. He's a piece of work, this Mark. A partner at some law firm, not anybody I'd be likely to know if not for the music. Andy either, as far as that goes. To be an assistant dean isn't scruffy, exactly, but at my age it's getting there. A late bloomer, you could call me, if I were blooming. I've been trying to get through one more winter with this coat by walking around with my hands in my pockets, thereby keeping the fraying cuffs tucked out of sight, except the edges of the pockets are fraying, too. When Mark first told me his address, I said, "Ah, where the neon madmen climb," and he obviously thought I was a babbling burnout. He's got a sleek, dark-haired wife and a pretty little blond daughter named Margit. Second wife, first child: you know the deal. Margit is four (Carrie's now eight), and at bedtime she'll pad in barefoot in her nightie and listen for a minute, eyes only for Daddy. And he'll be sitting there at his Steinway in his pink oxford shirt, playing this Jimmy Yancey shit he's learned note for note.

We're still looking for drums—hard to find anyhow, but especially for this music—and string bass. We'd prefer not to go the tuba route. Bass sax might give things an interesting feel, though more New York 1924 than I personally care for. If we had drums and bass, Mark wouldn't have to be holding everything together on piano. But the Hot Five got along fine without drums and bass—though they did have banjo, not to mention Louis Armstrong instead of Andy Kroll—so I suppose it's not crucial.

Not crucial. Jesus, *I*'ll say.

Last Thursday I left Mark's a few minutes after eleven and took the E train uptown to meet Jane. (You must have seen this coming, you ladies especially. Yes, even in his desolation—O lost daughter! O new-mown lawn!—he's managed to get himself a new one. So now you know her name.) Jane had called me at work that afternoon: could I see her, that night, didn't matter how late, kind of important. After a couple hours at Mark's the subway makes you feel poor and put-upon. Across from me sat an old woman, dozing, her possessions tied with yellow nylon rope to a two-wheeled cart. White-crusted sores that looked like salt deposits on her swollen shins. I caught myself regarding her only as another disagreeable feature of the mise-en-scène and not as a fellow traveler to the grave. One more way you know you've been in New York too long. Or maybe just at Mark's too long. Stop after stop, the doors opened and made the phoebe sound, and each time I clutched my clarinet case reflexively, though no one got on. While we were packing up, James had slipped me a sinisterly slender joint—"For you and your lady sometime"—and I was spooked about having it hidden in the case; it had been years since I'd carried anything around. Probably I should've been touched by James's friendly overture rather than creeped out by his inserting himself into my sexual life. Years ago, Laura and I had tried to make love stoned, and I couldn't control my mind. This was the time my brother and his grad-student cutie visited us at the farm. The two of them on the futon in the spare room. Jesus, the amount of stuff we owned back then. The lawn mower, the hibachi, the croquet set, the outdoor furniture, the *indoor* furniture. Most of it ended up going to a Scranton auctioneer who wore a cowboy hat and talked in a Bronx-like honk. I'll think of his name in a second. It occurred to me, sitting there in the subway car, that most of these things, still solid and serviceable, must persist somewhere in the world. In displaced self-pity, I reached across and stuck a five-dollar bill under the yellow nylon cord on the woman's cart. Which made me feel no better. Swapper Sam, that was the guy. We'd been regulars at his Saturday-night junk auction. Little thinking his box truck, with his smiley caricature painted on the side, would ever back up to our kitchen door.

I got off at Lex, the station deep, deep underground. I associate the name Lexington with the color green. Which, come to think of it, isn't such an uncanny mental leap. But Lexington, Massachusetts, aside, I also think of Lexington, Virginia, and Lexington, Kentucky, as green places. Like Old Lyme, Connecticut. Hell, Greenfield, Massachusetts. So it always seems to me that Lexington, not Park, should be the avenue with the grass down the middle. It was Laura's mnemonic that taught me the order of the avenues: Fat Men Piss Less, Fifth Madison Park Lex. A side of Laura that Greenfield will never know. The other day she told me there's now a place in Greenfield where you can get real H&H bagels; did you ever hear anything so sweet? I walked to the Third Avenue end of the platform, belatedly worrying about what Jane meant by *kind of important*, and belatedly wondering if she'd been counting on me to worm it out of her on the phone. I took the long, long stairs instead of the escalator, little as I felt like it. Good for the buns. A thing one thinks about these days.

The plan was, have a quick drink, talk about whatever this was, then get her home to her husband. You saw *this* coming too, no? His name is Jonathan. A something at WNYC, unless it's BAI. I need hardly add that I'm the Older Man. Back when Laura and I would sometimes have an adulterous couple out to the farm for a weekend—my brother Miller and, what was the name, Alix, were one of several—we used to feel parental. Well . . . what's the expression I'm looking for? Something in between *tempus fugit* and *mutatis mutandis.*

I found the place okay—a name like J. P. Donleavy's, Something Something Somebody's—and I just stood there staring at the door with its etched, frosted-glass panels. Not in the fucking mood. A panhandler played doorman, jingling coins in a cardboard cup. Shivering. To avoid his glance, I looked up: the sky was that corrupted pink you get from streetlights and neon in whatever combination. Snowflakes fell out of the pinkness, though not enough to amount to anything. You could hear Billie Holiday inside singing "Ain't Nobody's Business If I Do." So you had to give them a couple of bonus points for playing the Decca material: the Columbia stuff was a cliché, the Verve too depressing. So how much, I wondered, would their good taste inflate the price of their drinks? With that five gone to the subway woman, which I now thought was stupid—it might see her through, what, half a day?—I had twelve dollars, three tokens and maybe eight bucks in my checking account until payday tomorrow. I stuffed a dollar bill into the panhandler's cup and was told God bless you. I told him it was a cold night, which he already knew and which ungraciously implied that I wouldn't have been so munificent otherwise. Hey, you can't come out of every human transaction smelling like a rose.

I stepped inside and my glasses instantly fogged; dead Billie now sounded alarmingly loud above the chattering voices of the living. I stuck my gloves in my pocket, wiped the inside of each lens with a pinkie, and there it all was, exactly what the name and the frosted-glass door panels promised: the tiny square floor tiles, the polished brass, the polyurethaned oak, the stamped-tin ceiling painted glossy ivory. Had this evocation of whatever it was supposed to be an evocation of ever gladdened a single heart? Have I mentioned that I fucking hate New York City?

I spotted Jane sitting at a square table with a white tablecloth, on which was centered a clear glass bowl with a gardenia blossom floating. Perhaps to go with Billie Holiday, perhaps not. But it suggested—unless the mood forbade it—a bon mot to get things rolling. I would gesture at the gardenia and say, *Hey, this must be Lady Day Day.* No, too obscure. Was that even a gardenia?

"Sorry, you waiting long?" I said. "Cab got stuck in all this traffic coming up Lex." Will you find this pretense of being a cabber-about-town less contemptible when I tell you I kept it up partly for Jane's sake? It seemed sad that her Older Man should be one who had to take subways. How many Older Men would she be vouchsafed in this life? Jane was appealing—the overbite, the boy haircut, the Trotsky glasses—but nonstandard. But appealing. Christ, she could get all the Older Men she wanted. Some of the younger ones, too. I seemed to be dishing out displaced self-pity to all comers tonight.

But what was she saying? "Say again?" I said, and put my index finger behind my ear as if the loud music was the problem.

"I *said*," she said, "how can you go *up* Lex?"

"What am I saying? Up Park." I didn't go into my riff about how Park should be Lexington. "Here, where can I stash this? On the floor, I guess. Don't let me get hammered and forget it, okay?"

I set the clarinet case by my chair, craned around looking for a coatrack, then remembered to lean down and kiss her. She offered a cheek. I thought, *Definitely not the Lady Day thing*, then went and hung up my coat, arriving back at the table just as a waiter in a white apron set before Jane a grotesquely large snifter with a thimbleful of brandy in the bottom. I sat down and said, "You have Maker's Mark?"

"Gee, I think we're out," he said. I'm far from the only bullshit artist in New York.

"No problem," I said. "Jack Daniel's? Over ice?" *On the rocks* sounds old-time, like ordering a Rob Roy.

"So," I said.

"This has to be quick," she said. "I'm officially at the movies with Mariana."

"All ears," I said.

"It's weird," she said. "I feel like more of a shit lying about *that* than actually—you know."

"Well, better safe than sorry."

She looked down into her glass and said, "Yeah, right."

"So," I said.

"So," she said. She took a deep breath and let it out. "So yours truly thinks she's pregnant."

"You're shitting me," I said. "What do you mean you *think?*"

"Well, for one thing I'm like three weeks late. And I'm *never* late. Plus I've been sick to my stomach the last two mornings. I went out this afternoon and I bought one of those pregnancy things, you know, at the drugstore. Except I'm too scared to use it."

"Unbelievable," I said.

"Really," she said.

"How could it have happened, though?"

"If I knew *that,*" she said, "it wouldn't have happened. Obviously. I don't know. Some stupid thing, I'm sure."

Billie Holiday was singing "Baby Get Lost." I know; I didn't believe it either.

"Well, look," I said. "Let's not panic. For one thing, you've been under a lot of stress. Which can make people late. Which could also upset your stomach. Anyway, even if anything *was* wrong, I don't think, as nearly as I can remember, I don't think you'd be feeling sick in the morning this early on, would you?"

She raised her eyes and gave me the look I deserved.

My Jack Daniel's arrived.

I looked over at the rows and rows of bottles behind the bar, presumably doubled by a mirror. I looked back at Jane. She was looking down into her glass.

I said, "Whose would it be?"

She shrugged. "Up for grabs," she said.

"Have you told Jonathan?"

She shook her head, still looking down.

"Have you thought what you might do?"

"I'm a married woman," she said. "Married women get pregnant, they have a baby, right?"

"Yes, but when—"

"I mean, that's what you *do*, right?"

"But isn't this a tad more complicated?" I said.

She shook her head, still staring down. Not no to my question, just no.

"Look," I said. "First thing, you need to go to a doctor. Forget the kit thing. Until you actually see a doctor and actually find out something concrete, we don't even know what we're talking about."

Now she looked at me. "I know what we're talking about."

I woke up Friday morning, not to the alarm itself, but to the click you get just before the alarm goes off; I reached out and preempted it. Eight o'clock. In Greenfield, Carrie must have been out in the winter air, waiting for the school bus. Bundled up, I hoped. For all the good my hoping did. And on Eldridge Street, a twenty-three-year-old woman, vomiting perhaps, perhaps thinking, *Dear God, what now.*

I lay there, pain in my head, pain in my back, and stared at the ceiling fixture I would never have chosen: convex disc of frosted glass with this kind of wheat-looking design around the edge. I thought, *Surely there must be some good somewhere in the world that wouldn't exist if not for you.*

Well, Carrie, of course.

Problematic.

"How the hell do you live?" I'd asked Jane during our first long talk. Like a plutocrat indignant over slum conditions and about to start pressing ten-dollar bills into trembling palms. Jonathan, she said, made a little money each time they aired one of his pieces; that plus what she made working part-time in Graduate Records got them through. Later, when we'd begun taking cabs to my place at noontime, she told me Jonathan sometimes moved a little coke for people. One look at my shithole of an apartment should've put me in context for her. But maybe after Eldridge Street, Thompson Street looked passable. If you were twenty-three. Middle-aged lovers, listen up: if you're too depressed to change your sheets, at least stick the pillowcases in with the clothes you drop off on the way to work. The fresh-laundered smell will tell her, if only subliminally, that you're hanging onto your self-regard.

That first afternoon, in a student bar stinking of beer and pizza, I'd bent her ear about what I called "my band." She'd said, "Oh, neat." No italics, no exclamation point. "Did you know Woody Allen was into that?"

I knew.

"Do you believe he really did all that stuff to the little girl? I don't."

"I believe anything of anybody," I'd said. I mean, who had the luxury to give a fuck about Woody Allen?

"Ooh," she'd said. "Cynicism alert."

"Myself included," I'd said.

"I assumed," she'd said.

She, in turn, had bent my ear about how she wanted to transfer to NYU to do her thesis with some guy who'd done a biography of Cotton Mather. She hated our department's Early American guy, who—horrors!—had made a pass at one of her friends.

"Pretty late in the game," I'd said. "You know, to be changing."

"Sometimes people commit before they know what they really want," she'd said. I read this as being about her and her husband.

"I'll drink to that," I'd said, then thought to add, "he said tritely."

She wanted to do her thesis specifically on *The Wonders of the Invisible World.* Some feminist take, as far as I could make out. At least she wasn't deconstructing it, or I guess maybe she was. "It's like he *wrote* the thing, but as he's writing it you can tell he doesn't *want* to write it?" she'd said, setting down her beer to pull one of the straps of her tank top back onto her shoulder. "And of course he ends up getting incredible grief for it anyway."

"Least he had his fifteen minutes," I'd said. "You know, I'm embarrassed not to know this, but what *are* the wonders of the invisible world?"

"Well, basically devils," she'd said.

I rolled onto my side, worked my legs over the edge of the mattress and sat up. My headache seemed to balance my backache, as intellect balances emotion in the well-regulated soul. The one pain didn't exactly cancel out the other, but having *both* ensured that I wouldn't be homing in on just one, so there was that to be thankful for. I decided to skip the shower for fear warm water would make the backache better, which would make the headache seem worse. The way things were shaping up, I wouldn't need to be date-ready. Which didn't excuse me from shaving, though I wondered fleetingly (being half-awake) if it did. I went into the bathroom, ran some hot water and washed my face, trying not to look at Mr. Detestable. Then pushed the top of the can of Colgate: white lather came hissing out into a globule on my fingertips. The usual childish thought that this was like ejaculation. The related thought of bad boys in my high school masturbating their Adam's apples and making spit appear at their pursed lips. Particularly unwelcome thoughts this morning.

Obviously, if Jane did the sensible thing *(I know what we're talking about)*, one should offer to cover it, considering her meager budget. *Their* meager budget. I pictured limp bills tucked into a coffee can. A Maxwell House can, in honest workaday blue. But how does one make such an offer? How, for that matter, would one swing it on one's own meager budget if the offer was accepted? Beg off on child support for a month? I mean, since old Walt seemed to have things so well in hand up there in Greenfield. The alternative was unthinkable: another child of mine in the world, more lost to me even than Carrie, secretly scrutinized by its mother for signs of my features twitching up out of its generic baby face, as if in a horror-movie transformation. On the one hand, life forever with a mystery child; on the other, an abortion forever hidden from your husband. Not a choice I'd care to make. And guess what.

To dress and drink coffee by, I stuck in a Jimmie Noone CD. He's always intimidated me, and the idea, crudely put, is that if I listen every morning I'll somehow absorb Jimmie Noone, like learning French in your sleep. Of course it might also help to fucking practice. I was flipping through my shirts—the white with maroon stripes? the Classic Fit Poplin from the Gap?— when "My Daddy Rocks Me" came on, Jimmie Noone backing some tenth-rate singer. Chippie Hill or somebody. *I looked at the clock, the clock struck one / I said Daddy ain't we got fun.* And I thought it would be a natural for Andy to sing—just change "Daddy" to "Mama"—so I hustled into the living room to put my clarinet together and figure out what key they were in. Not because Andy would sing it in her key necessarily. Just so I could say, Well, *they* do it in whatever.

But where the bloody hell was the clarinet? Not on the table where I've taken to dumping stuff. Not in the coat closet where I used to put it. Not among the clutter on the floor. Bedroom closet, for some reason? Then of course it hit me: You left the thing in the goddamn bar, for Christ's sake. Fucking J. M. Barrie's, whatever it was. Third Avenue and something. I remembered sticking the case under the table, and I must've just up and walked out of there without it. Not hammered, by any means, but a decent buzz. Oh, Jesus, and marijuana in there, too. My name and address on the little card hanging off the handle.

Phone book. Except what *was* the goddamn name? Call Jane and ask? Right. Eight-thirty in the morning anyway; place wouldn't open up until lunchtime. Great. Well, this day was certainly shaping up. Christ, if only I'd left when Jane did instead of—well, no use. What I'd told her was, I hadn't had any dinner and I wanted to get a burger or something before the kitchen closed. What I'd told myself was, another Jack Daniel's wouldn't hurt a bit. Moreover, since we were both going downtown, I would've had to offer to drop her, in the cab I meant her to think I'd be taking. And moreover: my staying behind put her on notice that she was in this alone.

So the thing to do now was just get in to work. Jesus, five hundred dollars right down the toilet. I put on my overcoat, patted the pockets: the right-hand pocket was soft and lumpy, the left-hand pocket hard and flat. Terrific. So I hadn't lost either my five-dollar street gloves (*What, lost your mittens? You naughty kittens!*) or my *Portable Blake,* a gift from Jane. Back when love was young, a few months ago. I didn't have the heart to tell her I had an old Laurel edition kicking around, with everything anybody would reasonably want to read. The heart: ha.

Out on the street it seemed even colder than last night: sky clear blue, wind stinging. My breath made steam and my face was stiff and numb before I even got to the corner. At the bottom of the subway stairs, out of the wind, I stopped and pawed back my frayed left coat sleeve with my gloved right hand: quarter to nine. The usual line at the token booth, people looking over their shoulders toward the platform, huffing out their breath (no steam down here in the human-heated air), as an old geezer at the window took his sweet time over some bullshit with the token clerk involving a senior-citizen pass or whatever the hell it was. I felt smug breezing by them with my little store—three tokens left from the ten I'd bought on Wednesday—then realized that of course the fuckers count on that, on people like me thinking they're better than the down-and-outs who can only buy one or two at a time. They use it to divide us. Which doesn't sound so reasonable now that I write it down.

On the platform, people were packed shoulder to shoulder, meaning either a train coming any second or trouble on the line. I pushed through the turnstile, hearing in my head, as usual, *Drrrop the coin right into the slot/You gotta hear somethin' that's really hot.* Plus I have this thing where I always have to get through without the turnstile touching my ass when it comes around. I assume my unconscious thinks the spokes are dicks. Dicks going at your ass and another dick (the clarinet) in your mouth. No wonder you have trouble with women. Though I suppose I should cut myself some slack about the clarinet, since just about every other instrument is also a dick, no? I mean, the electric guitar is a well-known dick. The real interpretive problem this morning wasn't why I liked sticking a clarinet in my mouth, but why I had, in effect, thrown it away. Now, generally, leaving something behind someplace means either (a) you wanted to get rid of it or (b) you didn't want to go. I'd guess (a) over (b): after Billie Holiday they'd started Ella Fitzgerald, and I was only too glad to clear out of there. Okay, so let's agree that the clarinet *is* a dick: then you get something like *Wants to abandon his responsibilities as a man.* Like I say, what don't I know.

I'll give you an absolutely textbook instance of (b) that leaps to mind, the one where you don't want to go and what you leave behind is a stand-in for yourself. This happened the time my brother Miller came to New York for MLA with that graduate student. Alix. Big hair and tight jeans, but ultra-large glasses denoting seriousness: you could see why Miller bought the package. Miller was the charismatic Lacanian of his department; I was the dead-ender who had cannily crossed over into administration to become a rising young hack. We brought them out to Pennsylvania for the weekend, and it was painful to listen to him on the phone with Felice and the kids back in Indiana. After Miller got us stoned, this Alix and I locked eyes a couple of times, which I hoped Laura didn't notice. Which was *all* that happened. At any rate, when Laura and I and Carrie (she was three) came out again the following weekend, I was straightening up the spare room and found a copy of *Snow White* (Donald Barthelme's, I mean) with Alix's name inside. The old paperback with the naked girl on the cover whose buttocks had been blurred for decency, so naturally your eyes went right to the blur. On this copy, somebody had recloven the cleft in fine-point felt-tip. *Ah so*, I thought. But I was a faithful husband then. That copy of *Snow White* is on my shelf right now, next to *The Narrow Road to the Deep North and Other Travel Sketches*, which I might as well stop kidding myself I'm ever going to read. The *Snow White* Laura ended up with, in the Division of the Things, had been mine.

And since we're on the subject, there's one other story that goes with this Alix. One of those nights when they were out at the farm, it got to be Carrie's bedtime and Laura was holding her in the wicker armchair, about to read *The Tale of Squirrel Nutkin.* "Oh, Laura, could *I*?" said Alix. She'd plunked down on the couch between me and Miller. "That is just *such* a great book. It's like—*boundaries*."

"You'd have to ask Carrie," Laura said. Which I thought was fucking brilliant. We'd had drinks before dinner and wine with. (House rule: the dope came out only after beddy-bye.)

"Carrie?" said Alix. "Would you let me read *Squirrel Nutkin* to you? That's about my favorite book."

"No, I want *Daddy* to," Carrie said.

"You want *me* to?" I said. "Your mom's already got you."

"I want *you* to get me."

Laura rested her cheek against the top of Carrie's head, closed her eyes, smiled and said, "Loves her daddy."

"Pretty mutual," I said. I got up off the couch, knelt by the wicker chair and put my arms around the both of them, and just then old Alix could go fuck herself, her and her nice ass and her little eye games.

Alix, anyway. At some point one stopped hearing about her from Miller, and that was all she wrote for Alix. Call her a distant early warning. It was about a year later that Mickey crossed my path. Michelle, really: she'd renamed herself at age ten because the Beatles song infuriated her. One suspects that if it hadn't been Mickey it would've been somebody else, but at the time being with her seemed worth—oh, *boring.* To cut a long story short: there my wife and daughter are, in Greenfield, Massachusetts, and here *I* am.

I walked to the far downtown end of the platform where the crowd thinned out some, though even here I could've reached out and touched: two probable secretaries, white, each pretty enough to go to bed with once; a muttering black man, my age, whose checked pants were trodden ragged at his heels; a black teenager with a Raiders cap and a Triple F.A.T. Goose down coat. To assume that such a coat must have been bought with drug money was unworthy of me, a good man. I smelled human shit, glanced around, spotted the pile in the corner where the big trash bin met the wall. A residuum of modesty? Or a reversion to wary animality, shitting in a spot where you couldn't be blindsided? I stood in the stink and looked back up the platform at them all. Some read newspapers, others fat paperbacks. A few ventured to the edge and peered past me into the tunnel. But most of them watched others, looking away when the others saw. I took out *The Portable Blake.* Holding it up to read meant exposing my fraying cuffs. But I'd be straphanging any minute now, so what the fuck. And what the fuck anyway. I needed (meaning wanted) something between me and all of them. *How do you know but ev'ry Bird that cuts the airy way,* I read, *Is an immense world of delight, clos'd by your senses five?* Like I could give a shit. Eventually a train came along and took us all in. Shut its doors with that phoebe sound and brought each of us to where we did what we had to do, here in New York City.

I was going to leave it at that because I liked the cadence and the way it came around again to the phoebe thing. But you can't have all these loose ends. Did she go ahead with the abortion? Did he ever get his clarinet back? Or, I mean, you *can*, but. Plus, there are these two other moments I want to set down before I forget them. Or set down in hopes of forgetting them, whichever. Same principle as sticking stuff on a floppy that you don't want cluttering up your hard drive, if that's not too techno a model for that immense world of delight, the human mind.

Here's a short one. This is the first time Jane and I lay face-to-face. She runs a hand down my spine, then back up again to cup my shoulder blade in her palm, as if it were a breast, and says, "This is probably really a mistake. But I just really want to."

"I know," I say. Question remains: *Why* does she want to? Is it simply that being nonstandard has fucked up her self-esteem? Is it dismissive to add that her father deserted the family when she was twelve? The implication being . . .

"Oh, bullshit," she says. "You don't know the first thing. You are such a *fake*. Will you just please relax and make love to me?"

Did I give myself a whore's bath before? Get hammered after? Can't say. That other moment I wanted to put here is the same way: nothing before, nothing after. Also in bed, I guess a couple of weeks later.

She says, "I'm sorry I told you that thing."

"Thing," I say.

"About the coke," she says. "I shouldn't have told you."

"What am I going to do, have him arrested?"

"What I mean is, it's his business," she says. "And possibly my business. But it isn't anything you have to know."

"I care about you," I say. "I want to know what your life is like."

She rolls her head from side to side on the pillow. "Uh-*uh*," she says. "You're not my husband. If we even lose track of *that*—I don't know, forget it, it's stupid to even talk about ethics in a situation like this." She flops her naked body across me facedown, to stretch for her backpack on the floor (her buttocks, for all her nonstandardness, are more perfect than any I'm likely to touch again in this life), and comes back up with her hairbrush. She flicks two brisk strokes at her left temple, then flings the brush backhand against the wall. *My* wall. My landlord's wall. "This is so stupid," she says. "I don't know what integrity I think I'm trying to keep up. Why don't you hit me?"

"You're doing enough of a job on yourself," I say. I look at the wall. A tiny mark that might have been there already. "I wish we could go away," I say. "And just not come back."

"Please," she says. "This is the one thing I promised myself. Not to get into discussions about how I'm going to leave Jonathan and yat-ta-dat-ta-da. If this is going to be about sitting around saying I wish this and I wish that, it's like forget it, okay?" She gives me a quick, wide smile—the kind of facial cue an ape might use to signal submission. But there is no submission.

Now, maybe that right there is the cadence you want: *But there is no submission.* Over and out. God knows it's cold enough.

But I still haven't told how it all came out. After that we can worry about cadences. So under Loose Ends let's put (a) the clarinet and (b) Jane's little problem. (You want cold? Now that's *cold.*) Oddly enough, I did get the clarinet back. What happened was, I took the subway up at lunchtime, found the place, and sure enough: guy had it stashed behind the bar. He asked if I had i.d. and I thought, *Well, this is where you get busted,* but what was I going to do? I showed him my driver's license, he looked at the name tag and handed me the case. I opened it up, nodded when I saw all the pieces of the clarinet in their molded recesses, lifted out the bell and looked underneath. The joint was gone. The guy behind the bar had a white apron, clean except for a brown-red stain shaped like Mississippi. His blond hair was combed straight back. "Something missing?" he said. One more confrontation I wasn't up to.

Which brings us, by commodious vicus of recirculation— hey, the fun never stops—to (b). So here's the thing that happened today. Monday. No need to backtrack and give a blow-by-blow of the whole weekend: it got over with. Phone didn't ring once. Which really isn't a complaint. It wasn't until late this afternoon that I finally heard from Jane.

"I'm sorry to be bothering you at work," she said.

"What are you *talking* about," I said. "How *are* you? What's going on?"

She said, "I just wanted to tell you that you don't have any-thing to worry about if you were worried. I got my period."

"Thank God," I said. I fetched a sigh, too, but got my hand over the phone in time to muffle it. "That's really good," I said. "I *was* worried, to tell you the truth. That would've been just—"

"And," she said, "I also wanted to tell you. I don't think I'm going to be seeing you anymore, okay? So. It's like, I'll proba-bly, we'll probably run into each other around school and everything, but I really don't want to talk to you, like have a conversation with you. And I don't want you to call me. Okay?"

"Look," I said—but as I said "Look" she said " 'Bye" and hung up. I hung up too and said "Okay" out loud. I took a deep breath and let it out. Steady now.

I looked around and there it all was: file cabinets, books on shelves, cloth wall hanging of a vulpine Elvis in white jumpsuit, a lei around his neck. Camp fun from long ago, a gift from Laura, and what it was still doing up I couldn't imagine. Pic-ture of Carrie, in stand-up Plexiglas, smiling with all her hurt radiance, holding a kitten whose name I knew to be Mittens. As in *What, lost your.* I took another breath, let it out. Okay. See, the temptation would be to dwell on the possibility that she was lying about her period and had taken steps on her own. For all I know, she was calling from the pay phone at some clinic. And had been counting on me to see through her bullshit in the nick of time.

Vigil

It was the woman doctor who finally came out and told us we could go in. She said Bonnie came through the surgery fine, as far as they could tell, and not to be shocked when we saw her. We followed the doctor into the intensive care and over to a bed with an IV bag hanging over it. Bonnie lay flat on her back, in a white gown with short sleeves; they'd taped the needle end of the tubing to the back of her hand, and they had the hand strapped to the side rail in case she tried to move. But she wasn't moving: you had to look close to see her chest rise and fall. She had another tube up her nose, the whole top of her head was wrapped in bandages and her face was so swollen that she looked the way she had as a baby.

I picked up her other hand, stroked it and held it. The hand didn't do anything back. I said, "Daddy's here, honey. You're going to be fine." Nothing.

Dave Senior wouldn't come near the bed. Being her husband, it must've been even harder on him. He turned to the doctor and said, "*This* looks great. When the hell are you going to know what's going on?"

The doctor put up a hand, like she was making to guard herself. "Not before tomorrow," she said. "At the earliest." She was a small woman, pretty enough, with lines at the corners of her eyes and dark circles. To me, she seemed young for a doctor—she might've been forty—but for her I suppose it was a different story. I know when I was forty, I felt like an old man. Sylvia had run off to Phoenix with her boss and left it up to Bonnie either to go out there or to stay with me in Clinton. A teenage girl, with her school and all her friends? What do you imagine she's going to choose? So I had Bonnie to look after and the house to try to keep up, all the while putting in ten, fifteen hours a week overtime so I could set something aside for her college. But that's years and years ago now. I retired, sold the house and bought my little place up in Shelburne Falls. And Bonnie finally settled down and married Dave; they live over in Madison, not ten minutes from where we lived in Clinton. Sylvia and I will talk a couple times a year by phone, and I'll even chat with Harold if he happens to pick up. Hell, by now they've been married longer than we were. She claims to have cut way back on her drinking, which I think was half her problem. And I really *am* an old man now, though Bonnie says seventy-two's not old anymore. I don't *feel* old these days. I'm healthy (knock wood), I keep active and I'm not strapped for money. That's my good way of looking at it.

I left Dave in there with Bonnie and went back to the waiting room to use the pay phone. I'd managed to put off calling Sylvia for a whole day, just about. In the first place, Dave couldn't even get hold of me until a couple hours after he got word of the accident. (I'd been over trying to get Scotty Williams's ArcticCat running so he could put it in the paper; he hasn't been well the last year or so.) Then the drive down delayed things another couple hours. I meant to make the call as soon as I got to the hospital, but I found out they still had some tests to do, and by the time they finished up it was after midnight. Only ten o'clock Sylvia's time, but she would've been up the whole night worrying. I could've called this morning, but they started getting Bonnie ready at seven and I wasn't about to wake Sylvia up out of a dead sleep at five a.m. Why

Dave Senior left it for me to pass the word to his mother-in-law is another question.

So at least now I wouldn't be calling with all bad news, but it scared me to think what a chance I'd been taking. Imagine having to call to say Bonnie was gone—no preparation, nothing. I waited for a colored man to get done with the phone and tried not to listen—something about a transfusion. Then he went back and sat with his wife. It being a workday, we were the only ones in the waiting room. They were a nice-appearing couple, both of them starting to get some white hairs. She would look at the floor, then up at the clock. He kept hold of her hand.

Sylvia's phone out there doesn't ring like a regular phone; it sounds thinner and beepier. She says Harold likes to have everything modern. When she answers, she always says *Martin residence.*

"Syl, this is Len," I said. "I'm sorry to bother you. Now, Bonnie's all right, but I wanted to let you know she *is* in the hospital."

"Oh my Christ."

"No, now, she's going to be fine. The doctor—what happened, apparently somebody broadsided her when she was pulling out into traffic and they had to—they operated on her this morning and the doctor says she came through it fine."

"Oh my Christ. What are you saying?"

But all in all she took it okay; a couple more *Oh my Christ*s and that was about the extent of it. She even thought to ask who was looking after Dave Junior and how Dave Senior was holding up. I said he was doing fine. The only time he'd really started carrying on—I didn't get into this with Sylvia—was when he told me that where Bonnie was pulling out of was a motel entrance. As I told him, she was probably looking for a phone.

"You might as well sit tight for the time being," I said. "There's nothing much to do here at this point. Now, when they bring her home—"

"Are you crazy?" Sylvia said. "Are you out of your mind? You think there's any way I wouldn't be with my *daughter*?"

I could've said something about that. But I just said, "Well, I'll be here. If I'm not in the waiting room, I'm either at Dave and Bonnie's or I'm just down getting a cup of coffee."

"I hope you're eating," she said.

After I got done, the colored fellow's wife got up and made a call and came away shaking her head. They talked together for a minute, then went over to the elevators and pressed the DOWN button. *Ding*, and the doors slid apart to take them in. I don't know where the rest of the afternoon went to. The TV was on, a game show and then a talk show and then what I guess was a soap opera. I'm not much of a one for TV. Books, movies—anything where you just sit. Dave and Bonnie gave me a VCR my last birthday—a nice thought—but after I watched a half a dozen movies the novelty wore off.

The window had a view of the parking lot and a loading dock, and eventually it started to get dark outside. I was looking out, watching a UPS man hand boxes out of the back of his truck, when the pink lights came on.

I talked Dave Senior out of spending the night on the waiting-room sofa, thank God, and followed him to his sister's in North Madison to pick up Little Dave, then on to the house. When he unlocked the kitchen door, I got a smell of onion and garbage. They had dirty dishes piled up on the counter and toys all thrown around: trucks and hot rods and robots and space aliens. "You mind watching him while I try to get some of this shit squared away?" he said. "Housekeeping hasn't exactly been at the top of the list." But the truth is, their house doesn't generally look much better. Of course Bonnie goes to work, which Sylvia never did until Bonnie started seventh grade. (And we know what happened next.)

Dave Junior's three, and the way he gets more keyed up the tireder he gets reminds me of Bonnie at that age. I settled him down and let him pick out a storybook—not knowing what I was letting myself in for. I took him on my lap, opened up the book and, lo and behold, they had pictures but no words, the idea being you had to make up your own story. I thought, *Heaven help you if you don't tell him this thing the way his mama does.*

"Look at the mouse," I said. "He woke up the cat, see, and now look what happened, the cat's chasing him." It went along that while the cat's chasing the mouse a dog starts chasing *him,* then they knock over a big cake and that gets a man chasing the three of them, and so forth and so on. I could see now that it was a house-that-Jack-built kind of idea, though it would've been nice if they'd let you know beforehand so you could do a better job. But the way I told it seemed to suit him, except that one time he got impatient and turned the page before I was done talking about the picture.

Dave Senior came in from the kitchen. "How you making out?"

"We're doing fine," I said. "I think Grampa made a hit." I roughed up Little Dave's hair. It's so soft, softer, I'd say, than Bonnie's used to be. "You're going to see Gramma pretty soon," I told him. "You'll like that, I betcha. Gramma be plenty glad to see *you,* I can tell you that."

"Do you remember Nonny?" Dave Senior said.

"Yes." Little Dave has this way of saying his words exactly.

Dave Senior shook his head. "I would doubt he remembers. Let's go, partner. Past your bedtime."

I did this and that in the living room, piling up magazines, getting all the toys in one place. But the whole time I kept thinking, *If only*. You know, if only she hadn't stopped off there. If only she would've just pulled out five seconds later, or five seconds earlier. A good way to drive yourself crazy. You imagine all the things that could make five seconds' difference: fishing around for car keys, fiddling with your seat belt. Or, if she did stop off to call somebody, the phone ringing once or twice more. I could picture her turning the rearview mirror to fix her hair for a second, then taking another couple seconds to get the mirror back right. But what in the world was she doing out that way in the first place? Her supervisor told Dave Senior she went home sick—a turkey sandwich that didn't agree with her. She wasn't heading straight home, though, because where it happened was on the Post Road, almost over into Westbrook. She probably had an errand of some sort, then stopped off to make a phone call; motels generally have a pay phone outside the office.

I was trying to find where they kept their vacuum when Dave Senior came in and said he'd changed his mind and was going to take a shower and head back to the hospital. So I did my little song and dance again. The best way he could help Bonnie was to keep his own strength up, and so forth and so on. I told him, "She's not going to know you're out there, Dave. For all she knows right now, you could be on the planet Mars." Although I personally believe people *do* know. You hear of too many cases where they wake up and they can tell you what everybody said. But what was more important? Her maybe having that little extra boost now, or him being able to hold himself together over the next who knows how long?

I asked if he wanted the TV. He said he didn't care, but it didn't take him any time at all to get involved in some hospital program—not what I would've picked to get my mind off things—where a bad girl seemed to be making a play for a married doctor. So that when the phone rang he jumped a foot. He listened for a second, then said, "Hang on, I'll let you talk to Len," and held out the phone to me. It was Sylvia, calling from the airport out there. She couldn't find a nonstop to either New York or Boston, so she was about to get on a plane for Atlanta, where she'd put up overnight and fly to New York in the morning and then hire a rental car. I hated to think what all this was going to set old Harold back.

"Be careful driving," I said. "Just take your time."

"Hah," she said. "You'd just as soon I didn't come at all. You think I won't be on good behavior."

"That's not so," I said.

"Hah. You never were much of a liar."

I could've said something about that, too.

When the commercials came on, Dave Senior looked over. "I get you a cold one, Pop? I could sure as hell use one."

"Guess you could twist my arm," I said. I was glad he felt like he could call me Pop. His own father died years ago; from what I can gather, he was hell on wheels when he drank. They say it's one in ten; seems like about one in two sometimes.

We cracked our beers and I got him talking about Little Dave and what he could and couldn't do—lately he was trying to learn to tie his shoes—until the hospital program came back on. I remember when Bonnie was about four, she used to tie her shoes with a special knot she made up herself, and you had a hell of a time undoing it. I'm ashamed now to think back, because I sometimes lost my patience. Not knowing that afterward the time would seem so short. On the TV, the bad girl tossed her head to get her hair out of her face, then clinked her glass with the married doctor.

"Pop, can I ask you something?" Dave Senior said. "What do you honestly—I don't know, shit, forget it. You're not really the person to ask."

"Hell, go ahead and ask. What is it?"

"Well, I guess you knew we'd been having trouble."

"No, I had no idea." Though Bonnie had said some things. He took a long swallow that finished off his beer, and put the empty can on the table next to him. Then he turned back to the television, so I did, too. That girl tossed her head again and gave the doctor a look, and I wouldn't have been in that doctor's shoes for a million dollars.

"Doesn't seem like you're too curious," he said.

"I don't want to stick my nose in your business," I said. "But if—"

"Nope. Nope, I think you're smart," he said. "I think we might as well leave it right there."

He turned in after the news, the best thing he could've done for himself. I found sheets and blankets in the linen closet and pulled out the hide-a-bed, but I wasn't tired—I mean I wasn't sleepy—so I put the TV back on with the sound low, hoping that might do the trick. Letterman had some actress on, and the two of them kidded back and forth. I'm guessing she was an actress; he didn't say. The point was she was young and pretty, had a lovely figure, full of fun. Something to keep old men watching TV.

I got disgusted and went out to the kitchen for another beer, in hopes that might put me under. But I noticed there was no milk for the morning, and not much of anything else in the icebox. Pudding snacks, yogurts, hot sauce, jar of dill spears, open can of black olives. I lifted the lid of a covered saucepan—leftover Spaghetti-O's—then hunted up my jacket, wallet and car keys.

Everything's changed in this part of the world, but you were bound to hit a 7-Eleven or something down on the Post Road. Turned out I didn't even need to go that far: the Mobil station on the corner had a Mini-Mart, pretty well stocked. I picked up a half gallon of milk, plus a pint of half-and-half as an extra treat for the coffee. A dozen eggs, a package of bacon. Quart of grapefruit juice. Loaf of bread, pound of butter. And a six-pack of Bud Light so Dave wouldn't run short. I put it all on my debit card, and stuck the receipt in my shirt pocket so I wouldn't forget to write it in my checkbook. That's the damn problem with those cards.

Then I figured since I was out, I might as well swing by and have a look at where it happened. A motel on the Post Road, in Clinton, but over toward Westbrook: shouldn't be too hard to pin down. I switched the radio on and picked up an oldies station—what *they* call oldies. Back when Bonnie was growing up, these songs used to scare me: so cheap and raw, and all tied up with drugs and whatnot. Now I kind of like to hear them, though I'd be ashamed if anybody caught me listening. They played a Little Richard number—*Gonna tell Aunt Mary about Uncle John*—then "Angel Baby," then that "96 Tears." About half a mile before the Westbrook line, I saw a place up ahead on the left—the Nautilus Motor Court—that I remembered from years ago. If it had a bad reputation back then, I never heard about it. Sure enough, you could see skid marks on the pavement and the burned-out stub of a flare; safety glass still sparkled on the shoulder under the streetlight. I slowed down, pulled over to let a car full of teenagers pass and looked across at the motel. They'd painted the cinderblock wall white and planted geraniums along the top; seemed like they kept the place up nicely. I couldn't see a pay phone by the office, but they might've had it inside, or back along where the rooms were. Anyhow, it didn't mean anything one way or the other. She could easily have pulled in thinking there might be a phone, not found one and tried to pull out again. Or maybe this wasn't the spot after all. I crossed into Westbrook, then made a U-turn in a car wash and started back.

In the center of Clinton, I thought, *Why the hell not,* and took a right under the railroad underpass. It was lower and narrower than I remembered; I hadn't been up this way in how many years? I drove up 81 and crossed over the turnpike, glancing down at white headlights bound for New York and red taillights bound for Providence and Boston, then took a right on Glenwood Road.

The house looked pretty much the same—same shutters with crescent moons cut out—but they'd put up a split-rail fence along the driveway, and the little shrubs I'd planted on either side of the front door had grown to four or five feet wide, and somebody'd squared them off with a hedge trimmer. We bought the place the year after Sylvia went to work for Martin Real Estate and Insurance, the year before she ran off. It was too much house for us, really—three bedrooms and a finished basement—but Sylvia had talked in terms of another baby. I was hoping for a son; meanwhile, she must have had Harold Martin on her mind. I don't doubt it was true love—look how long they've been together now—though at the time I know certain people assumed otherwise, seeing that he had his own business, was president of the Lions Club and so forth, when I was just a machinist there at the Wahlstrom Company.

After Sylvia left, Bonnie used to work on me about getting myself a ladyfriend. Or I'd go over to somebody's house for supper and the wife would want to introduce me to this one or that one. But with Bonnie and the house and my job, I had enough to do as it was. And then later, when Bonnie went off on her own, I got used to coming and going as I pleased. I rewired the basement and set up my shop—lathe, drill press, milling machine—and if I felt like spending the whole weekend down there working on some project or other, there was nobody to complain. When Bonnie would tell me it wasn't normal not to have what she called an outlet, I'd always say I had plenty of outlets—put 'em in myself.

Vigil

I sat with the motor running for a minute, just looking, then used the driveway to turn around. I don't think anybody was home; the windows were all dark, and they'd left the outside light on over the kitchen door the way we used to do.

Sylvia showed up the next afternoon, looking like a million dollars for a gal her age. Last time I saw her was when Dave Junior was born—this same hospital, as a matter of fact. She gave us each a two-hand squeeze and a peck on the cheek, asked if anything had changed since she'd phoned from LaGuardia, told us about her trip. But when they called Dave Senior into the ICU, she started up. Did these doctors know what they were doing? Shouldn't we get Bonnie to someplace in New York? I finally told her, "Look. You and I don't have a thing to say about it. This is all up to Dave now."

"They could put her on a helicopter and have her down there inside of an hour." A fellow in a green hospital outfit was walking right past when she said it.

"You want to keep your voice down," I said. "Listen, I forgot to ask: how's Harold getting along?"

"Harold," she said, "is won-derful. By the way, he said he'd be glad to help out any way he can."

"Tell him that's much appreciated, will you?" But I thought, *To the tune of a couple hundred thousand dollars?* Because where Bonnie worked they had no health plan at all, and when I'd asked Dave, he'd said his plan only covered her up to a certain amount. "Cocksuckers inch that deductible up every year and bring the cap down," he'd said. "Sons of bitches." I told him not to worry over the out-of-pocket because I had more in my checking than I knew what to do with. True, up to a point.

"Had the boy been drinking?" Sylvia said.

"What boy's that?"

"The boy that *hit* her."

"It wasn't any boy," I said. "This was a man thirty years old. Sure, of course he was drunk." He'd been killed instantly, and there'd been some talk of charging the bartender who'd served him. Typical.

"And what about Bonnie?" Sylvia said.

"How do you mean?"

"Hel-*lo*?" she said, in that new way that means you're thick-headed. I'd thought it was a thing only young people said. "Bonnie? Your daughter? Was *she* drinking?"

"Of course not," I said. "She was on her way home from work, for Pete's sake."

"But she pulled right out in—"

"Here's Dave," I said. "Maybe he's got some news."

He came over and sat down in the chair next to mine. "They got the nurse in with her now. Be about fifteen minutes, they said."

Sylvia leaned across me. "Is she awake?"

"Not yet."

"Shouldn't she be awake by this time? What are they *doing* in there?"

"Probably just, you know—I don't really know, to tell you the truth." He ran his hands through his hair, scratched the back of his head.

"Well, what did they say when they called you in?"

"Not a hell of a lot," he said.

"Tell you what," I said. "Why don't we all go down and get some coffee? Wouldn't kill us to stretch our legs."

"I think I'll just sit," Dave said. "Why don't you two go ahead. Bring me one back?"

"Cream and sugar, right?" said Sylvia.

"Good memory," he said. "I better have it black, though. I need to cut down. Couple Sweet-and-Lows?"

"Well, they must have skim milk here, for pity's sake," Sylvia said. "It can't be *that* primitive."

Vigil

Dave shrugged. "If they got it."

On each of the tables in the cafeteria they'd put a carnation in a water glass, with greens to set it off. We got our coffees, Sylvia fixed an extra one to bring to Dave and we sat down.

"That's a nice thought," I said.

"What is?"

"Putting flowers. You know, they didn't have to do that."

"Oh," she said. "Funny, you know what it makes me think of? Pink carnations on the table? That place where we were that time."

"What place would that be?" I reached in my pocket and felt around to see if I had enough change to get some Raisinets from the machine. Nothing at the counter looked all that appetizing.

"*You* know." She touched the frilly edge of a petal with her fingernail, coming up under it the way you make friends with a strange dog. "Where we stayed that time."

"Oh, sure."

"It's funny," she said. "I don't mean it's *funny.* But that's where she—you know, where we really *made* her."

"Well," I said, "that's a natural thing to remember." She was talking about the place we'd stayed at in Cape May the summer before Bonnie was born. Truth to tell, I'd never been as absolutely convinced as Sylvia that *that* time was the time, but it wasn't anything to argue about anymore. "Matter of fact," I said, "I was thinking yesterday about the way she looked when she was a baby." I didn't go on to say what particularly had brought that to mind.

"She was the most *beautiful* baby I ever saw," Sylvia said. "Not just because . . ." I looked across. She had her napkin up to her face and her shoulders were shaking. "Oh dear," she said. "Oh my goodness."

I wasn't any too thrilled to have her sitting there breaking down, but it was more to the point than helicopters and all.

"You don't need to hold back," I said. "It's the most natural thing in the world."

"I'll be all right in a sec," she said. I looked at this lady, fairly well along in years—like I am, sure—pressing a wadded napkin against her eyes, and I thought, *I was married to her.* I sometimes get the idea that old Harold didn't turn out to have as much money as he let on. Though of course she'd never say so. Sylvia turned out to be loyal as the day is long—though a little late in the game, from my point of view. She looked at the black stuff on the napkin. "I better go fix my face again. I wanted to look nice for her."

"You look fine." In my pocket, I ran my thumbnail over the ridges of a quarter to make sure it wasn't a nickel. "I wouldn't expect her to take too much note anyhow. You know, the first few days."

She unwadded the napkin and tried to smooth it out flat with her fingertips. "Have they said anything at all about the long term?"

I shook my head. "I don't believe so."

She worked some more at smoothing out the napkin, then said, "I wonder if I hadn't better start looking for a reasonable place to stay."

"But aren't you—I just assumed you were staying at Dave and Bonnie's."

"Aren't *you* staying there?"

"So?"

"Well? Don't you think that would be . . ."

"What?" I said. "Christ, they got a big enough house. I can take the den and you can have the hide-a-bed. Or vice versa. I think Dave was sort of counting on you helping out with the baby." I stood up. "You want anything from the machine? I'm going to get some Raisinets."

"Is that what you've been eating?" She shook her finger, which was an old joke between us: my mother had a habit of shaking her finger, and I'd told Sylvia how I used to hate it. "What am I going to do with you?"

We finally got Sylvia settled in, though we had a little go-round about who slept where. I was bound and determined that she should have the hide-a-bed. I'd slept on it the night before and my back was fine; I hated the thought of her trying to get comfortable on that sofa in the den. I was just going to put a couple quilts down on the floor in there. But she said she'd rather have her privacy.

After supper Dave Senior went back to the hospital, leaving me and Sylvia with the baby. She had a cocktail before supper, but just the one. Afterward, she gave Dave Junior his bath while I cleaned up, then asked me to watch him while she went into the den to finish unpacking. Now she had him on the couch—the hide-a-bed, folded up—trying to zip him into his sleep suit while he wiggled and giggled.

"What would you like Nonny to read, punkin?" she said, once she finally got him squared away. "Your daddy said you could have one story and then off to bed."

He went and got the mouse book from the coffee table and put it right in her hands. "*That.*"

"He loves that one," I told Sylvia. "Just so you know, they don't have any words in it, so you have to sort of make it up as you go. It's kind of along the lines of the—".

"Oh, I think Nonny can manage." She had him up on her lap, playing with his hair. "What do you think, punkin? Does Nonny have it under control?"

"Just telling you," I said.

Sylvia opened the book, flipped through the first few pages, then nodded. "Now, once upon a time," she said, "there was a little mouse. And one fine day, this mouse happened to meet up with a kitty cat who was as big as a *monster.*"

I shot her a look—the idea was to put him to sleep, not get him worked up. When she pointed at the picture, I got up from the recliner and came over and sat down beside them, and my God, you could smell her breath three feet away. *Unpacking.* She must have been into it hot and heavy. "So the mouse said, 'Can't we even talk about it?' " Little squeaky voice for the mouse. "But the kitty cat hated all mice in the world, and he began to run after the mouse. See? 'Come back, I want to eat you *alive.*' " A big bass voice.

I looked at Dave Junior, but he was smiling away.

"So the mouse ran into her hole, and when the kitty cat went after her, he tripped over a *grrreat big dog.* And there's the dog, see? And that dog was as big as a *monster.*"

"Syl?" I said. "I don't know about too many monsters."

She put a finger to her lips and hissed. "Quiet in the peanut gallery. Now, the dog, who was as big as a *monster,* hated all kitty cats in the world, and when the kitty cat tripped over him, he took off after her just as tight as he could go. 'Come back, *I want to eat you alive.*' "

"You said *her,*" Dave Junior said.

"Uh-huh. And there's the kitty cat."

"But before you said—"

"Sssh. So they ran and they ran and they ran and they ran and they ran. *Aaaand*—they ran!"

Dave Junior giggled.

"And then guess what?"

He did a big show-off shrug.

"They *ran!*"

Another giggle.

"Until pretty soon what should they come upon but a man and his wife. See? Now, the wife had just gone to all the trouble of making the most beautiful cake in the world for her husband, and there it is right there. Can you guess what's going to happen?"

"The kitty's gonna run under the chair and they're gonna go *pow* and all go flying."

"That's right. Completely ruined. So watch, she's bringing the cake in, and he's not paying any attention. Just sitting there with his face in a newspaper. You're not going to be like that, are you?"

"*I* don't know," said Dave Junior.

"What kind of an answer is that?" she said, in a way that made me look at her. "That's no answer. Let me tell you something. You turn out to be like that, I'll come back from the grave and cut off your penis."

He squirmed around and stared up at her.

She began to laugh. "Oh, my Christ. Oh, Sylvia. *Now* you've done it. You have *done* it."

I got up and picked him up off her lap. "C'm'ere, young fella. Time to hit the hay. We got a big day tomorrow."

"No," he said. "I don't want to, you didn't *finish*."

"Here we go." I got up as he tried to wrestle out of my arms. "I'll tell you the rest of your story in bed."

"No, *Nonny* has to tell it." He started kicking.

"You run along with Grandpa, sugar," Sylvia said, just sitting there on the couch smiling, not even looking up at us. "He's going to give you your milk because Nonny got tired. She's going to have *her* milk and go to bed, too."

I carried him out to the kitchen, squirming and screaming his head off, and managed to get the icebox open and pour him a cup of milk one-handed; I put it on the table and sat him down in front of it. He gave me a dirty look, drank it in one big gulp and instantly got quiet. I led him by the hand into his room, put on his night-light and tucked him into bed. He lay quiet while I finished up the story as best I could, but when I left, shutting the door behind me, he started up again.

I went back into the living room; Sylvia was gone and the door to the den was shut. I sat down on the couch—still warm where she'd been sitting—and listened to him carry on. He was just all keyed up, and probably wouldn't keep at it for long. Basically he's a good boy; Bonnie did a fine job with him—or I better say *does*.

Jesus, I thought, *imagine having all this to do over.*

That night I dreamed the accident was just a false report, and that Bonnie and I were grocery shopping in the Big Y in Greenfield (where I go once a week). I was pushing the basket and she was riding in it, standing up, even though she was a grown woman, and pulling down boxes and cans and throwing them on the floor. Actually, she was sort of Bonnie and Sylvia both. I woke up and it was just starting to get gray outside the picture window. It took a second to understand that none of this was true.

I thought about getting up and pulling the drapes closed, but once I'm up I'm generally up. For me, a couple hours is a good stretch, and I don't seem to need more than four or five hours a night. Which can make for a long day unless you've got some project going.

When I first retired up to Shelburne Falls, I figured I'd do some hunting and fishing, not having fished for maybe twenty years. I got a license and borrowed a pole and some tackle from Scotty, but it was all I could do to poke the hook through a nightcrawler. If they're so backward they can't feel pain, why is it they start wringing and twisting when the hook goes in? I knew right then that if I was that sorry for a worm, I wouldn't be much of a hand at shooting deer anymore. You change, you know?

The one smart thing I did, I moved my shop up. My basement's only half the size of the one in Clinton, but without the rec-room furniture and Ping-Pong table I've got more space. I still turn out some piecework for Wahlstrom—last month I cut two hundred and fifty cams—which gives me a little mad money. We could do everything back and forth by UPS, but it makes a good excuse to drive down and get together with some of the old gang. A few of them still work there, and I guess Fred Wahlstrom'll outlast everybody. Eighty-one years old and he still comes in at seven-thirty every morning. We have an early supper and I drive back up the same night; somebody always offers to put me up and put up with me, but it's a straight shot up 91 and I like to sleep in my own bed. Sometimes you sit there at the table and they'll be talking about how so-and-so did such-and-such the other day, or what a fuddle-dee-dud old man Wahlstrom is, and suddenly you feel like you've died and you're looking on from the other side. Like you can still hear and see them, but if they were to reach out a hand it'd go right through you.

I must've fallen back asleep, because I woke up again and the room was brighter. What woke me up this time was a hissing and the smell of bacon. *I'm at Bonnie's house*, I thought, *and she's fixing breakfast.* Again, it took a second for it all to come back. I sat up and saw Sylvia out in the kitchen, poking a fork around in a skillet. Dressed to the nines, too, in plaid slacks, white blouse, her hair just so. She saw me, smiled and waved. As if that business last night had never happened. Well, I wasn't about to bring it up. Old Harold was more than welcome to deal with all that.

I pulled my robe on over my pajamas, stepped into my slippers and went to use the toilet and brush my teeth. I hadn't thought to bring toothpaste, and when I opened the medicine cabinet looking for theirs I noticed a prescription vial with Bonnie's name on it. VALIUM, 5 MG. How long had she been on that stuff? Well, it could've been something a lot worse. It was, when she was younger. I guess some people have a couple beers to relax and some people take one of them. I got the cap off (childproof, thank goodness), shook one out, looked at it—it was just a little bit of a thing—then slipped it into the pocket of my pajama top.

Back in the living room, I folded away the hide-a-bed and replaced the cushions. Now you could smell coffee, too. Sylvia was pouring grease out of the skillet into the dispose-all, and she'd laid the bacon out to drain on paper towels; she'd turned on the coffeemaker, and coffee was piddling down into the glass pot. I'm getting a little hard of hearing, but I could've sworn she was humming. Sylvia never could carry a tune in a bucket.

She didn't seem to know I was watching—maybe she's hard of hearing, too—and I felt like I knew every move before she made it: put the skillet in the dishwasher, scoot over to the ice-box, get out the eggs. When she opened an overhead cabinet and started reaching for the juice glasses, I could see the muscles of her calves under the pantlegs. This was a woman seventy years old. Supposedly she plays golf and tennis; that's all since my time.

I picked out slacks and a sport shirt, and went back into the bathroom to get dressed. I took the pill out of my pajamas and set it on the edge of the sink while I got my shirt on, then put it in the breast pocket. When I came out again, Sylvia had the table in the breakfast nook set for four. "Look at all this," I said.

"Good morning," she said. "*You* certainly look spiffy. I've got coffee ready. Any signs of life down the hall?"

"Not a peep out of either of 'em," I said. "You look nice yourself."

"Makeup covers a multitude of sins," she said.

"Sleep all right?"

"Like a rock. I was so bushed I can barely remember getting into bed. How about you?"

"Not so bad."

"I thought I heard you get up a couple of times."

"While you were sleeping like a rock?" I said.

"Oh, well," she said. "You know." She picked up a cup and saucer with one hand, pointed to it with the other and raised her eyebrows. Her hands were steady enough that the cup and saucer didn't rattle.

"Sure," I said. "Please."

She filled the cup and handed it to me, saucer and all. Damned if I could keep *my* hands that steady, and I'd had one Bud Light—one!—to get me to sleep. I remember many a morning when Sylvia'd be fixing breakfast after a rough night, just as fresh as a daisy. Which scared me more than anything.

She was pouring a cup for herself when little Dave came in, dragging his stuffed dinosaur. "Well, look who's here! Good morning, punkin."

"Where's Mommy?"

"You remember, punkin. Mommy had to go in the hospital?"

"Want her to come back." He dropped the dinosaur and grabbed Sylvia around the leg with both arms.

She stroked his hair. "She'll be back. I bet you like bacon, don't you?"

"Yuck," he said, making a scrunched-up face I bet a nickel he'd been told was cute. Then he cocked his head, like he was listening to something. "No, wait, I like it."

"Well, here." Sylvia handed him a piece. "That should hold you for a little while." He stuck it in his mouth: gone in two bites. "My goodness. You're hungry, aren't you, punkin? What do you usually like for breakfast?"

"Yogurt."

"Okay, let's have a look." She opened the icebox and bent over. "Oh my *goodness*, yes. We've got peach, wild berry . . . peach and wild berry."

"Wild berry," he said.

"By God, he's an opinionated little cuss," I said. "Ain't'cha?"

"Can I hear a *please?*" said Sylvia.

He stared as if she was talking Chinese.

Sylvia looked at me, I shrugged and she handed him his yogurt. He took it over to the table and started right in making a mess. The telephone rang, and I thought, *Oh my God.*

Sylvia picked it up. "Carter residence." She listened for a few seconds, then said, "Well, I was going to, lover. But things got a little hectic."

I let out my breath.

She turned her back, which I took as a hint. Carrying my coffee into the living room, I heard her say, "Yes, I made a point of it. What? Yes, of course."

I put the TV on and sat down on the couch. The Big Bird and all were on, and of course that fetched Dave Junior; he was on my lap in two shakes, purple yogurt all over his face.

"This your favorite program?" I said.

"*I* don't know," he said, not taking his eyes off the screen for a second.

Dave Senior came in, his hair wild, in his undershirt, zipping up his trousers. "What happened? What's going on?"

"Go on back to bed," I said. "It's just Harold."

"Jesus. What the fuck time is it?" With the boy right there.

"Early," I said. "Go back to bed." It was only seven-thirty, quarter to eight. I counted back: out in Phoenix it wasn't even six in the morning.

"And what the hell's this?" He was giving little Dave a dirty look. "What'd I tell you about eating on the good furniture, Mister? You get in there right now." He pointed to the kitchen.

"But I want to see—"

"*Now.*"

Vigil

Dave Junior got down and stomped off with his yogurt.

"And get a better attitude," he called after him. He shook his head. "Too early in the morning for this shit."

"I didn't mean to get him in trouble," I said. "I didn't know he wasn't allowed."

"He knows better. He's trying to see what he can get away with because he knows something's up."

Sylvia hung up the phone and stepped in from the kitchen. "Good *morning.* How would you gents like your eggs?"

"I usually have scrambled," I said.

"You used to like a three-minute egg."

"God, that's right. I don't know, I guess I just got out of the habit. Egg timers and all."

"Men," she said. "What about you, Dave?"

"Bowl of Total, I guess." He rubbed his eyes and passed his hands back through his hair to smooth it down. You could see where he'd zipped his pants but not buttoned them. He *was* starting to put it on. "Christ, it can't be but about five in the morning out there. What the hell's Harold doing up at this hour?"

"I was supposed to call him last night," Sylvia said, "and I forgot all about it. He's such an old fussbudget. He *said* he was calling to make sure I'd gotten credit for the frequent-flier miles. But I think he just wanted to know I was safe."

"He's up at five in the morning thinking about frequent-*flier* miles?" Dave said. "He scared the piss out of me."

"You ought to just go back to bed," I said.

"I'm up now." He looked into the breakfast nook. "Hey! Will you watch what you're doing, Mister? You're getting it all over the table."

"It'll clean up," said Sylvia. "You ready for some coffee? I'll get you a bowl for your cereal."

"Don't bother, I can get it." He went into the kitchen and I thought, *No time like the present.* I took the little pill out of my

shirt pocket, glanced in to make sure neither of them was looking, popped it in my mouth and washed it down with coffee.

Dave Senior came back in with a bowl of cereal and flopped
down on the couch. I guess the rule didn't apply to him. "Five
o'clock in the morning." He put a spoonful in his mouth and
started watching the Big Bird dance with a bunch of children.
"I didn't *want* this day. And here it fucking is."

I said there was no sense in taking two cars this morning—I
wasn't sure what that pill would do to me—so Dave drove us in
the Caravan. We dropped the boy back in North Madison for
the day, then went on to the hospital.

When the nurse on duty saw us walk into the intensive
care, she brightened up. "Hi," she said. "They're moving her
right now."

"Oh, shit," Dave said. "*Now* what the hell happened?"

"Oh, they didn't tell you?" She was still smiling; they must
train them to breeze over any bad words from people under
stress. "She was awake and talking this morning, and Dr.
Chambers thought she'd improved enough to go into a semi-
private. And they might try to get her up for a few minutes this
afternoon."

"Hell *no*, they didn't tell us." Dave Senior shook his head.
"That's about par for this place. If she isn't here, where the
Christ *is* she?"

The nurse stopped smiling.

I took a big breath and let it out. "Thank God. Thank *God*.
You know, they probably called the house when we were on
our way here. *Jesus*, isn't that wonderful." It was like the weight
of everything lifted up off of me—my arms actually felt light,
like there was air under them. And then, just like that, it hit
me that this little time, with all of us together, was rushing to
an end.

Vigil

The nurse ran her fingernail up and down a clipboard gracefully, searching. It seemed to take longer than normal. "She's being moved to five-seventeen B. That's in the other wing, fifth floor. You can take the elevator by the waiting room." Dave Senior turned around and tromped out without so much as a thank-you. Sylvia stared at him. I told the nurse thanks for everything, that she'd been a wonderful person to us, then Sylvia and I followed Dave out. He'd been under all that stress for so long, you see, that having it suddenly let up—I don't know, you can understand how it must have discombobulated him.

The waiting room, where I'd spent so much time the last couple of days, looked strange to me, like some place you haven't seen in years—it could've been that pill starting to take hold. I hadn't noticed before that it was all shades of green in here: green walls, green carpeting, green couch and chairs. To calm people down. I thought, *With all this green around, plus a Valium pill, you ought to be ready for anything they throw at you.* Dave Senior was over at the elevators; he touched his finger to the UP arrow, and it lit up green. The colored couple was there on the green couch—I was pretty sure it was the same couple—and I was going to nod at them except I wasn't a hundred percent sure. And what for? We were in different boats now: them still here and me just passing through one last time, really a million miles from it.

When Sylvia and I got over to the elevators, Dave Senior pounded the lit-up arrow with the side of his fist. "Let's go. Son of a bitch."

Sylvia laid a hand on his arm. "It's all right. She's going to be okay—thank *God*."

"Fine. *You* thank God. God'll shit his pants when he hears from *you*." He shook loose of her hand and pounded the arrow again.

She took a step back. "What's the trouble? I should think you—"

"What's the *trouble?* That's beautiful. That's a classic. That should be the family motto. What's the trouble. You whored around on *him*"—jerking a thumb in my direction—"your daughter whores around on *me*, and you—"

"No, now you're out of line now," I said. The colored fellow was looking over at us, trying to make believe he wasn't. "I can understand if—"

"What brought *this* on?" Sylvia said.

Dave Senior looked at me. "What, you didn't tell her? That would figure. That's about par."

"What didn't you tell me?" Sylvia said.

"The great peacemaker," said Dave Senior, shaking his head. "The great cover-up artist. Okay, what happened to your daughter, Syl, she got creamed when she came barrel-assing out of the motel where she was shacked up with somebody *else's* husband. This shit's been going on for—"

"Don't listen to this," I told Sylvia. "He's all hipped on this thing because he's upset. As near as I can make out, she just went in there to use the telephone."

"Where do you get that crap?" said Dave Senior. "She had her car phone, for Christ's sake."

Ding, and the elevator doors came open and we had to step aside for a gurney with an old, old lady flat on her back, asleep or in a coma maybe. All there was to her, poor soul, was just ragged white hair and poor thin, wrinkled skin over her skull; her closed eyes stuck up in their sockets like knuckles. I had a foolish thought—probably due to that pill, because I could feel it coming over me pretty strong now. I thought that she'd lived a good long life and for that reason she'd been chosen to take Bonnie's place. I stole a look at Sylvia on the million-to-one chance she might be thinking the same fool thing. But Sylvia

was looking at her watch, and I could tell just as if she was saying it out loud what she was *really* thinking: if Bonnie was truly
out of the woods now, what's the soonest you could get a plane
to Phoenix? They wheeled the old lady off toward the intensive
care, and we stepped into the elevator. My ears were humming
and my legs felt like they had no bones. I fingered the coins in
my pocket: okay, if this one's a quarter, then *this* one has to be
a nickel. So I couldn't be too far out there yet. Dave Senior
pounded the 5 button with his fist, the metal doors slid shut on
everything that had happened until now, and up we went.

Beating

He says, "I'm entitled, am I not?"

I say, "Whatever helps."

The bartender sets a Johnny Walker in front of Tobias and a Diet Coke in front of me; he takes away Tobias's old glass, drained to the ice cubes. My Diet Coke's got a slice of lemon, for festiveness and sophistication, like they stick a Maraschino cherry in your ginger ale when you're a little girl. I am so much not in the mood.

It's Friday and I'd been looking forward to just going straight home and popping into the tub. But Tobias called me at Helping Hands and said could I meet him at the Little Finland when I got off work, and I just quickly said okay fine since I didn't have time to get into a big thing with him. He called right in the middle of the preschoolers putting on *The Three Little Pigs* for the toddlers, and Margaret wasn't thrilled with his timing. Neither was I. But I thought, *Well, he's had a hard couple of days, apparently.* Something happened yesterday at the march on city hall, from what I could gather over the phone; last night he didn't get in until after I was asleep, and he was still asleep when I left this morning. So I just thought, *Okay, obviously he needs to talk.* Plus the Little Finland was a place we used to go.

Beating

I want to tell him about *The Three Little Pigs*, though this clearly isn't the time and anyway Tobias makes me feel—well, no, that's not fair—*I* feel like my stories go on too long for him. The play just sort of evolved in the course of the day; one good thing about Helping Hands is, it's the kind of place that allows for this. At Morning Story we were reading this junk Disney book of *The Three Little Pigs* that Josh had brought in, and Gwendolyn (who else?) said, "Can we put on a play of it? I have to be the wolf—no, Max has to be the wolf, and I have to be Fiddler Pig." Nothing seems to drag Gwendolyn down: not the Laura Ashley dresses, not the waist-length hair that's been trimmed but never really cut, not the moon-child name. Depressing that even Gwendolyn, at four years old, has already gotten it that bigness and badness are male things, but it was brilliant what she did playing Fiddler Pig: absolutely *reveling* in how stupid it was to build your house out of straw. She just completely upstaged poor little Max, who did his *I'll huff and I'll puff* in a naggy singsong, and when he blew the house in it came out spitty. I mean, no balls at all. Gwendolyn had decorated her paper-bag pig mask with tiger stripes and glitter glue around the nostrils. (Margaret vetoed strap-on snouts because they'd be too frustrating to make; Gwendolyn argued and got a time-out.) She danced around playing air fiddle as she sang, to the tune of "Who's Afraid of the Big Bad Wolf":

> *My-y house is o-okay*
> *O-okay*
> *O-okay*
> *My-y house is o-okay*
> *Fiddle fiddle fiddle all day*

I thought, *Now, before you go crazy on this, remember this is basically a happy little girl. Maybe her house* is *okay.* I guess I have an attitude because the mother comes in with her chopped-off hair and her power suits (so you wonder what weirdness causes her to make her daughter look just the opposite), and the father is this long-haired narcissist in a leather jacket that must have cost eight hundred dollars. He picks her up like once a month, and I have yet to see him drop her off in the morning.

Anyhow. Trying *not* to be a bitch about being in this actually kind of scrimy little bar instead of home in the tub. And trying not to get started on quality-of-life stuff in general: e.g., coming in the door just now, I had to get around this babbling homeless man thrusting a shopping bag at me, God knows why. I thought I knew most of them who hang around the neighborhood, but this one seems to be a new acquisition. Though of course with Tobias the last thing you want to do is complain about what a drag the homeless are.

"Heave-ho," Tobias says, by way of toasting me, and drains off half the glass. He was here when I got here, and already long gone inside himself. I mean he's still talking and everything, but I could be anybody, you can just feel it.

"See, this is the thing that kills me," he's saying. "Everybody saw the *Times*, right? And so they all assume, I mean I *assume* they assume, that this is the way it went down. I don't know, everything is like that movie anymore. You know. Oh, fuck. Famous Jap movie. *Rosh Hashanah. Rosh Hashanah Mon Amour.*"

This is one of Tobias's things. Not a joke, exactly. But like the way he calls a yarmulke a Yamaha, or he'll say, "Whatta we got in the Norhay?" meaning our refrigerator. That one took me weeks.

"See, I was there," he's saying. "I mean, not that I was any more there than the *Times* guy. But he came with his agenda, which we all *do*. You know, me the same as anybody." He takes a smaller sip, like he's already home free and anything he drinks now is just for the luxury. "But what I saw," he says, "what *I* saw, was a bunch of cops just zeroing in on this one black guy and absolutely hammering the living fuck out of him. It was fucking Rodney Two, man." Back when Rodney King happened, Tobias taped it off the news and for days he'd be playing it over and over, saying, *Unbelievable, unbelievable.*

"You mean using their sticks?" I say.

"You better *believe* using their sticks. You know, okay, I can see it, he was yelling shit, all right? But Jesus Christ. I'll tell you something, it took my breath away." Sip. "And the fucking *Times* reports it 'marred only by minor disturbances.' "

"Maybe the *Times* person just missed it," I say. "If you're one reporter, you can't be everywhere."

"Yeah, right. Maybe. *Possibly.* But I also kept checking News 88 and WINS. And they also had jack shit."

"The *Post* didn't have it this morning?" I said. "Sounds like right up their alley."

"You know I won't buy the *Post*," he says. "Look. Doesn't matter. The *New York Times* is what people read who have the power to get anything done." Sip. "What I'm saying is, all the information about this is being very, very adroitly fucking managed." Sip. "Fuck it, what are we even talking about it for?" He waves his glass for the bartender.

"It's just extremely obvious," he says, "that the word was put out, high up. I call the police guy I've been dealing with all week, okay? And suddenly, 'We have no record of that.' Imagine this shit? I call the guy in the mayor's office—and I *don't* assume he's a total asshole just because he works for Giuliani—and it's like, 'Well, the police say they have no record.' And so now this becomes the truth. It's like *There is no war with Oceania. We have never been at war with Oceania.* And of course the way they sell it to the media, *Now we certainly don't want to have another situation like L.A. on our hands here, DO WE, GENTLEMEN?* So word goes out, everybody gets with the program and everybody's happy except some *nigger* who was asking for it anyway."

"Could you keep your voice down?" I say. I sneak a look around, but there's nobody black, thank God.

"If anybody had a camcorder yesterday," he says, "that tape got bought for major, major bucks. *You*'ll sure as shit never see it." Another glass of whisky arrives, the old glass goes. "Well, hey, not to worry. Bernie's on the case. Going to blow their whole game wide open. He *thinks*. Anyhow, he was there when I left last night, working on his letter to the *Times*. Bernie Adler, the Undefeated. Faxed it to them and everything so they'd be *sure* to get it in. *Oh, yes, Mr. Adler, certainly.* Another little thing you're never going to see. *Gee, we had to hold it for space reasons*, or it's like *Our computer must've eaten it.*" Sip. "Fuck it. What I'm going to do, I'm going to get stinko."

No kidding, I want to say.

When I can finally get Tobias out of the Little Finland, I take him around the corner to Biagio's, where I keep passing him the bread before our food arrives on the stupid theory that bread soaks up alcohol. (He really doesn't do this very often.) He tells me about five times that we have to eat in a hurry because I have to get him home in time for the news at ten. It's now like eight o'clock.

But instead of going straight home, he says we have to walk past where he parked the car, all the way over between York and East End, to make sure it's okay. It's like, what more could happen to it? Last week we found the driver's-side door handle wrenched up halfway out of the door and papers from the dash all over the front seat. This pathetic '81 Honda Civic. Maybe it would be better not to keep locking the thing; this was about the eighty-fifth time. So now the key won't open Tobias's side anymore and his window goes down only partway. Which is especially a drag because one thing he used to actually enjoy was driving in the summertime with his elbow out the window. This is one of the ways you know Tobias isn't really a New Yorker at heart despite what a New Yorker he is. He always says he'd never have an air-conditioned car for just this reason. (I can see it, right? Tobias Baker, man of principle, turning down the Lexus somebody's trying to give him because you can only hang your arm out the window of a shitbox car like we have.) Anyhow, there's Old Betsy up ahead, between a Cherokee (which I personally would love to have) and a something else.

"Looks much the same," I say. Chain holding down the hood so they don't get the battery again, and the red thing on the steering wheel—not The Club but this thing Tobias says is just as good as The Club. "Actually, I sort of feel sorry in a way for somebody that would pick this car to break into."

"Yeah, well, I don't," he says. "You know, a lot of the time lately? I visualize coming down the street and I see some son of a bitch fucking around with the car and I would pound their fucking head into the pavement and kick their balls in. I am really fucking sick of fucking crime."

"I know, I'm sick of it, too," I say. "What I guess I meant, it's like it would be somebody so beaten down that they wouldn't even *presume* to break into a Grand Cherokee or something."

"Right, they're animals. They *smell.* I could smell it the other day when they broke in and they were sitting going through the glove compartment. That smell. You know, you start out telling yourself that this is what *you* would be inside of a week if you couldn't bathe, you didn't have anyplace to shit—but the brute fucking fact is that you're *not* that, man, you're just *not.* I can't even believe I'm saying this, but you know? I mean, I think back when I first went to work for Bernie, and he even told me, he said, 'We're not going to work miracles here,' but I—okay, now check *this* out."

He tosses his head at the car going by: a glossy little Jeep thing with music thudding out of it and two black guys with baseball hats, the rear license plate framed in glowing purple.

"Couple of brain surgeons, probably," he says. "Mustn't jump to conclusions, right? You have any idea what a rig like that *costs*? I mean, beaten *down*, who's beaten down in *this* situation, man? You know, you can completely see how it happened."

"How what happened?" I say.

"The *thing*," he says. "No, World War Two. You know, the cops just had *enough* of it. At that minute. And something fuckin' *broke*, you know? I mean it could've been me. Easily. Easily." He snorts. "Hey, confront your racism, right?"

Upstairs at last, he lies back on the futon, breathing through his mouth, eyes rolling. I untie his work boots and tug them off, getting not a lot of cooperation though not a lot of re-sistance either.

"And another evening bites the dust," he says. "At least we got away from *that* shit for a couple of hours."

"Which shit is that?" I say.

"*That.*" He points to the window giving onto the air shaft. "You don't *hear* that?" Only now am I aware that the music, so-called, from the next building has started up. Boom-badoom, boom-badoom. The air shaft is only about that far across, and they keep it up eighteen hours a day. "I live here," he says. "*Why* do I live here? Even fucking Bernie Adler couldn't hack it—Mr. New York. In his fucking co-op in Riverdale."

"Wasn't part of it that they were sending Winnie to Horace Mann?" I say. That "I" of his is echoing.

"Fucking Riverdale. I mean, isn't that what the place was in Nancy Drew? Riverdale?"

"River something," I say. "I wasn't all that big into Nancy Drew."

"The blue roadster," he says. "Sometimes I just want to fucking scream."

"I think we're both sort of burned out," I say.

"Oh, so sorry, have we been neglecting *your* problems? Nap time and its discontents?"

Fuck you.

He sits up and starts his thing of running fingers through his hair, hard. "I am disgusting," he says. "I'm so fat now I'm out of breath coming up the stairs."

I glance over. He's got just the teensiest little roll, about that big, above his belt, the way anybody gets if they're sitting. "You're the same as you were," I say.

"I smell like a pig, too. Come home and I take a bath and it's like I can't get clean."

"What is *this* about?" I say.

He says, "I can understand why you would lose interest."

"What?" I say. "Correct me if I'm wrong, but—oh, God, look, it's late, I'm exhausted—"

"I need to talk to Bernie," he says.

"Okay, fine," I say. "Talk. You can pick up a phone."

He gets the phone and starts jabbing numbers. "I know Bernie, he'll still be there." He listens for a long time.

"It's after nine," I say.

"He should *be* there. Jesus, if even Bernie is in on this thing."

"What thing?" I say.

"Dinah. What have we been *talking* about the last three hours? Jesus. I feel like I'm going out of my mind here. I mean, maybe I should be insulted that I'm not *important* enough for them to even try to *get* to. What do *you* think? Should I try to call like Mike McAlary?"

Mr. I-Don't-Read-the-Tabs. "I don't know what to say about it," I say.

He shakes his head. "This is some serious shit going down in this city."

He's in bed, asleep, by the time the news comes on. No follow-up about the march: it might as well have happened a year ago.

I zap the thing off when they say sports is next. I get up and go into the kitchen and open the Norhay (I mean, it *is* funny, kind of) and have a good long slug of Tropicana HomeStyle, right from the carton. Then I mosey back out and over to the bookshelves, hands clasped behind my back like Prince Charles or something inspecting the royal guards. Queen of all she surveys. You wouldn't believe what's here. I mean, *Journey to the End of the Night*? Chaucer, Chesterton, Dickens, the complete everything of T. S. Eliot, Faulkner Fitzgerald Freud, what looks like all the Hemingway in the world (which would figure), Langland Lawrence Lorca, Melville, Nabokov, O'Connor O'Neill Orwell, Peacock Plato Pinter Poe Pound. If they bombed all of New York but miraculously not us, you could start Western civilization all over again. Though lately Tobias's intellectual life is mostly turning on the TV and complaining about how stupid it is. Which I guess is better than Rodney King over and over, or when Bernie gave him that tape of *Koy-aanisqatsi* and we had that for the next month. But what really pisses me off as somebody who's Jewish is all this Ezra Pound: the big fat *Cantos of, Literary Essays of*, I mean it goes on. Who but Tobias would have *Jefferson and/or Mussolini*? Plus not one, not two, but three biographies, *plus* two books just on the treason thing that he got locked up for and rightly so. Sometimes when Tobias isn't here I'll read around in these books just to give myself a good hit of how totally unbelievable this man was.

I mean, every other word out of his mouth is *kike*, and this is the great poet supposedly, and what Tobias thinks is a good idea to have in what after all is my home, too. I fantasize sometimes about making a big stink and demanding that he at least put Ezra Pound away where I won't have to see it every day of my life. I'd be like *Hey hey, ho ho, Ezra Pound has got to go*. But I can't really imagine having the energy to get into a big hoo-ha with Tobias over Ezra Pound, or anything else, like having no sex life. What I think is that he should know not to have books where every other word is *kike* without my having to say anything. So I don't say anything.

Actually, I don't know why I'm even bothering to look at the books, because I already know what I'm going to do: I'm going to go rent *Beauty and the Beast* again. When Tobias is out he's *out*, and RKO Video doesn't close until eleven. This is truly a stupid obsession, but harmless, I guess. I mean, by comparison. I get my purse and duck my head into the bedroom: Tobias's shoulder is rising and falling. I'm out the door.

Same as every Friday and Saturday night, crowds of hooting white kids wander this neighborhood because of the bars. I say kids; in their twenties, really. In packs and couples. Bare-legged girls, noisily drunk—you can tell they're going to be sick and sorry—held up by what look like frat boys who probably all work on Wall Street and could buy and sell you by snapping their fingers. And in front of every bar and deli, some homeless man shaking a paper cup. I go into a Koreans' for my usual thing of M&Ms, pay with a dollar bill and, back on the sidewalk, drop the change into a dirty hand.

RKO Video is bright and empty; except for the clerks I'm the only one here. They've got *The Shining* on the overhead TVs, right at the part where Shelley Duvall is looking at the huge stack of pages Jack Nicholson has typed. I go straight to Children's: sure enough, three copies of *Beauty and the Beast*. You never have a problem renting *Beauty and the Beast*, which I thought was weird until I realized everybody with kids already has it and who else would want it. Strange feeling, bringing it up to the counter. It seems sicker than something from Adult X.

I went to see *Beauty and the Beast* when it first came out because I wanted to know what the kids at Helping Hands knew. It's like if you had a real job you'd read *Crain's New York Business.* Anyhow, it blew me away: I was like crying and crying. Of course I asked myself why. I mean, am I not Dinah Keltner? So okay, you got your buttons pushed by really, really expert moviemakers who know that everybody wants perfect love. At least Tobias wasn't on hand to see me lose it. I think I keep going back and renting the video because I'm into the way it just dependably rips me open. I sort of knew this afternoon, when I was helping Gwendolyn on with her backpack (she'll get one arm through and just flail with the other), that if I got any time by myself over the weekend I'd probably watch it again.

Back in the apartment, I look in on Tobias—dead to the world—then close the bedroom door. I tear the corner off my M&Ms and zap the TV on, but when I try to push the tape into the thing there's already something in there. Tobias says one of these days I'm going to wreck it, just shoving something in without checking. I hit EJECT and out pops the tape with KING BEATING hand-lettered on the label. Great, so we're back to this. I stick *Beauty and the Beast* in, hit PLAY and go sit on the sofa. The FBI warning comes on and then it really hits me how stupid this is. You're going to cry when they start to fall in love and cry more when the Beast dies (or maybe it's supposed to be a near-death experience the way he's sort of floating up) and then *really* lose it when all the stuff in the castle goes back to being real. So you have your big cry, and so what. I pick up the zapper and zap the thing off and get a screenful of snow and a snowy roaring. I zap it back on and it picks right up where the FBI warning turns color, and it's like it was just waiting for me and would have waited and waited. I rattle the first M&Ms into my palm. A yellow, a brown and a brown.

Around four in the morning I wake up when I hear Tobias moving around. The toilet flushes and that line pops into my head, *Watch waterfalls of pity roar.* Now, that dates you. If I don't watch it, I'm going to be wide awake. I hear him out in the other room fooling with the VCR, and then he's walking this way and the door closes. I can't remember him getting back in bed, but there he is when I wake up in daylight, one foot with a dirtied white sock poking out from the comforter. My first thought of the day is: *And we are supposedly good people.*

Tobias and I got married in 1981, both of us having had our grand passions: mine a husband, his somebody named Dorothy who he said went crazy. (I actually found out a little more than that, but it was like pulling teeth.) Our first date he took me to Cinema Village to see *The Parallax View.* "It's basically a Hollywood piece of shit," he said, "but you should probably see it." It turned out this was his fourth time going. Afterward we went to the Little Finland Bar and talked about movies, having agreed that telling life stories was a cliché. Not that movie talk wasn't. He said his favorite film was *Blow-Up,* though he said he knew he was supposed to say it was *The Searchers* or something. I forget what I said mine was: I certainly at that point wasn't going to admit to *The Way We Were.* I married him because:

It was charming that he had asked me out to a movie he called a piece of shit. Still more charming that this wasn't calculated.

He was a romantic.

He was a *left-wing* romantic. I think he thought of himself as like a John Wayne with good politics. He used to say, "Get your ham and eggs over here." You know, one wanted to be wanted.

These days I can't even bear to think about stuff we did in

bed, some of which I got him into doing. What I used to love was him getting his pleasure, which of course I'm sure now was probably just a power thing on my part, bitch that I am. I would watch his face scrunch up and then go blank. He would say, "Oh, this is the only time I ever really and truly relax." Of course in two minutes he would be like, *Can I get you something? Washcloth? Glass of water? Get you a drink?* We were the best, that's what's killing. The best for us. Which is why it's just so weird that he would turn around and stop. Gee, you don't think he's passive-aggressive, do you? I'm ashamed to even remember this, but I actually at one point bought this book on living with the passive-aggressive man. My first and only self-help book, except for one about depression. I hid it under the mattress like pornography: I think the last time Tobias made a bed was when he went to sleep-away camp. But I used to fantasize that he *would* somehow find it and know because I'd hidden it that it must be super-important to me and bingo, we'd begin to talk. I eventually put the thing in the garbage. So it's now in the Great Kills Landfill, where archaeologists of the future can find it in the same undisintegrated bag with our undisintegrated junk mail. They'll know our names and what our problem was and be sad that the answer (now found by science) had been so simple all along.

Tobias in those days got his hair cut short at a real barbershop and said that while he once thought drugs were revolutionary (having been stoned, he said, for the entire Nixon administration, 1969–1974) he now considered them decadent. When he did anything at all (which really wasn't that often), he drank like a tragic proletarian. At the time I met him he was running the local assemblyman's office, a storefront around the corner from where we live now, which later became a David's Cookies that went out of business. The assemblyman fired him for wearing a FREE JOHN HINCKLEY button in the office (this made the papers at the time), which Tobias claimed was protected political speech. What was actually happening, he was all set to go to work for Bernie Adler, who had started this thing for the homeless and who everybody thought was a saint because he'd worked for Allard Lowenstein, and Tobias just wanted to—his words—go out in a blaze of glory.

I at the time was just trying to get over my divorce and waiting tables and taking one course a semester at Hunter toward a teaching certificate because it was too late for anything better. (I'm still nine credits short, and will be when I die.) So one day I was complaining to this friendly woman in one of my classes (who turned out to be Margaret) about the rats in my building and she said her husband knew somebody in the assemblyman's office. Well, I was a woman who knew my rights, so in I marched. The first thing I remember Tobias actually saying beyond, like, *How do you do*, was when I told him who owned the building and he said, "What, are you shitting me?" Apparently this landlord was well known to everybody on the East Side except me for being some judge's brother-in-law or whatever he was; his buildings had rats and lead paint and drunken supers and no heat for weeks on end, and what your recourse was, Tobias said, was not to live in his buildings.

If you ask Tobias what it's like working for the homeless, he'll be a real prick and tell you he works *with* the homeless. But mostly he doesn't talk like your usual lefty, and that was another thing I thought was great about him. Don't get him started on the word *empowerment*. He's even down on *African-American*, though he wouldn't say so to anybody but me. Movement types were already into this kind of talk when I met Tobias, except you didn't have the expression PC back then; Tobias called them college pussies. I thought it was cool that his friends were relatively no-bullshit people like Bernie Adler, who actually grew up working-class. It *wasn't* cool that the worst insult he could come up with was calling someone a vagina, but I gave him credit for what I thought was the meaning behind it. He would talk about college pussies, and yet just about the only films he would go see were foreign, and his idea of decor was (still is) brick-and-board shelves with every book he ever had in college plus the hundreds he's picked up since.

But in the past few years he's stopped going to any movies at all. He wouldn't even go see *Schindler's List*, and I worry about him getting out of touch. But he's still the only man I personally know who wears a beret, which he says is because in the wintertime he can pull it down over his ears, but what I think it is, it's because he wants to make sure you know he's an intellectual. So then he has to go around saying fucking this and fucking that to compensate. Growing up in Binghamton and graduating from Penn State, that was how I used to read it all—and of course the usual male thing where if you're sensitive you have to not seem to be, which is the meaning behind *pussy.* I wonder how he read me back then. I was there and okay-looking, that was probably about the extent of it, why lie. He's a hard worker, Tobias, but lazy about his life.

Lugging the laundry, I squint against the morning sun. I need to get something in my stomach, but there's a homeless man with a shopping bag in front of the Koreans'—same guy from last night?—so I decide to put the clothes in first and maybe he'll be gone. Saturday mornings you can pretty much always get a machine if you come before eight-thirty; after nine o'clock, forget it. If you thought about it in a victimized way you could think of going to the Laundromat as part and parcel of everything else, like having the tub in the kitchen and parking on the street. Tobias absolutely forbids paying someplace to wash and fold, not so much because of the twenty dollars it just about ends up being but for class reasons: paying somebody to handle and smell your dirty clothes perpetuates the division between the clean and the unclean or something. Which I basically agree with, though I don't see *him* ever doing the wash. But mostly I don't mind because at least it gets me up and out. Saturday morning used to be our morning in bed; Sunday morning, we agreed, was a cliché. Plus for me additionally, spending Shabbos in bed was a fuck-you thing. Yet also in some slantwise way reverent. Now I'd just as soon get something accomplished.

And although I know what he's saying about the wash-and-fold, I don't go all the way with Tobias in seeing absolutely everything as being about class. Like we got into this huge thing at the time Margaret asked me if I wanted to come to work at Helping Hands. For me, the class reasons against working at a day-care place that costs like a thousand dollars a month were canceled out by the feminist thing of women getting into the workforce. Except of course that they're already *in* the workforce because they have to be because the whole economic system is so fucked, which Tobias would say comes right back to the thing of class again, so where did your feminism get you? And at a thousand dollars a month, these are not beaten-down women. Okay, Tobias is right: my politics aren't all that thought-out. But on the other hand, I get something out of being with the kids, and I don't really feel like arguing the point.

I told Margaret that Tobias and I didn't have children because we can't, which I think was okay to say because I'm pretty sure she would never bring it up with him. The truth is, I always used to think I might someday want to do something and then not be able to do it if I had a kid. That plus Tobias's political problems about it: too many children already starving globally and so forth and so on. Though since I'm going to be forty in addition to not having sex anymore, I guess you could say that at some point it got decided. One of those hard-to-pinpoint points, like the thing about when does life begin. As it's worked out, I get a lot of the good stuff that goes with kids of your own and get spared the worst, like being afraid every minute that they're going to die. What I end up with is the moderately precious moments. At nap time, Gwendolyn is usually too wired to sleep and, quote, helps me by going around and patting the other children, though I discourage her made-up lullabies, which tend to get loud. Then we go into the big playroom, where I can watch them through the doorway, and we read. But deep down we both know what the deal is. I mean, what childless woman *hasn't* had her life brightened, temporarily, by some other woman's child? It's the oldest, most disgusting story in the world.

I flomp the laundry bag down in front of the row of top-loaders. One thing that's feminist about doing your husband's wash plus your own plus the sheets and towels, you have to be strong to carry it all. I untie the knot in the drawstring and start tossing whites into one machine, bright colors into another and dark stuff into a third. Between us, Tobias and I have a lot of black jeans and T-shirts. Lately he's even been getting on my case about stuff like tying up the laundry bag, supposedly I'm being anal. "You tie the drawstring again every time you put in a pair of socks?" he said the other day. "Christ, it even *looks* like a puckered asshole." This is the man who used to sing, *Every night/why do I/quake with fright?/'Cause my Dinah might/change her mind about me.* Sometimes I'm afraid there's something wrong with him, like he has a brain tumor. I mean, not just his moods but the way he sleeps. I just try to bite my tongue when he gets evil, which really probably isn't as often as I tend to think it is.

I get the stuff going, then head back to the Koreans' to pick up a *Times* and something to put in my stomach. I've quit hovering over the machines waiting to add fabric softener when the rinse light goes on: Dinah's little protest. The homeless man is still in front of the door, so I first go over to this sort of diner place to get coffee. One of Tobias's things is to call the man who runs the place Mr. Mippippippippopopolos (not to his face), which does strike me as being not funny. I always say *milk no sugar,* and Mr. Mekos always drops four sugar packets into the bag. I suppose you could take it as not listening; I take it as wishing you more sweetness in life, like a Mediterranean thing. I pick up the *Times* at a little news and candy store that keeps the papers outside so you don't have to go in and see all the sex magazines. The homeless man is *still* in front of the Koreans', so I figure okay, fine. I hang back until he turns to this woman in running shorts coming out with a bottle of Evian, and I dart in past him. But when I come back out with my banana I'm the only one around, and he says "Spare *anything?*" in this odd voice, so I give him three quarters and say "Good luck." My usual.

I walk up to what used to be a block of 91st Street and is now this mall with benches, and sit with my back to the little park we herd the kids into every nice day in the warm weather. It's great having a job right in your neighborhood, except sometimes it makes you crazy, like you can't ever get away. Already children are yelling and running through the sprinklers.

I take the lid off the coffee and say "You and me, pal," to the mostly naked discus thrower on the cup. His crudely drawn muscles look like the squares on a turtle's shell. I sip gingerly so I won't burn my mouth. Then I peel the banana partway down and break off a bite.

I always read the *Times* the same way: scan the front page, go to the editorials, then the columns, then see if there's a letter about anything interesting or from somebody famous. What stops me is Bernie Adler's name, at the bottom of a letter headed WE'RE ONE COMMUNITY.

To the Editor:

Thursday's peaceable and mostly amicable march on City Hall has reminded New Yorkers of what we're too apt to forget: that we're one community and not (ideally) a welter of warring entities at each other's throats in a zero-sum game.

Can it be that even the Giuliani administration, once so cynically adept at other-ing homeless New Yorkers, demonizing the so-called "squeegee men" and putting the police at odds with a segment of the public they exist to serve, is feeling the winds of change?

We of the New York Homeless Alliance wish to acknowledge the cooperation of the mayor's office in facilitating the people's exercise of their right "peaceably to assemble," and to express our gratification at the measured police response to the (very) few potentially provocative incidents. May this march serve to put on notice all those who would polarize and divide us: The men and women of the NYPD are working people (they work for us—for *all* of us), and the vast majority of the homeless *would* be working people under the aegis of more enlightened social and economic policies.

> Bernard Adler, Chair
> New York Homeless Alliance

I'm like, *What?*

But I know. I mean I guess I sort of *did* know. But here it is in black and white. Real words in a real newspaper that a million people are reading in the real world. Now I feel my heart start to pound, like it took a few seconds for the idea to get through to my body: that I live with a man whose mind's gone wrong. Take out the clothes, dry the clothes, fold the clothes— but sooner or later you have to go back to where he's waiting.

Beating

I smell the homeless man before his shadow darkens the page.

"Excuse me for intruding." I look up, thinking, *Oh, shit.* It's the same one: white stumblebum, teeth with gaps in between like a syphilitic, carrying a dirty white paper shopping bag. "D'y'know Jim Morrison?" he says. Sort of an Irishy accent: hint of a *d* among the *r*'s. *Mawdison.* "Of The Doors?"

"Yes," I say, and look back down at the paper. Not streetwise of me to answer at all, but I believe you give each person their dignity until they ask you for something.

"There's been a slaughter here!" he sings, or more like chants, in what he must mean to be Jim Morrison's voice. *Been* comes out *bean.* I don't recognize the line: I don't know any more than just the normal about Jim Morrison, having been a Dylan person.

I get to my feet and walk away, telling myself not to run, leaving coffee, banana and newspaper behind. I wouldn't look in that bag for anything.

There's a phone if I can make it to the laundromat. But who would you call? The police, to report that a homeless man said something crazy? Your husband, to say you're afraid and could he please come make it right? Save your quarters for the dryer. Let him and the thing he's got in there, the thing he's following you along the street with, the thing he's now yelling about, the thing that probably isn't anything, melt back into the Great Whatever. I'm walking faster now, he's dropping back. And this will be just another New York story I'll tell.

The Intruder

They had the air conditioner on HI COOL, and the whole downstairs smelled of roasting turkey. Friday afternoon. Finn sat in the blue armchair, which rested on Teflon wafers to protect the floor he'd finally gotten around to sanding and refinishing. With spar varnish, not that damnable polyurethane. He was reading, of all things, *Timon of Athens*, which he'd remembered as being much better. So this would probably be the last time in his life he would read *Timon of Athens*; that made it seem sad and precious, if not especially enjoyable. As he read, he worried: that there would be too many leftovers, that Thanksgiving dinner in July wasn't charming but simply outré, that none of the guests would know he'd been interested in American cooking before it had become fashionable, and that he had been boring James by saying so repeatedly.

James sat cross-legged in the burgundy armchair with his earphones on. Among the few possessions he'd brought along when he moved in was his collection of books on tape. Lately he'd been reading—if that was the word—Edgar Allan Poe.

"Plugged in and passive," he'd said. "I'm the first to admit it. The MTV generation. Before your very eyes." Affected decadence was one of James's comic turns.

"But *Poe*?" Finn had said.

"It's camp, what can I say?" said James. "I thought *all* faggots were into camp back in your day."

On the floor by his chair James had set a sweating glass of seltzer. He was forever setting his glass on the floor, and Finn was forever nagging; today especially he should just bite his tongue. He'd invited Peter and Carolyn, of course, and people from the department—Bill and Deborah Whitley, Byron Solomon—although he'd told no one it was an occasion. An anniversary, for James and Finn, could only be the anniversary of one thing, and Finn was ... he called it considerate, James called it chickenshit, about shoving in people's faces what they didn't want to know. They'd decided to make today their anniversary, although it could also have been yesterday; by the time this had become important, it was too late to pin it down. James had gone to the library and looked in the microfiche to check the movie ads in the paper that week. *Rebecca* and *Notorious* had been Wed-Thur, but they couldn't decide which day they'd gone. For once Finn hadn't been teaching summer school, and James said (his decadent routine again) that he hadn't cared what day of the week it was since the last time he'd held a job.

James's sister Carolyn lived on the next street, one house over from Finn's: their backyards touched at a single point. A year ago today—or yesterday—Finn had been out back taking down, at long last, the swing set that had been there when he'd bought the place. With a sledgehammer he'd pulverized the concrete plugs that anchored the supports in the ground; the swing set now lay on its side like a dog killed by a car, two stiff legs in the air. He was trying to decide if it could be knocked apart with the hammer or if he'd have to take a hacksaw to it when he noticed this "young man"—Finn hated the expression—dressed only in shorts and running shoes mowing the Sykes's lawn. Finn nodded and received a nod in return. Carolyn had forewarned him that her brother would be coming up to stay in the house for a few days while she and Peter were in

Umbria, and encouraged him to go over and introduce himself. It seemed uncivil not to make use of this opportunity, but the brother's very good looks made Finn feel disinclined. That night, Wed or Thur, he went to what he still thought of as the Central but was now called the Symposium: the town's musty, velvety old theater had become a revival house with air-popped popcorn and a beer-and-wine license, run by a graduate-school dropout convinced that civilized people were getting tired of VCRs. Ahead of him in the ticket line stood the young man. When he turned away from the window with his ticket, he saw Finn, smiled and nodded, and walked over.

"I think you're Finn McCarthy," he said.

"Well, that makes one of us," said Finn. "However. Yes. And I think you're the person who was so diligently mowing the Sykes's lawn this afternoon."

"James Chase." The young man stuck out a hand. "Carolyn's brother."

"Yes, Carolyn had prepared me," said Finn, taking the hand. "Somewhat." Should he have? Well, it was said now. "I ought to have come over to say hello, but I was preoccupied."

"You did look kind of menacing with that sledgehammer," said the young man.

"That was my John Henry mode," said Finn. "Otherwise I'm harmless enough. So Peter and Carolyn euchred you into looking after the old homestead while they traipse around sunny Italy."

"It didn't take much euchring." James Chase pushed up the sleeve of his T-shirt and scratched a shoulder. "It was this or muggy Manhattan. Carolyn told me I should be sure and look you up."

"Ah," said Finn. "Here, why don't we go in?" Was he over-reacting, or was this a bit gauche of Carolyn, to have steered this obviously gay boy in his direction? The first move, if any, ought to have been Finn's. On the other hand, he couldn't afford to think ill of Carolyn Sykes: except for poor Byron Solomon, and of course now the Whitleys, Peter and Carolyn were as close as Finn had to friends in this community. As Carolyn undoubtedly knew. Which was why she had taken such a liberty. Although she had surely meant well. (There: he was coming around already.) And as to the boy's being obviously gay, would that have been so obvious to a less knowing eye? Did Carolyn herself know it? One's family had a gift for not knowing these things, or so it had been in Finn's family. This brother of Carolyn's was certainly presentable—whatever that meant—and obviously conversable.

When the lights came up at intermission, Finn turned to him and said, "I'm going to give *Rebecca* a miss, I think. I remember this as being the better of the two, and it's starting to show its age. All this malarkey about how *magical* the two of them are together. Didn't seem so bloody magical to me. Ingrid Bergman reconciles me to living in the age of Julia Roberts."

"It really wasn't all that hot, was it?" said James Chase. "God, I feel like a heretic."

"Bracing, isn't it? I'll tell you what, since you're new in town. There happens to be quite a wonderful diner here. A lot of the old features pretty much *intacta*. They make a mean rice pudding, and there's a jukebox thing in every booth, with all sorts of marvelous old songs. It still has 'Ring of Fire.' Do you know 'Ring of Fire'? Johnny Cash?"

"I must've heard it," James Chase said. "But, you know. I'm into Garth. Mr. Va Va Voom."

"Well, then," said Finn, "we must educate you. Are you game?"

"Always," he said.

From the diner they went back to Finn's house to hear "White Circle" by Kitty Wells, which Finn insisted was a minor masterpiece. He opened a bottle of Montalcino, and soon he heard himself calling Willie Nelson a "filthy toad," and was aware for the millionth time that he tended to sound like an old queen when he'd been drinking. And so to bed—a surprise to them both. Finn had stopped doing this kind of thing years ago, and James had promised himself that he hadn't come up here to cruise. And he'd sworn off older men.

Later that same night—actually, it was beginning to turn gray outside the windows—when they got around to comparing stories, Finn's misgivings came back more sharply. James had been vague about his involvements in New York, but from what Finn could gather it was clear that he might really have been taking his life in his hands with this boy. But truly, wasn't AIDS simply the extreme, the mortal, instance of what had always been the case: that your new love's irrevocable past determined your future? But this James was his first adventure—was it possible?—since he'd moved here. Finn didn't even have a condom in the house. James, thank God, had come equipped, despite what he'd promised himself; he carried them in his wallet, like the flamboyantly heterosexual boys of Finn's high school days.

Finn found James's coming-out story unsettling, too. His own announcement to his parents (he'd been forty; they'd been too old to hear it) had been like something out of a made-for-TV film: the father's anger, the mother's self-castigation. James had been in his last year of high school; he'd stuck a video called *Top Sergeant* (randy Marines in the barracks) in a *Sound of Music* box, wrapped it and put it under the Christmas tree. As James told the story, his parents waited to watch it until his Aunt Addie showed up for Christmas dinner, and she'd been so shocked that her dentures fell out. Finn suspected that at least part of this was invented: Aunt Addie was clearly a stock character, a Margaret Dumont or an Edna May Oliver. And it might or might not have been true that his father's slapping him across the mouth had been the pretext for James's quitting school and moving to New York. But true or not, the story made Finn feel both excited and intimidated, much as he'd felt when Ricky Morrison had seduced him into playing with matches. From the can Finn's father had kept in the toolshed, Ricky had poured a circle of gasoline onto the Mc-Carthys' lawn and tossed match after match until it roared up. Finn rubbed in vain with the soles of his sneakers at the telltale ring of charred grass; he'd caught holy hell, named his accomplice, and that was the end of his friendship with Ricky Morrison.

That first night, with Kitty Wells keening, it had been James who committed himself first: he took a deep breath, put a warm hand on the back of Finn's neck and pulled him close. Yet it had also been James who'd said, "I want to put this on you, can I?" So neither of them, Finn reminded himself, had all the power. That is, if you believed it was all about who fucked whom.

James's Walkman gave a snap. Finn looked up from *Timon of Athens* and saw him take off the earphones, stretch his arms up over his head and stand up. "The willies," he said. "So what time are people supposed to be arriving?"

Finn stuck a finger in the book and rolled his wrist to check his watch. Ten after four, which of course had no bearing on the question. "I told 'em all six o'clock," he said. "I hate this nonsense where you have one coming at six o'clock and one at six-fifteen and so on." Endearing that anyone could still get the willies from Edgar Allan Poe.

"Six o'clock," said James. "Listen, if you don't mind, I think I'm going to nap for a little. Could you come wake me up?"

"What time?" Finn said, hoping he didn't sound disapproving. He'd gotten up at three in the morning to take a piss; when he came downstairs he'd found James in the study watching *Star 80*. The room had stunk of pot.

"I'll leave that," James said, "to your discretion."

Oh.

"Actually, I might come up and join you," said Finn. "I'm pretty much at a stopping place. Just let me baste Junior again."

"Don't feel obliged," said James.

"Now, what's all *this*?"

James shook his head. "Nothing. I must be on the rag."

Oh, fine, Finn thought. So now it was up to him whether to allow James to get in a jab for free or whether to turn this into another battle royal. Since there were guests due in a couple of hours he should just drop it. But. But but but.

"Am I being unreasonable?" said Finn. Like a damn fool. "To want to know what I'm being told?"

"You're never unreasonable."

"And what's that supposed to mean?"

"Just what I said. You're never unreasonable. *I'm* unreasonable. As we all know so well."

Finn closed his eyes for a count of three and blew out his breath for James to hear.

"Now I've done it," James said. "Enter the Bickersons."

"*Why* are you doing it?"

"What a reasonable question," said James. "Why doesn't James just go take his nap and wake up cheerful and refreshed? If there's anything the world doesn't need it's another scene with the bitchy *faggots* trying to keep it together in front of company."

"That's not what I'm concerned about," Finn said.

"Oh, right." James started up the stairs, then stopped and looked back. "Hey, Finn? You *would* be welcome to tuck me in."

Finn decided. "Okay. Just let me deal with Junior."

James continued up the stairs. As his feet disappeared from sight he called, "Don't be too long."

Finn put the book down, not bothering to mark his place. Truly, that turkey smelled splendid. On his way to the kitchen he picked up James's Walkman from where he'd left it on the floor. Which story had given James the willies? Finn hit EJECT and saw it wasn't Poe at all but just a tape tape. On the label someone had written WORKOUT MUSIC/MADONNA ETC. The writing was faded, and it wasn't James's.

Finn McCarthy made documentary films. Or had until six years ago, when he was looking for a place to land and was approached by the college's Department of Communication Arts. That was the year his film about children's street games had been nominated for an Academy Award. He'd meant to show these children (filmed in Newark, Liverpool, Mexico City and Connecticut) as members of a savage tribe with alien customs and ceremonies; it had bothered him, therefore, that two of the three reviews he'd gotten had called it "sensitive." For whatever reason, he hadn't been able to get going on a new project since. It was his course load, his inability to travel. It was the too-comfortable life here: dinner parties with tolerant acquaintances in a tolerant college town. It was his house, the first he'd ever owned, which had needed everything done to it. It was James.

But at long last he had a new project in mind. Which would damn well not be called "sensitive," either. And which would get him once and for all, at the age of fifty-two, out of the closet. (James gave him guff about that, but that was just James being James.) Finn had ignored the whole Stonewall business and everything thereafter; bully for them, of course, but. He was damned if he'd be ghettoized as a quote unquote gay filmmaker; anyway, his work wasn't political. Lately, though, he was beginning to wonder whether avoiding the subject in his films—well, not avoiding, just not obsessing—hadn't been a mistake, esthetically. When he looked at his old work nowadays (which wasn't often), it felt impersonal to him. Put together to a fare-thee-well, of course. Surely there was a way to get closer in without being either confessional or, God forbid, polemical. Assuming he wasn't too old to want to.

What he'd come up with was a film about the makers of gay porn videos. Which, if it worked—if he could get the time and the funding and of course the access—would be a sort of oblique self-portrait in addition to whatever else. His films had always been about subcultures: American Indians who worked building skyscrapers, a leprosarium in what was then Southern Rhodesia, country music fans. The children and their street games. But a subculture based on being homosexual and making films: how could this not end up being his best work? Or so he sometimes thought.

He'd gone so far as to begin collecting videos; he'd also written part of a first draft of an essay on the implicit formal conventions of film pornography. If he could finish this and get it decently published—he'd try *Film Quarterly* first, then *Sight and Sound*—it might help with the funding. The biggest problem, aside from outright censorship (the Mapplethorpe business still had everybody running scared) was that these days such a subject could only be a downer: even safe-sex porn had a "Masque of the Red Death" aura. Which was all to the good as far as the film was concerned. But it made the project a tough sell, even with his Oscar nomination. Which was now a long time ago.

Another problem was that James hated the idea: it would set things back twenty years, he'd said. "What if you were a black person? Would you make a movie about welfare cheats eating watermelon in their Cadillacs?"

Finn was flattered that James thought a film of his could have any impact at all in the world. "Hell, yes," he said. "If I could get a grant from General Motors."

James looked at him. "It's not funny, man. You ever stop and think about where you *are*? You drive ten minutes outside this town, man, any direction, and you're in fucking Bible country. They don't *like* faggots out there, or haven't you heard?"

"You've lived in New York too long," Finn said. "I've never encountered the least—I mean, I don't go to workingmen's bars on a Saturday *night*, but who in his right mind *does*?"

James was still looking at him. "You are so blind, man."

Finn had never seen him this exercised. And only once before had he called him "man." When James first moved in, he'd gone down to the city for a weekend to pick up the rest of his things, and the weekend had lasted until Thursday. When Finn had gone to get him at the airport in Albany, James's explanation had been so carelessly thin that Finn (who'd drunk a half-carafe of vile Paul Masson red while waiting in the lounge) had called him a slut.

"Listen, man," James had said, "this *slut* was good enough for you when you picked me up at the movies."

"*I* picked *you* up?"

"You don't know how lucky you are," said James. "You're getting a live-in slut all your own, man, complete with checkered past. Just don't push it."

This, of course, was nonsense. Finn knew what it was to be excited by beautiful bad boys, but at his age he also knew better than to let any of them move into his home. To take a lithe, treacherous animal to bed was one thing; to wake up next to such a person was something else again. James's good looks, in fact, had bothered Finn until he got used to them. (It humanized James a bit when Finn walked in on him spraying Right Guard into his Nikes.) In fact, after the first few days, Finn had been about to hint that it was getting time for James to go back to his sister's house. He changed his mind the afternoon he came inside from mowing the lawn and found James in the darkened study. On the TV screen, the little black girls from Newark were jumping double Dutch. James looked up, saw Finn in the doorway, thumbed the remote and froze a little girl with her teeth bared and both feet in the air. "This is amazing," James said. "How did you get this to be so scary?"

Finn dropped into his Zen pedagogical manner. "Just by looking at it."

"Gol-*ly,* professor." James looked back at the frozen image. "I wonder how you look at me," he said. "I'd like to be looked at with kindness."

"Of course, when I first saw it listed," Byron Solomon was saying, "I was quite humiliated."

"Why?" said Bill Whitley. "God, to be able to say you worked with John Ford."

"*Worked?* I'm afraid that flatters the case," Byron said. "At any rate, I nearly made a great fool of myself by calling them up and lacing into them about it. Jeannette, of course, talked me around. She said, 'Good heavens, how were *they* to know?' Because naturally, for mere *movies* I never used 'Byron Solomon.' Never sullied the great name." He laughed. It didn't sound bitter, and Finn wondered if that was even more depressing. "So she said, 'How were *they* to know, for heaven's sake?' You remember how she was."

"I wish I could've known her," said Bill Whitley, apparently meaning it as a tactful reminder.

"God, yes, I can hear her now," said Finn, throwing in a chuckle to boot, though in fact the imitation had sounded more like Marie Dressler than Jeannette; Byron Solomon, after all, hadn't been much of an actor. Bill Whitley, like the other newer faculty, tended to treat Byron as if he were senile, which was terribly unfair. True, he had slipped a bit since Jeannette died. But the man had to be sixty-five: who didn't slip? Really, Finn should have exerted himself more to find Byron a dinner partner. But one no longer worried about pairing people off for dinners, just as one no longer worried about going boy-girl-boy-girl at table, although Finn in fact had seated Carolyn between himself and Bill Whitley, and Deborah Whitley between himself and Peter Sykes.

"At any rate," said Byron, "my curiosity of course got the better of me, and down I went. And you know, I thoroughly enjoyed myself. In *both* senses. I was on-screen for all of three minutes, and let me tell you, I was as bad a bad guy as ever chewed the scenery." Finn had heard Byron tell this story before, in exactly the same words. "And do you know what happened?" Finn knew. "A rousing cheer went up! The house lights came on! And there stood my entire class, applauding. Jeannette, it seems, had called one of my students—Finn, you remember her, a Susan somebody? Lovely girl—who in turn had called the fellow at the theater and arranged the whole thing. Jeannette had been prepared to drag me there bodily if necessary, sick as she was. Well, let me tell you, it was like *The Ed Sullivan Show. Toneet in air steeyewdio audience . . .*" Even Byron's Ed Sullivan was no good.

James was staring down at his plate through all of this, mixing together his turnips and mashed potatoes with his salad fork. Must he show his boredom so plainly? Finn had civilized him in some respects—he no longer drank Kahlúa, for instance—but his table manners were still an embarrassment. Not just the elbows, but the face hanging over the plate and the clumsy business of having to switch his fork to his right hand after cutting a piece of meat because no one had ever taught him to use his silverware properly. Well, that was a lost cause nowadays.

James began mixing in his cranberries, turning the whole mess gray. Finn leaned over to Carolyn and whispered, "I think your brother's attention span has reached its limit. I should never have put him between Byron and Bill." Before Byron had gotten the floor, Bill Whitley had been holding forth on Simon Callow. Which Finn couldn't help but think was punningly appropriate, though to say so later to James would be a cheap shot.

"But God help me," Byron Solomon was saying, "if there's a kinescope floating around of my episode of *Judge Roy Bean*. Also pseudonymous. 'Law West of the Pecos.' Now, that's one I do *not* care to see revealed."

"Edgar Buchanan!" cried Bill Whitley. Everyone but the Whitleys had heard this, too.

"Suppose I mobilize him to help me clear," Carolyn said to Finn. "Meanwhile you can rescue poor Deborah."

Deborah Whitley, whom Finn had seated at his left, had her golden, mostly naked back to him, leaning into her conversation with Peter Sykes. Who had filled his and Deborah's wine-glasses twice now, and was speaking too low for the rest of the table to hear. He made a fist, then stretched forth the fingers like a tenor hitting a high note. Muscles bulged in his forearm: Peter Sykes was a sculptor who'd spent the past three months working in an auto body shop to sharpen his welding skills. Deborah Whitley laughed.

Finn admired Carolyn for her civilized pretense that her husband was a bore, bending the unwilling ear of the large-breasted, precariously halter-topped Deborah Whitley. Carolyn's intelligence would probably get her through until her looks began to go. Good Christ, one's friends.

After dinner, Byron nodded off in Finn's armchair; then his eyes flew open and he said he guessed he'd better toddle along. The Whitleys had brought him, but Bill looked so crestfallen—Finn was flattered that he was enjoying himself, but appalled by his bad manners—that Peter Sykes offered to drive Byron home. This jogged Bill into a belated sense of the decencies, and that was it for the evening; one couldn't very well ask Peter and Carolyn to stay on with the Whitleys standing right there.

Carolyn offered to help with the cleanup, but Finn wouldn't hear of it. She said she'd be glad to. Finn said they had things well in hand.

"Oh, don't be such a macho man," she said. "You'll be up till all hours."

"Well . . . ," said Finn.

"Shoo," James said. "No girls allowed."

"If you're sure," said Carolyn.

James rolled his eyes. "Ve vant," he stage-whispered, "to be alone."

Carolyn looked down at the beautiful wood floor.

After closing the door on all of them, Finn turned to James. "There was no need to be brutal. Couldn't you see she was upset?"

"What?" said James. "What are you talking about now?"

"Oh, come," Finn said. "Even *you* couldn't have missed what was going on at dinner. I assure you, your sister took note."

"What, Stanley Kowalski and Little Bo Peep? Oh, for God's sake. Parties are for flirting. That's what they're *about*. I mean, if there's anybody there under *fifty*. Or wasn't it like that back in your day?"

"This was a social evening," Finn said, hating this tone he was being maneuvered into taking. "I don't regard that as giving people license to hurt other people's feelings."

"Ooh," said James. "Well I guess that tells *me*. The Queen of Feelings has spoken." He walked into the kitchen with that walk Finn hated. That goddamn faggot walk, where the shoulders didn't move. The fourth bottle of Montalcino—Finn also hated white wine—had only about that much left. He picked it up, glanced at the kitchen doorway and polished it off. What would the Italian be for *À même la bouteille*? He carried the dead soldier into the kitchen, not even looking at James (who fetched a loud sigh as he bent over the dishwasher), and on through into the mudroom, where he dropped it, clank, in with the green glass. All this environmental malarkey was accomplishing exactly nothing except to give a bunch of small people the power to tyrannize you when you went to the dump. Even grocery bags had turned self-righteous: WE RECYCLE, with the arrows going around. Finn hated that "we."

On Saturday morning the phone rang while he was standing at the refrigerator eating cold stuffing with his fingers. "Hi," said Carolyn. "I hope I'm not calling too early."

"No no no, I've been up since seven-thirty." Finn looked at his watch: eleven on the dot. "Didn't you see me out back with my trusty wheelbarrow? That bloody sandbox is finally going the way of the swing set. This time next year we'll have a backyard suitable for grown-ups, by Jesus." He hated saying "we" to Carolyn, but "I" would've been even worse. "Did the O'Donnell children really play on that flimsy little swing set?"

"And everyplace else," Carolyn said. "*Four* of the little monsters. From sunup to sundown. Peter and I used to *pray* for a rainy day."

"Ah, but sure and they were precious souls for Holy Mother Church," said Finn.

"Listen, Finn?" Carolyn said. "There's something—listen, James isn't right there, is he?"

"Christ, no. Lazy little son of a bitch is still asleep." The lumberjack mode, he felt, compensated for that "we." "You want me to call him? It's about time he—"

"No," she said. "No, what I mean is, could I talk to you about something?"

"Of course." He edged over to the kitchen table, watching the coils of the telephone cord stretch, and sat down. He put his hand to his shirt pocket as if pledging allegiance. Only the rattle of a matchbook.

"There was a message on our machine when we got home last night," Carolyn said. Finn was scanning the room: damn it, his cigarettes were over there on the counter, far out of reach. "My father went in for some tests a couple of weeks ago. And now they want him to go back and have more done. And—you know, it just doesn't sound very good."

"Tests," said Finn.

"See, he's had, you know, rectal bleeding . . ."

"Right," said Finn.

"And I just thought James ought to be told."

"Right," said Finn. "I agree. Do you want to, or shall I?"

"Well . . ." she said.

"I'll be glad to," he said. "I take it there's been very little contact."

"I guess it's been a little better since—you know, since he's been living up here. If anything, they're—"

"Would you excuse me just a second?" Finn put the receiver down, wedging it between the heavy cut-glass vase and the dinette-style metal napkin dispenser so the tension in the cord wouldn't pull it off onto the floor, then went over and fetched his cigarettes.

"I'm back," he said, holding the receiver to his ear with his shoulder as he struck a match. "Carolyn, I'm very sorry to hear this about your father." He took a deep, welcome drag and considerately raised the mouthpiece as he blew out the smoke. "We'll hope it turns out to be nothing serious. And I'll speak to James as soon as he comes down. Now, are *you* all right?"

"I guess," she said. "I'm just trying to, you know, wait to hear something concrete and not panic until there's actually something to panic about."

"Good girl," he said. "It's a harrowing thing, I know. I went through this with *my* father." Hardly a reassuring thing to say, on second thought. "I can't honestly tell you that the waiting is the worst part"—Christ, he was getting himself in deeper— "but in your case I truly hope it will be." He had extricated himself by inspiration.

"So do I," she said. Then she said, "I'm sorry about your father."

"Oh, this was years ago. So meanwhile. What do you recommend? Should James go down there, do you think? Are *you* planning to go down?"

"No," she said. "I think at this point all it would do is get everybody more upset. You know, people showing up like . . ." Had she been going to say *like vultures*? "Besides, Fort Myers isn't all that divine in July. But I do think that if he would call or write—I don't know, I just think it would mean a lot. If only for his own sake, you know? Like later on."

"Right," said Finn.

"I think he really is very ill. I just—something just tells me that."

"I'll go upstairs right now. And you'll let me know if there's anything else I can do."

"I will. Thank you."

"*Ciao*," he said, and stood up to put the receiver back in its cradle.

"So what's going on?" Finn turned: James was standing, barefoot, in the archway leading to the dining room.

"I didn't realize you were up," Finn said. "That was Carolyn. It seems your father has gone in for some tests, and they're not certain at this point, what if anything, is wrong. But apparently your mother's quite upset, and your sister seems to think it sounds serious enough that you ought to get in touch with them."

"And say what?"

"I don't honestly know, Jamie. That would be up to you."

James went to the refrigerator, took out a bottle of seltzer and drank from it. "Sort of tests are we talking about?"

"Again," said Finn, and spread his hands, palms up. A long ash fell off his cigarette, and he saw it shatter softly on the floor. "It seems to be some sort of colorectal thing."

"That figures," James said. "So we're talking cancer."

"Again," said Finn.

James said, "I want to call my sister."

The test results weren't in until the following Friday. On Saturday morning Finn drove James to Albany. He put James's round-trip ticket on his Visa and got him four hundred dollars, the daily limit, from a cash machine. After a goodbye hug at the gate, Finn walked back out to the car, sat on the front fender and watched the plane out of sight. Watched himself watch the plane out of sight.

The drive down to JFK used to take Finn four hours; today it had taken four and a half. He no longer had the energy—no, the foolhardiness—to roll seventy and seventy-five all the way. Even so, he was half an hour early, so he tried to get comfortable on the narrow aluminum ledge of a giant window near the security station, and to involve himself in the last act of *Timon of Athens.* He'd deliberately brought nothing else: damned if he'd allow himself to get that far and not finish. But how was he to concentrate? About fifty people were clustered here, whole families with whining children; they sat against the wall, paced, stood shifting their weight from foot to foot. Only ticket holders were being allowed to go through security and down to the gates where there were seats. So decent, ordinary people, waiting for their loved ones, were denied a modicum of comfort all because—well, enough. It was unattractive to be querulous.

He'd driven all the way down here because James couldn't find a direct flight. Flying to Albany would've involved shuttling from JFK to La Guardia, sitting at La Guardia for two hours . . . ridiculous. If the lights started to bother Finn's eyes on the drive back, they could always stop and put up at a motel. He'd also driven down because he needed to make another foray into Times Square.

James had seemed in fine fettle on the telephone, but now that it was certain the old man (five years older than Finn) had only months to live, God knows what buried feelings were bound to come up. Finn was truly sorry for James: he himself had been forty-five before he'd had to go through this. But he hoped that whatever James had to endure over the next few months—and he was ashamed of how selfish this sounded—it would not prove too disruptive. During the week and a half James had been gone, Finn had written another three pages of his essay and had composed the covering letter. No doubt James would be upset that he intended to run an errand—particularly this errand—before going home. Had Finn not taken so much wine last night, he would've been able to get up earlier, to finish picking up the house earlier and to make his stop before coming to the airport. But if there had to be a showdown, then a showdown there would be. This was his only life, and he had only so much of it left.

He couldn't concentrate on *Timon of Athens*.

At last passengers with suitcases and garment bags began appearing. No one had even bothered to announce the arrival: the slipshod way everything was run nowadays would make a saint querulous. Yet he mustn't visit this querulousness on James, who would need his support. And would find his bitching and moaning unattractive. And there was James now, his canvas duffel slung from his shoulder, and in his other hand—what? A net bag of oranges.

Finn gave him a brotherly one-armed hug. James bent to lay the oranges down, straightened up, gripped the back of Finn's neck and kissed him on the mouth. "This is New York City," he said. "Remember?"

"Forgive an old man," said Finn. "When ye git my age, sonny . . ."

"If," James said.

Finn looked at him. James's tan, he noticed, was even deeper than when he'd left. So more had been going on, apparently, than just the compulsive TV-watching and the silent family dinners James had re-created so amusingly on the phone. "Ah, nature's bounty," he said, bending down to pick up the oranges.

"My mother insisted," James said. "And she was very particular that they were for both of us."

"Well well well," said Finn. "God and sinners reconciled. But wouldn't pink grapefruit have been more appropriate?"

James began walking. The sight of his firm buttocks under his white shorts made Finn suddenly furious.

"Your tan looks splendid," he said, catching up. "So how are the beach girls down there? Really *stacked*, I'll bet."

James stopped. People passed by on both sides, paying no attention. "Hey, Finn? Why don't you give it a rest, okay? I'm just really not up to it. This has not been a good week."

"Yes, I can see it must've been hell," Finn said, appalled that he couldn't shut up.

"I can't believe this is happening," said James. "I've been off the plane for all of two minutes, and already we're in one of these *things.*"

"I'm sorry, Jamie. I don't know what the hell's wrong with me."

"Can we not stand here in the middle of all this?"

"Sorry. Here." Finn touched James's shoulder to guide him. "We're parked down this way."

They walked a few steps toward the escalator and James stopped again. "Look," he said, "would you rather I just took a cab into the city and got out of your life?"

"Jamie, I'm truly—"

"Because I don't seem to be making you very happy, and you're driving *me* out of my mind."

"You're shouting," said Finn.

"What, these people have never seen a pair of bickering *faggots* before?" Well, he was shouting now, at any rate.

"James," said Finn. "For Christ's sake."

"You want to know about my tan? Well, my parents have a *pool*, man. In their *backyard*. Which is where I sat for nine days, man, watching game shows with my mother. She keeps a TV out there so she can work on *her* tan. She looks like distressed leather. My father, meanwhile, sits in the den with the blinds closed, watching—I'm not kidding—old Super Bowl games on his VCR. He's got tapes of all but four of however many fucking Super Bowls there are. And he's scared shitless and he eats so much Valium his flesh is turning to balsa wood."

"I'm so sorry," said Finn.

"Look," James said, "do you mind very much if we get out of here?"

In the parking garage, Finn unlocked the passenger door first. James in turn reached over and unlocked the driver's door, which Finn took as a sign of conciliation. He decided not to nag James about his seat belt. He reached over and stroked the back of James's head. James allowed it.

When they came out into the sunlight—it was still only five o'clock—Finn put on the air conditioning. James had taught him that it was more fun to keep the windows open when the air was on, even if less efficient. On the Grand Central, traffic in the other direction was halted, but inbound it was moving right along.

"I hate to backseat-drive," said James, "but shouldn't we be in the other lane?"

"Ordinarily," Finn said. "But I need to make a quick stop-off in midtown."

"For what?"

Finn drew a long breath, let it out. "For something you don't approve of."

"Oh." James looked at his watch. "You know, it's going to take *hours* to get in and out of Manhattan at this time of day. You couldn't have done this on your way?"

"I'm sorry. I'll make this as quick as I possibly can, but I get to the city so seldom that I really mustn't pass up the chance."

"So that's why you were so hot to come down and pick me up," said James. "Tell me something. Do you ever think your tastes might be a little depraved?"

"We've been over this," Finn said.

"Then let me put it in another light for you. Did it ever occur to you that it might be insulting to *me*?"

They were caught behind a huge yellow school bus. The lanes on either side weren't moving any faster, but Finn cut to the left in front of a cab—the driver leaned on his horn—just to get behind something he could see past.

"You're not going to provoke me," he said. "We disagree about this project. I respect your view. I'm asking you to respect mine."

"Project?" said James. "What project? This isn't a *project*, for Christ's sake. It's one more old queen who likes to watch young dudes get it on. You can dignify it because you used to be some hot-shit filmmaker."

Finn looked over at him, this idle boy with his dirty blond hair blowing. Who made him waste his time and now had contempt for him because of it. He had let himself become an aging man with no family, who no longer prepared before meeting his classes and whose taste for good wines was giving him broken veins in his nose. He was this young man's sugar daddy. He turned back in time to avoid ramming the BMW ahead of him by lifting his foot quickly from the gas pedal: to hit the brakes would call James's attention to his bad driving.

"For whatever reason," Finn said, his heart beginning to pound in delayed reaction, "I have done almost no work in the time I've known you. This is going to come to a screeching halt."

"You haven't done any work for five years, man," said James.

Seven, thought Finn. "I'm not putting it off on you," he said. His heart was pounding harder. "But I won't allow you to interfere with what I need to do."

James said nothing.

"And I might add that it's probably time for you to start thinking about what you're going to do when *you* grow up." The pounding began to subside. "It's a waste of life, and it depresses me severely."

"Would you like me to go to night school and become a hairdresser?"

"That, my dear, is up to you," said Finn. "What I mean to do is to make a stop in midtown. For one hour, no longer. And then we'll be on our way. If you're coming."

"Finn," said James. "It's your car, it's your life. I don't really have anything to say about it."

"Now, if you prefer," Finn said, "it *is* getting late-ish. We could have dinner in the city, leave when the traffic's thinned out and maybe put up for the night somewhere along the way."

James didn't answer. Finn looked and saw that he was crying. Not sobbing, just letting the tears go down his face.

"Just please do what you're going to do," James said at last. "All I want is to get home."

The Intruder

. . .

James had been back almost a week before Finn had time to sit down and go through the videos he'd bought in Times Square. *Made* time, he corrected himself. But James had come down with a summer cold, and Finn did have to nurse him, bring him ice cream and ginger ale and magazines, go to the drugstore for cough syrup and Comtrex. And they did have to ask Peter and Carolyn over to hear James's report and to discuss what might have to be done in the time remaining. Which of course involved preparing a decent meal, and what with the shopping and the cooking, that was *another* day shot to hell. And the lawn had needed another mowing. He'd neglected it while James was gone.

But now, at last, a quiet day. James, recovered, had borrowed the car for the afternoon. Acting mysterious about it, too. Perhaps out buying a thanks-for-taking-care-of-me gift, since before leaving he had—wonder of wonders—done the breakfast dishes and straightened up the bedroom. So Finn, having run out of distractions, sat alone in his study with a notepad, watching something called *Hellfire Club*. Two men lay side by side on a bed as cheap, nasty music went *wacka wacka wacka* on the soundtrack. One, with mustache and short hair, decked out in leather jacket, leather pants and motorcycle boots, was propped up on a pillow, angrily puffing a cigarette. The other, with a platinum-dyed Mohawk, wore only a black leather collar with diamond-shaped silver studs. He lay facedown, his body a uniform dingy white; you could see sores on his legs. (At least this film wasn't arty.) The leather one took a final drag, tapped off the final ash and stubbed his cigarette out on the Mohawk one's white buttock. The Mohawk one twitched, then lay still again.

Finn suddenly felt sick to his stomach; and these were only the opening minutes of a sixty-minute film. He hit STOP and the screen went snowy. Was his discomfort a sign that here was something worth his attention? Had he needed to turn the thing off because it was too powerful? Or was it just ugly and frightening, period, without any significance? Why did these films fascinate him? *Did* they fascinate him, or was he in fact burned out and desperately willing himself to be fascinated?

Well, good: simply to ask such questions was to work. Unless it was another way of not working.

Perhaps the thing to do was to look at something less harrowing and allow his unconscious to process some of this.

He ejected *Hellfire Club*, put it back in its case and looked through the rest of the new ones. Well, what about *Sean in Love*? If nothing else, it ought to be sensitive. Perhaps instead of films that were manifestly sordid, you wanted to look at the capital-*S* sensitive ones and spot the details that showed they were sordid, too. Or was that too easy? Probably.

The premise of *Sean in Love* was that "Sean," a Wall Street type—there was some malarkey at the beginning about "mergers"—took an island vacation and kept falling for lifeguards, Rastas and suchlike. He would gape at them, then the image would go wavy and dissolve (harp glissando on the soundtrack) to show that what followed was fantasy. In the third such fantasy, he was in a sauna getting fucked by a Nautilus instructor—it seemed to Finn that the wooden bench must've been hell on his back and shoulders—when there was a cut to outside the door (through which their stagy moans could still be heard), where a third young man, in tight shorts, was reaching for the door handle. (This annoyed Finn: up to now the fantasies had been presented scrupulously from Sean's point of view.) "Oopsy-daisy," said the intruder—and Finn leaned forward. Cut from the fuckers' surprised faces to the smiling face of the intruder: James, of course, of course, of course. Younger, but still James. Finn had never been fool enough to think that particular smile had been turned on no one but him. He watched the scene through to the end, with its combinations and recombinations. All very predictable.

Finn was still sitting in his study when he heard the car pull in. He'd smoked all but one of the cigarettes that should have lasted him until sometime tomorrow, and he'd tossed the pack with the last cigarette onto the floor just out of reach; that way he wouldn't smoke it until he really needed it. Well, he would take the keys from James—who he now hoped wasn't bringing him a present—say as little as possible and drive over to Stewart's for a fresh pack. Maybe by the time he got back he would've figured out what to do next. He heard the screen door slap and James calling, "Hey, anybody home?"

He stood up and felt suddenly lightheaded. He'd been sitting there ever since . . . ever since. He opened the door and saw James coming through the kitchen. The living room between them, with its narrow, glossy floorboards, looked as vast as a basketball court.

"So guess what?" said James.

"Suppose you just tell me," Finn said.

"Okay. Brace yourself." James wasn't picking up Finn's mood at all. Or he was choosing not to, in order to make his own mood prevail. "You're looking at a productive citizen."

"A productive citizen," Finn said.

"Well, a soon-to-be productive citizen. I've got a job."

"Do you." Finn remained standing in the doorway. James went over and sat in the burgundy armchair, draping one leg over the side and letting the foot swing.

"So aren't you curious?"

Finn said nothing.

"I would've thought you'd be pleased." James now seemed to be catching on.

Finn thought for a second. "I can understand that," he said.

"What's going on?" James said. His foot stopped moving. "Oh, Jesus," he said. "My dad."

"Say again?" Then Finn remembered. "No," he said. "No, there's no news of your father."

"Jesus, you scared the hell out of me. So listen, do you want to hear this or not?"

Finn stretched forth his hands as if supplicating, then let them drop. "Fire away," he said.

"Okay, there was an ad in the paper that they were looking for an assistant manager at the Symposium. So I went down and checked it out? I thought it would just be like running the popcorn machine. But it's actually a serious job, like book-keeping and stuff. I *will* have to run the ticket window, but he said I'd have some input on programming, and I'll definitely be writing the little synopses in the schedule, and it's just—I think it's really going to be good."

"You've taken a job," Finn said.

"Assuming the reference I gave him checks out." James laughed.

"Right," Finn said.

"So anyhow, I promise that every July I'll get them to run our Hitchcock movies again that we didn't like. God, I'm getting sentimental in my old age."

"Perhaps you could make it a triple feature," said Finn. "With *Sean in Love*."

James cocked his head. "I don't get it."

"*Sean in Love*," said Finn. "It's a video I picked up in Times Square. I think it would interest you greatly."

James took a deep breath and let it out. "Oh," he said. "Always wondered what they ended up calling it."

"So what do they pay for work like that?" Finn said.

"I don't know. They paid *me* a hundred dollars. Which I needed very badly at the time. It was my first year in New York."

"A hundred dollars," said Finn. "Did you enjoy your work?"

"Did *you*? What do you want me to tell you? That they were holding a gun to my head like Linda Lovelace? You know, I was eighteen, and this friend of mine asked me if I wanted to be with him in this movie that—"

"Which friend was that?"

"He was supposed to be playing this exercise teacher or something. He actually *was* an exercise teacher. I used to go to his workout."

"I can imagine," said Finn.

"Maybe you ought to sit down," James said. "You look really pale."

Finn walked to the blue armchair—his footsteps seemed to echo, and the journey seemed to take a long time. He sat down. Sparkles swam before his eyes.

"How many of those *friends* of yours," he said, wishing he had that last cigarette, "are dead?"

"How would I know?" said James. "This was one afternoon, like five years ago. Don't you think I think about it every day? Plus all the other stupid shit I did?" He reached into his jacket pocket and tossed Finn first a book of matches, then an unopened pack of Merits. "You know, everybody's got dead friends. Except you, right? Since you don't *have* friends."

Finn got the pack open, worked a cigarette out of it, lit it, took a first deep, wonderful drag and glanced around for an ashtray. The late afternoon sun glinted off the varnished floor. He became conscious of the faraway drone of somebody's lawnmower; for a second there he thought of nothing at all. Then he realized he was staring at the overlapping white rings by the side of James's chair.

"So," he said. "I suppose this explains why you were hell-bent on getting me sidetracked from my project."

"One reason, yes," said James.

"Why didn't you simply tell me?"

"Because look at you. You know, I know about men who like naughty boys. And the bottom line is that they don't like 'em to be *too* naughty. So." Quick shrug. "What? Do you want me to go over and stay at my sister's while I make other arrangements?"

Touching up just that little bit of floor, Finn thought, would be simplicity itself.

"I don't know what I want at this point," he said. "I want to believe that none of this really happened."

"Oh," said James. "Well, if that's all. You can manage that okay, whether I'm around or not. I imagine you've already started."

The Crazy Thought

The year was round, a millstone turning slowly clockwise, and even on this Friday afternoon in August, Faye could feel it moving down toward Christmas. There were points on the circumference whose approach she always dreaded: Ben's birthday and their wedding anniversary, both in June and safely past this time around; her own birthday, in January, when he was likely to call or send a card; May 21, the projected birthday of their aborted child; October 17, the day it died. They were like the songs she must never never listen to: "Devoted to You," or "These Foolish Things" or "The Long and Winding Road." She had been able to date the conception exactly, because it had been the only time for weeks. She had wept afterward, and Ben was put off, probably understandably; the next week he moved out, and never touched her again. When she went through her mystical thing about it, both her shrink and her sister Karen had explanations: she had gone off the pill because it was killing her (to increasingly little purpose), and having sex with him that afternoon was a fleeting self-destructive impulse. But lately she hadn't been bothering to fight away mystical ideas. At this point, what harm could they possibly do?

Karen had called Wednesday night, out of the blue, to ask if she and Allen could come for the weekend. And would it be at all possible to pick them up in Burlington if they took a plane Friday evening? Because if they rented a car, it looked like they couldn't possibly get there until after midnight. Not a problem, Faye told her, if they didn't mind Paul coming to get them in the truck; the car was in the shop, and she still hadn't learned to drive a stick.

"A *truck?*" Karen had said. "Allen will be thrilled."

"I'm always thrilled when people are thrilled," Faye had said. The car was in the shop because after front-end work to the tune of four hundred dollars they couldn't afford to get it out.

Faye had never met the new husband. In the wedding pictures he looked like a pretty standard product. Richard Dreyfuss in *Close Encounters*. Well, why not. Karen had relocated to L.A. just after Faye had moved into Paul's place on Laight Street, and she'd married Allen around the time Faye and Paul had clinked glasses at the Ear Inn to toast their plan: Paul would quit teaching and make the down payment on the farmhouse they'd found, and Faye would take that newspaper job in Burlington while he stayed home and wrote. By the time Karen talked Allen into moving back to New York, Faye and Paul had been up here for two years—during which time Faye got laid off and Paul began working for the town. Then another year just sort of went by. Faye and Paul never left Vermont, and Karen and Allen both had new jobs and couldn't always get away on weekends. When Allen had surgery on the knee he'd damaged playing squash, Faye almost went down to lend moral support but let Karen talk her out of it. *Moral support:* a weird expression. Was the assumption that people's morals needed shoring up in time of stress? Or was it moral of you to lend support? This was one of the many things that flew apart if you looked too closely.

The Crazy Thought

. . .

Across the road, above the green hills, the sky had turned
black. She'd better take the clothes off the line and hang them
in the woodshed. Paul had offered to get her a dryer, but Faye
wouldn't have it: she was living in the country now, and she
wanted that fresh smell. If he wanted to get her something, she
said, he could start with a wicker clothes basket to replace that
horrible green plastic one. "A *clothes basket?*" he said. Misun-
derstood Provider was one of Paul's favorite roles these days.
He was taking on the local accent, too, flattening certain
sounds and giving others an odd depth: the *a* in *farm* was
somewhere in between the *a* in *ah* and the *a* in *hat*, while the *i* in
wife was something like the *uy* in *Huysmans.* He had learned to
treat the kitchen as a living room, and to operate a chainsaw.
He had his truck, which he had taken to calling his "rig," and
half a dozen adjustable caps—the fronts thin foam rubber, the
backs nylon mesh—which still smelled after they'd been
through the wash. To have adopted such an esthetic so convinc-
ingly was a real accomplishment for someone who knew perfectly well who Huysmans was.

She had just got the still-damp clothes safely into the woodshed when the sound of rain came up out of the silence as if
somebody had turned up the volume. She walked to the open
door and watched it pelt down in slanting gray lines through
which waves of intensity swept back and forth; already the
driveway was a pair of muddy streams running side by side
with a strip of grass between. Paul would be home early: the
road crew certainly couldn't work in this.

It looked so touching, rain falling on all that green. And she
liked it in the woodshed. The rough-hewn beams, the sweet
wood smell. When they first moved in, she'd found a box of
shotgun shells out here, on a shelf next to a can of motor oil.
She brought the oil can to Paul but threw out the shells with-

out telling him, hiding them near the bottom of a trash bag;
then she'd worried for weeks that they might explode in the
compactor at the transfer station. All in all, things were better
up here. More coarse, yes: oafish locals sitting around her
kitchen table, six-packs torn open. More coarse, less harsh—
was that a meaningful distinction? New York was harsh. After
her divorce from Ben, she'd moved in with Karen on East
Third Street. Because she had a thing about poison, she'd
vacuumed up the boric acid Karen had put out, and bought
roach motels. A couple of days later she'd picked up one
to check inside, and it struck her that she was looking into
hell: tiny, starving creatures struggling to free themselves, or
just feebly waving their antennae. Later, when she took it up
with her shrink, she could see that it was explicable as a
projection of her guilt and not necessarily a message from
God. But at the time she'd screamed, and poor Karen had
come running.

It was sometime around then that Paul had come along.
Completely different from Ben, one hundred eighty degrees,
which was exactly what she needed. Somebody completely
right-brain, or whichever side it was that made you verbal as
opposed to whatever Ben was, with a lot of books, some of
them the same as hers, a novel-in-progress, a funky old Saab
and a failed marriage of his own. She'd gone to hear Cynthia
Ozick at the 92nd Street Y and started chatting with this man
in line who was wearing a nice-smelling leather jacket; when
they announced that all the tickets were sold, everybody
groaned, but he shrugged and said, "Minor disappointment.
I'm not sure I wouldn't rather have a drink anyway. Care to
come?" Karen had been greatly in favor of Paul. "You should
grab him," she said. "*I* would." This sounded like a threat, but
it turned out Karen wanted to move to California but was
afraid to go unless Faye had somebody. At first it made no
sense, being in bed with this bearded man whose hair didn't

smell like Ben's, or driving around up in the country staring at the fall colors out the window of this man's Saab.

She looked through the slanting rain at the green hills. Beyond them was the long and winding road that led to Ben's door, in Leavenworth, Washington. Then, down at the foot of the driveway, Paul's truck appeared, its lights on, edging close to the mailbox; she saw his arm stretch out of the window, pull open the box and reach inside. Now he gunned it up the driveway toward the house, and pulled onto the grass by the kitchen door. The wipers stopped, the headlights went out and she watched him trot into the house, hugging the mail to his chest with one hand, his other elbow shielding his head from the rain. She listened to him calling her name.

For once they got to eat in the dining room. Karen and Allen had brought four bottles of a better-than-okay California Merlot, and cheeses, olives and bread from Zabar's; Faye made sauce with their own tomatoes, which had just started to come in, and fresh pasta with her pasta machine. Paul's contribution was to keep the music going, though Faye thought she detected an edge of something when he put on Merle Haggard. He filled his wineglass again—they were already on bottle number three—and claimed Merle Haggard looked like King Hussein, which no one was prepared to dispute.

"Okay, Famous Look-Alikes," Paul said. "For ten points: Mama Cass."

"You mean think up somebody that looks like her?" Karen said.

He nodded. "Famous writer."

"Who was Mama Cass again?" said Allen.

"Mamas and the Papas," Karen said. "Faye used to have their album when I was in fourth grade."

"So ten points," said Paul. "Looks just like her. Famous, famous writer." He glances around the table.

"Would I know this person?" Allen said.

"I would hope so. You want another hint? Eighteenth century."

"You'll have to tell us," Karen said.

"Samuel Johnson."

"I don't see that at all," Karen said.

"I'm not really familiar," Allen said.

"Allen's more into John Le Carré," said Karen.

"Come on, I read good stuff, too."

"Nothing wrong with John Le Carré," Paul said. "I'd a hell of a lot sooner read him than fucking John Updike. If we're talking about Johns here."

"You realize that's the second mean thing you've said about John Updike?" Karen said. "Why do you have such a thing about him?"

Paul snorted. "I wonder."

Faye swirled the sediment in her wineglass. Alcohol was so interesting, she thought. Interesting just to sit here with all this loud talk going on around you and yet to feel safe. She'd probably feel even safer lying down on the bed, and maybe in a while she'd get up, excuse herself and go do just that. The dishes could wait until morning: no cockroaches up here. And Paul could flirt with her sister all he wanted because Karen's husband was on hand.

"Hey, actually I've got one," Allen said. "I'm thinking of somebody that looks just like Cecilia Bartoli."

"Who the hell is that?" said Paul.

"Cecilia Bartoli? Opera singer?"

Paul shrugged. "I heard of the Three Tenors. That's what opera singers you get up here in the boonies."

Now, what was this about? Paul never missed the Metropolitan Opera broadcast on Saturday afternoon—unless his redneck friends were in the house. His all-time favorite tenor was Jussi Björling.

"But you get PBS, don't you?" Allen said.

Faye poured herself more wine—just a touch. Karen's husband was going too far with Paul, but she was too drunk to imagine how to warn him.

"I told you," Paul said. "This is the fuckin' boonies, right? I *like* it to be the fuckin' boonies. Because all that crap is interchangeable. You know? Spaghetti-bender of the month. I mean, after a certain *point*"—waving his hand, he knocked over the current wine bottle, then quickly righted it, leaving just a splash of maroon on the white tablecloth.

"Good hands," Allen said. "So you give up?"

"I don't give *up*," Paul said. "I just don't happen to know what the hell you're talking about."

"*I* give up," Karen said. "If that helps."

Paul turned to her. "You don't believe me about Samuel Johnson. Don't go anywhere." He got up and headed for the living room, walking surprisingly well.

"Does *anybody* want to hear my thing?" Allen said.

"I do," Karen said.

Faye took another sip.

"Your sister," he said.

"What? No way," said Karen. "Okay, you're cut off."

"But it's true," he said. "Am I crazy?"

Faye closed her eyes and began to count. Maybe to fifty, she thought.

"There. Check it out," she heard Paul say.

She opened her eyes and saw him laying a book beside Karen's plate: a gray paperback whose cover showed a fat, peevish-looking, full-lipped man in a wig.

"Okay," Paul said, "now picture Mama Cass."

"I am," Karen said. "I think you're as nuts as my husband."

Faye closed her eyes again and considered proposing Richard Dreyfuss, but she couldn't tell if the game was over or not. Anyhow, it might take things someplace weird.

"What's it like for you, living here?" Karen said. They were walking up the path to where Faye knew there were blueberries, both swinging Medaglia d'Oro coffee cans. Faye had made holes in them with Paul's electric drill and attached pieces of clothesline for handles.

"I don't know," Faye said. "It's like—I don't know. I mean, it's like living anyplace, except it's . . . I don't know what to tell you."

"Sorry," Karen said. "I didn't mean it to be a tough question."

"Oh no, it's a legitimate question. I just, I don't really think about it. I mean, is it better than the city? You know, sure, in some ways. Having the space. Plus just being able to just go out your back door."

"Allen and I talk about it sometimes," Karen said. "I mean, we eventually do want to have kids, and it would be so much better in a place like this. But right now there's no way."

"You don't think? I bet if Allen played his cards right *he* could get a job on the road crew."

"Right. How's Paul dealing with that?"

Faye shrugged. "Like a pig deals with shit. He's running the grader, he's running the backhoe, the bushhog—whatever it all is. The big roller. Last winter he was on night call for the snowplow. All he needs is a gun rack for his pickup."

"He doing anything on his book? Wasn't that part of the idea?"

"The magnum opus? You never hear about it anymore. I assume it's fallen by the wayside."

Karen shook her head. "Waste."

"I don't know," Faye said. "Waste of what? He claims he's happy. Gets him outdoors, plenty of exercise—hasn't he given you the whole rap?"

"What about you, though?"

"What *about* me? I'm here, no? If I ever think of something else, I'll think of something else."

"There aren't any other papers or anything?"

"Sure, this is the land of opportunity. Can't think why *everybody* isn't up here."

They climbed over a tumbledown stone wall into a field of thigh-high saplings. A jay screamed. Faye squatted and stretched out her hand, palm up, to touch one leaf in a patch of low, tidy-looking bushes.

"A blueberry bush," she said, pronouncing the article like the letter *A*.

"God, look at them all," said Karen, getting down on her bare knees. "You weren't kidding."

"No, not my style. You can pick here. I'll hit the other side." The first berries started *ping*ing into the coffee cans. Then only the rustling of the bushes as their hands tore at the berries, and the screams of the jays.

"It's so quiet here," Karen said. "I actually had trouble getting to sleep with nothing but the katydids."

"Yeah," said Faye. "This is the time of year you start hearing them. I still have trouble myself. It's like, the one thing stands out more when there's just silence. Though I personally didn't hear jack shit last night."

"I bet. I was worried you might be sick, but Paul said you were okay."

"Paul should know."

Karen shot her a glance. "Are you guys fighting?"

"That's a quaint enough way to put it. No."

"Oh." Karen went back to picking, then stopped and stared

at Faye. "At the risk of being put down definitively," she said, "I would like to note that (a) I'm your sister, (b) you do not seem happy, and (c) if something's wrong I'd be glad to listen."

Faye shook her head. "It's not really any one thing. Just the usual."

"I know I shouldn't ask this," Karen began.

"No, you shouldn't. Whatever it is. I'll tell you one thing: about sixty-five percent of the problem is that I'm hung over and this sun is giving me a headache. We must have about enough. Let me see what you've got." Karen tilted her coffee can toward Faye. "Well, not quite. We want to make two pies, and these things cook down."

"You make them in twos?"

"The frugal hausfrau," Faye said. "Costs money to run that gas stove, you know. Actually, one is for you guys to take with you."

"Really?"

"No," Faye said. "I'm kidding you again."

By the time they got back to the house they were both sweating, but it was cool in the kitchen. Karen lifted the tightly rolled bandanna from around her head and shook her hair out with both hands. It struck Faye that she'd only seen this style in magazines. Then it struck her that Karen obviously had been wearing the bandanna all morning.

"Okay, if you'll wash those, I'll start the piecrust," she said, opening the cabinet and handing Karen the colander.

"What happened to the boys?" Karen said, looking out the window. "I don't see the truck."

"Probably went someplace to measure cocks with the locals. Saturday in Vermont. You go buy a case of beer, then go over to somebody's house and watch him work on his car. Paul is nothing if not assimilated."

"Allen must be in seventh heaven," Karen said. "He'll have some real Americana to lay on everybody back at Time Warner. So is Paul serious about all this? Or is he just collecting material?"

"Material for a beer belly, maybe. Which he's already getting. I don't know, you'd have to understand Paul. Question is, does anybody *want* to understand Paul."

"Well—you, presumably."

"Right," Faye said. "There's always me. Listen, let's get these pies in the oven, and maybe we can go for a swim."

"That would be great." Karen poured blueberries from the coffee cans into the colander, began running water, then turned the faucet off. "Wait. Why am I doing this?"

"Don't go philosophical on me."

"I mean, what are we washing off? They don't use insecticide up there in the woods, do they?"

Faye looked out the window. "How would anybody know? If it's not insecticide, it's acid rain or God knows what. The deer come through and piss on them, I don't know. Actually I think New York's the only place a nature lover should really live. Put up your Ansel Adams calendar, and you're in business." She dug the measuring cup into the bag of flour, held her palm against the outside of the bag to level it off and dumped the flour into the mixing bowl. "Could you get down the Wesson oil? Up in that cupboard?"

Karen stood on tiptoes and craned her neck, tilting bottles to look behind them. "Canola oil?"

"Sorry, that's what I meant. See, this isn't the boonies. A mere twenty miles to the nearest supermarket." Faye measured oil into the cup and dumped it over the flour. Then she held the cup under the faucet and measured water.

"Are you sure this is going to work?" Karen said. "I thought you were supposed to mix the oil and water first and then keep adding flour to it."

"It all ends up together anyhow," said Faye. "I can't put it together—it *is* together." She measured out salt and baking powder. "Okay, we need room on that counter to roll this stuff out. Have you picked over those berries?"

Karen started moving junk off the counter. "You've got amazing counter space," she said. "Even on the West Side the kitchens really aren't big enough."

"Counter space," Faye said. "Sounds like what's inside a black hole." She fluttered her fingers and intoned the word in *Twilight Zone* baritone: "Coun-ter-space."

Karen laughed.

"There's a rolling pin in that drawer," Faye said. "By the fridge? God, I actually own a rolling pin. If I had a bathrobe and curlers, I could give the boys a real American welcome."

"This really *is* America, isn't it?" said Karen. "The women-folk in the kitchen and the boys out God knows where. Is this really what it's like here?"

"Honey," Faye said in her hillbilly voice, "this rot year is jes' the tip of the osberg of what it's lock year. It's th'unstable suf-face thoo which th'unwayry"—now she'd slipped into her black radio preacher voice and was rolling her eyes—"is lahble to fawel, at enna instant. Now, sistah—" Karen was laughing again. Faye stopped and looked out the window. "I don't know," she said in her own voice. "It's a good question. I really have no idea what it's like here."

Faye sat on the bed and dug her right heel into her left heel to work her shoe off without having to untie it, pried the other shoe off with the bare toes of her left foot and stretched out on top of the quilt. She'd told Karen she was still feeling iffy, given her a towel and explained how to get down to the brook; she was going to lie down for half an hour, take the pies out, and maybe afterward she'd come join her. But the hangover was only part of it. She hadn't seen Karen in, what, four years? Shouldn't she be able to endure two days? It was quarter after one. She could nap until quarter of two, take the pies out, pick up around the house a little. That still left a lot of hours. She made a fist and started sticking out fingers: quarter to three, four, five, six . . . God, nine or ten more hours today, and at least another, what, five or six tomorrow. A minimum of fourteen more hours, and you've only gotten through—let's see—maybe four hours last night and three or four today. Like a third of the way through.

She closed her eyes and started watching for the crazy thought, the one that meant she was asleep. Although examining each thought to see if it was crazy made it harder for the crazy one to come. She realized she was clenching her eyelids, relaxed them and felt her face get longer, all the way down to her chin: her jaw dropped, her teeth parted. This was the way your face needed to feel if you were to receive the crazy thought. She went down through her body, checking for tension; she found it, then relaxed it, in the neck, in the shoulders, in the stomach, in the buttocks, in the thighs, in the knees, in the feet. What was the term for them, those head-to-toe descriptions of women in medieval literature, in which lovers itemized their ladies' attractions?

English 242, Beowulf to Chaucer. A seminar room with cinder-block walls, and windows you pulled down to open; like an oven door, except they stopped at an acute angle. Outside, blue sky, trees starting to turn. Fall semester, her junior year, first day of class. She waited to learn what name he would answer to, the one with the violin case and the wrinkled oxford shirt and the full lower lip, unsmiling. Then three unforgivable weeks of catching his eye and simpering. In those days, Ben practiced six hours at a stretch, and he dropped the class before midterms. But by that time—well, not what you want to be thinking about. This much was clear: she had been married to him, but he had never been married to her. It had all been an invasion of his privacy. And it had meant nothing the time he'd come with her to the vet's to have poor, sick, old Bootsy put down; on a plastic sofa, in a waiting room that stank of disinfectant, he'd turned to her and said, "There's always me." So when he left and she learned that he was still growing inside her, she'd had him uprooted. She was still uprooting him, every day.

She checked for tension again, found clenched fists. So puzzling that after being in this body for thirty-odd years you still don't know how to shut it down. Yet somehow it happens: the crazy thought comes, and that's the last you know.

Faye set the pies on the counter and turned off the oven. She felt worse for having slept: the inside of her mouth tasted foul, and a pinpoint of headache was coming and going high on the left side of her forehead. She washed the mixing bowls and the rolling pin, ran water through the colander, wiped off the countertop. She took Paul's book off the dining room table and reshelved it in the living room, between *The Golden Bowl* and *The Penal Colony.*

Down at the brook, Karen was sitting against the big beech tree, her hair wet, her shorts and T-shirt dry.

"Hi," said Faye, seating herself on the big rock. "Looks like you found it okay. How's the water?"

"Muddy. But nice. You going in?"

"No. I was being polite. What are you reading?"

Karen held up Jung's *Answer to Job.*

"Yikes. How is it?"

"Muddy. Entertaining, in a weird way. He's trying to psychoanalyze God. I think." She picked up a beech leaf to mark her place, and set the book on the ground. "You *are* being polite."

"Okay," Faye said, "I'll stop. If you want Paul, you can have him."

"*What?*"

"Oh, shit. Forget I said it. Please? Sometimes I just get the impulse to say something completely insane just to see what happens next."

"Faye. What is this? Why would you think—"

Faye shook her head. "You don't get it. I mean, I don't blame you." She stood up and brushed off the seat of her jeans. "I'm sorry, Karen. Really. Look, it would be a mistake to take me seriously. Really. I just say things all the time now."

Karen got up and put an arm around Faye's shoulders. "You're really not doing so hot, are you?"

Faye shook her head. Karen moved in front of her to put both arms around her.

Faye twisted away. "Really. Don't. Karen, just please don't." She walked to the edge of the brook and squatted to put a hand in the water. "Too cold," she said. "You about ready for a drink? It must be almost happy hour."

"Look. Would it be better if Allen and I left tonight? If we can't change our plane tickets, there must be a bus or something."

"Karen, no, really. Absolutely not. Could you just forget it? Just"—she cut through the air with her hand at chest level—"*canceled.* Really. Okay?"

"Do you want to tell me what this is about? It's not about Paul."

"No," Faye said. "I guess it's not about Paul. Poor Paul. Then again, poor Paul can take care of himself."

Karen looked at the water. "I was going to ask you before if you still heard anything from Ben."

"Card on my birthday. With a note. *There* was a shitty day."

"Where is he?"

"Leavenworth, Washington. I looked it up on the map. The nearest big place is Wenatchee. It's on Route Two. Which happens to be the same Route Two that goes through Burlington. What you came here on. He said he's living in a cabin and building violins. I assume he's there with somebody. He said he still thinks about me."

"Bastard," Karen said.

"I don't know," Faye said. "Yeah, sure. On the other hand, why not say what you feel like saying? It's just that it's so fucking unfair. I mean, I have to take Route Two to get to the fucking supermarket."

"Listen," said Karen. "Just one piece of sisterly advice and I'll shut up, okay?"

Faye shrugged. "Shoot."

"Wouldn't it be better all around if you just let go of him? And tried to repair what you've got with Paul?"

"Right. Absolutely right. Now shall we go get that drink? Time's a-wasting." Faye stood up and motioned with her thumb. Karen sighed and followed her up the path.

They'd gotten all the way up to the road when Karen said, "Crap. My book. You don't have to wait for me." She started back down the path, and Faye watched the sunlight and shadow make zebra stripes on her long legs until she disappeared into the trees. Faye ducked through the fence between the strands of barbed wire, pushing the top one up, away from her hair and her back, and keeping her calves clear of the bottom one. Then she straightened up, looked across the road at the house and saw Paul's truck parked in the dooryard, alongside Thurston Martin's. She decided to pick wildflowers and wait for Karen.

She'd gathered a few Indian paintbrushes and black-eyed Susans and was looking for ferns to set them off when Karen came squirming through the fence.

"Lucky you," Faye said. "You get to see the Thurston Martin show."

Karen fanned herself with her book. "Will I like it?"

"*De gustibus non est disputandum.* As Thurston might say."

She could smell cigarette smoke through the screen door. The three men were sitting at the kitchen table. Faye said, "Hello, Thurston," and breezed past to get a Mason jar for the flowers. Then, remembering her manners, she turned to introduce her sister and saw Karen staring. A shotgun lay across the table, on top of its zippered case, among the beer cans. One, unopened, had the plastic thing still attached: five empty circles. No opera today.

"Oh, for a camera," Faye said. "Wouldn't I give Diane Arbus a run for her money."

Paul's face was red, maybe from the sun, maybe from drinking. "Thurston's going to sell me his shotgun," he said. His accent got thicker when Thurston was around.

Faye shot him a quick fake smile. "Oh. And what will *Thurston* do for a shotgun?"

"Hell, I got two, three over to the house," Thurston said. "This one here, this used to belong to my father." He took a last drag of his cigarette and stuck it into a beer can. Hiss.

"What do you intend to do with a shotgun, Paul? Shoot hippies?"

Thurston laughed.

"It's hunting season coming up," Paul said. "And I been thinking it might not be a bad idea to have something around anyway. Just in general."

"In general?" Faye said.

"Plus that woodchuck's been at your garden."

"Christ," said Thurston, who pronounced it to rhyme with *floor joist,* "you don't want to go after *him* with a shotgun. Tear up the friggin' plants. You want a twenty-two if you're looking for a varmint gun."

"Oh, *do* get a varmint gun," Faye said. "You could get rid of all the undesirables."

"Hey, Allen?" Karen said. "Come here a second, I have to show you what Faye's been doing in the garden." Allen looked puzzled, but he stood up and Faye watched them walk out the screen door hand in hand, Karen in her little shorts. She turned back to the table and saw Thurston looking.

"That your sister?" he said, wrenching the plastic off the last beer.

"That's right," Faye said. "And if we were all as diplomatic as my sister, I could be talking with Paul right now."

Thurston popped the beer open, stood up and looked at Paul. "You want me to—" He pointed his thumb at the shotgun.

"Just leave it," said Paul.

"Be outside," Thurston said.

When the screen door slapped behind him, Faye said, "I won't have that in the house. You can tell your friend the sale's off."

"The hell's this?" Paul said. "It's not your money. You sit in the goddamn house feeling sorry for yourself while I'm on the goddamn truck all day. So *you* don't tell *me.*"

"What is this, the 'Working Man's Blues'? Give me a break, Paul. I mean, this is a game: we live in this house because you closed out an IRA and plunked down fifty thousand dollars. So don't hand me this Merle Haggard bullshit."

"You think it's a game? We come here on the strength of God knows what, you get laid off and you decide to have a breakdown. Where, exactly, do you think the mortgage payments come from every month? Not from *you*."

"You love to think you're a helpless victim," she said. "Because it absolves you of any and all responsibility."

"*I* love to think *I'm* a victim?"

"And then you get to say, 'She's a castrating bitch, she humiliated me in front of my friends,' and everybody is *so* sympathetic. Why don't you go out and talk to Karen? I'm sure she's just dying, just *itching*, to listen to all your little marital problems."

Paul stared at her. "You're psychotic," he said.

"Oh, he's talking better all of a sudden. Are we dropping the mask? What happened to the working-class hero?" She stuck out her lips and put on a deep voice. "You got it, bitch?"

"Okay," he said. "End of discussion. I am buying, this gun, from Thurston. Clear?"

"Paul," Faye said. "In view of everything, do you really think it's a good idea to have a gun in this house?"

"Fine," he said. "I'll keep it in the truck, how's that? I'll go the whole route, the gun rack and everything. And that way you can have the pleasure of complaining to your sister that I've gone native."

She gave him the finger, then said, "It smells in here."

Out in the garden, she found Karen and Allen, her arm around his waist, talking with Thurston Martin, who was squatting by one of the zucchini plants. The three heads turned, and Thurston got to his feet, dangling his beer can between fingertips and opposable thumb. "Just saying you ought to pick some of these big ones," he said.

"Thanks for your concern, Thurston," Faye said. "You can go back in now. The little woman has been put in her place."

Thurston looked at her, then started for the house.

"Faye?" said Karen. "Allen and I think we should head back tonight. Allen's got a bunch of work to do before Monday."

"Oh," Faye said. "Should I be gracious? That's clearly what's called for here."

Allen looked at the ground. Karen said, "He really does have work. And it doesn't seem as if our being here is helping things any. I mean, we obviously didn't pick a very good time."

"Aren't you diplomatic," Faye said.

"Not really," Karen said, "But I just want you to know, if you ever feel like coming down, either by yourself or—"

"Yeah. Well. Thanks. Look, you're both handling this very smoothly, and old Faye intends to hold up her end. I'll tell Paul what's going on so you don't have to go through all that again, he can drive you over to Burlington, we'll find a shopping bag so you can carry that pie, and we'll just have this whole thing together in no time."

"Faye, I'm really sorry."

"Oh, come on," she said. "Come on, come on, you're taking this way too seriously. This will all blow over. You guys can come back in December and we'll have an old-fashioned Christmas, what do you say? Paul can kill us a goose with his shotgun, and we'll all sit around and drink smoking bishop."

Faye sat on the doorstep looking across the road. She had listened and listened, following the sound of the truck into silence; by now it had been silent for God knows how long. Here and there the scream of a jay, and that was all. She tried to wish that if the truck were going to crash it would wait to crash on the way back, so only Paul would die. It wasn't actually a heavy thing, wishing people dead; she had learned this during her analysis. Everybody did it. Obvious example: children wishing their parents dead. Of course they feel guilty if that wish should appear to come true—the child is angry with the parents, the parents coincidentally die in a car crash—and then they need to enter analysis to straighten out the misunderstanding. But what about when parents wish their children dead? "These are not children," her shrink had said, when she told him about her abortion. He'd said it angrily, unless she'd misperceived. The *quality* of the life, that was his concern. "We are physicians," he had said, full of indignation at human suffering. In his work with teenage mothers, he'd seen what damage could be done. Yet damage was the foundation stone of his practice. So it all went around and around and around.

Down the driveway, beyond the mailbox, across the road, the land dipped down to the brook, then rose again to a grassy hillside, belonging to somebody—Paul must've said the name a hundred times—whose black-and-white cows stood in a complicated arrangement against the green. The phrase *effictio portrait* came into her head. Above the pasture, the wooded hilltop, a deeper green in which she already saw flecks of red; it was crazy to pretend she didn't. Strange and terrible powers were available to us, no matter what her shrink had said, but in most cases you could wish and wish and wish—wish people dead, wish the leaves green again, wish your husband, your real husband, back in your arms and babies beyond number issuing from between your legs—while everything just stayed silent and inert, exactly as it was.

She stood up and went back inside. Her wildflowers lay on the kitchen counter; better get them in water. She lowered her palm above the remaining pie until she felt heat, then edged it back up, feeling for the boundary where the heat left off. Then she walked over to the table and touched the shotgun, still lying on top of its fake-leather case. She touched the stock, then the barrel; why should metal feel colder than wood? She couldn't imagine an explanation that wasn't mystical. At least touching this thing took away some of the awe. After all, it was just an object: its presence probably wouldn't change things much, unless you allowed it to become an emblem of something. She sat down at the table and started lifting the beer cans, found one that was nearly full, examined the edge of the hole for cigarette traces, sniffed, took a sip. It was so quiet in here that her whole body jerked when the phone rang. She jumped up to get it, then sat back down and let it ring and ring and ring, thinking: *As long as I don't pick it up, it isn't anybody.*

A Wronged Husband

alf awake, pawing at the night table for *The Book of Great Conversations*, I knock the bottle onto the floor. The sound hangs there: a ringing part, a shattering part, a splashing part. I smell the gin. Fine. It can stay there until I feel like getting up and dealing with it. Nobody here to be scandalized, nobody to be protected. A mouse, I suppose, might scamper across and cut its dainty foot, but that's the mouse's lookout, no? I remember when we first moved in here, we felt sorry for them, darting along the countertop to cower, bright-eyed, beside the toaster. So tiny, so dear: couldn't we all just *live*? It took a month for you to agree that something had to be done. But no D-Con. So, like what? I said. A resettlement program? "Well, couldn't we?" you said. "Couldn't we try?" And finally I went out and bought the Hav-a-Heart trap. Humane, enlightened. That was only last fall. Less than a year ago. As I remember it, we were all right then.

Kid noise through the open window. Sunday morning, quarter to eleven, already hot. I lift the sheet and shake it out to make it feel cool as it floats back down to rest on my legs. The coolness doesn't last. I prop both pillows (yours and mine) together against the headboard, sit up, put on my prescription sunglasses and turn to the Great Conversation in which Shaw loses his temper when Chesterton calls him a Puritan. Shaw says Chesterton has no real self, no firm place to stand, and Chesterton calls Shaw a Puritan for thinking that was necessary. Trying to understand these ideas is waking me up. I put the book back on the night table—carefully, though now there's no need—get out of bed, step around the glass (I can't wholly avoid the gin puddle), go to the window and tug the shade to make it go up. Down in the street firemen have put a sprinkler cap on the hydrant—otherwise the Dominican kids just open it up and let it gush—and pencil-thick streams of water come arching out. A little boy stands at the edge of the widening pool, undecided.

But hang on: didn't I park the car in that first space to the right of the hydrant? What's there now is a rusted-out station wagon, cloudy plastic duct-taped over where the passenger window used to be. So now I know: they tow after a week of tickets. Well, fine, more power to 'em. Unless of course somebody stole the thing. In which case, also fine. But isn't it weird. You were always the one who said it was insane to keep a car in New York. I was always the one who said I wanted the feeling I could get out.

And your suddenly having to go to D.C. (yes, well, supposedly) gave me a blame-free opportunity. Drive up to New Hampshire, get away from the heat and noise, spend some time with my brother. We hung out at the house mostly—Joey was still depressed about throwing his marriage away—though one afternoon we did get over into Vermont, to a used-book store run by a lady with cats. Joey beat her down on the price of some old compendium of myths he wanted for the engravings; to atone, I picked *The Book of Great Conversations* off the twenty-five-cent table and told her it came from the dollar table.

He called yesterday, speaking of Joey, to say he was doing a lot better. In case I'd been worried. I said I was doing a lot worse: that you had gone to live in Boston, that I hadn't left the apartment for a week, hadn't called work, didn't know if I had a job anymore and, even if I did, couldn't face going back and having to see Kate every day. I said I couldn't sleep because of the car alarms and sirens. Kate, he said: refresh me. I refreshed him. Hm, he said. But the Kate thing was already over with, I said. Discussed. Worked through. Resolved. Hm, he said. Well, he said, as far as the job, they were probably just assuming I was taking two weeks instead of the one; if they were seriously upset, they would've called, no? He said he was sorry about your leaving, but guessed he'd seen it coming when we'd been up there at Christmas. What do you mean? I said. Why do you say that? Well, for one thing, he said, you never touched each other. He said, speaking as somebody who'd been through the same thing, that he knew I was going to come out of this stronger. Said at least in my case there were no children. Said maybe I could start seeing this Kate again. Joey. He runs off to the Outer Banks for a mad two-week interlude with his old used-to-be, she ends up going back to her husband (many tears), he comes home and Meg and the children are gone. And now he discovers there are no great new women in Peterborough, New Hampshire.

The night I arrived, in fact, he tried to talk me into getting back in the car and driving down to Boston to pick up college girls. Just as big as real women, he said, but stupider.

"Joey," I said. "I just drove five hours."

"So I'll drive and you can sleep on the way down. Listen, I got a teensy thing of coke left. And we can absolutely get more once we're in Boston. Fuck, let's do some coke, you want to?"

But as of yesterday, he'd gotten the north side of the house painted, which badly needed it, he'd started cutting wood for the following winter—he likes it to dry for a year and a half—and he'd patched the leak in the woodshed with roofing tar. He'd probably just needed some physical exercise. Said he'd

begun a new series of silkscreens, which were absolutely going
to be the best things since those ducks he was doing a couple of
years ago. They're going to be—whatever the plural is of
phoenix. But getting back to my thing: he'd always said that
Gordon Conway was scum, and he was glad at least that now
everybody would see it. Said as it turned out he guessed it was
a damn good thing I'd talked him out of driving down to
Boston that night. He'd planned to hit Gordon up, since
Gordon generally kept enough coke around to sell, and it
would've been an absolute mess if we'd knocked on the
door and so on. Said he thought you might come back once the
dust had a chance to settle. If that was what we both wanted.
Said it seemed to him that despite everything there'd been a lot
of love there.

Or something.

I remember speaking the vows and thinking, *Maybe*.

The day before the ceremony, we'd had that huge thing
about whether Meg's sister Jodie should be there. "What am I
supposed to do?" I said. "Turn around at this point and disin-
vite her? You know, she drives down with them, thinking
everything is cool, and—I mean, Cindy, this was literally *years*
ago. She's now a *friend*. Okay, what should I have done, *not*
told you?"

"Yes," you said. Then you said, "No." Then you began to cry.

But then there were the times when, deferring to my choice
of a movie or a restaurant, you used to take my hand and kiss
it like a courtier. What were the proportions of sweetness and
irony? Not that I ever wanted to pick it apart. This gesture was
still in your repertoire as late as a few weeks ago, the night you
felt like going down to one of the Indian joints on Sixth Street
and I felt like going someplace where we could count on air
conditioning. In retrospect, this last handkiss makes me wonder

whether or not you and Gordon Conway had already made your arrangements.

As far as I know, you hadn't met him before this spring, when you went up to Boston for Lynnette's show. The three of you having lunch at some health food place. Which seemed fine: a friend of your friend Lynnette's. I remembered him, of course, from when he'd been at Pratt with Joey, and I decided not to be gratuitously unpleasant by saying he'd always struck me as a poseur, and therefore just the kind of person who'd fasten onto Lynnette. Or vice versa. This must have been in April. (It was the weekend Kate and I broke our rule about each other's apartments. She came here; we rented Syberberg's *Parsifal*, ordered in from the good Chinese place, marveled at how Armin Jordan, playing Amfortas, had lip-synched so undetectably in close-up.) Now, at that point, I assume, you were telling me everything, or why would you have told me as much as you did? Well, maybe to preclude my hearing it from somebody else. Or maybe just to get some relief—I know, I've been there. I used to make a point of telling you what I hoped sounded like everything: how Kate and I, say, had spent half an hour on hands and knees wrenching misfed paper from increasingly deep places in the innards of that chronically misbehaving copier. Such truths, told forthrightly, kept the rest of the truth away; while telling them, I could almost believe that Kate was just the funny woman who worked two offices down. With the husband who sounded so interesting.

Now, the next thing I heard about your new friend Gordon was the following week: he and Lynnette were both bringing work to show to some dealers in SoHo, and could we all have dinner? This was the point, I decided, at which to get myself on record. "As you know," I said, "Lynnette is not one of my favorite people. And I truly dislike Gordon Conway."

"He speaks well of *you*," you said.

"He's a ferret," I said. "Are he and Lynnette an item?"

You said nothing.

"So where are you dining?" I said. "Elaine's?"

You put your glass down. "Oh, fuck you."

"Or, hey, there's always Greenwich Village," I said. "Where the *real* artists hang out. Now, me, there's nothing I like better than *real* artists, you know? Getting together and being *real*. Should I bring a rose and eat it petal by petal?"

"I thought you weren't going."

"Are *you*?" I said.

"Yes."

"Well," I said, "have a *marvelous* time."

"Thank you." You picked up your glass. "I intend to."

And then nothing (meaning nothing I was told about) until two weeks ago, when the phone rang on Sunday morning. Me at the kitchen table, drinking coffee.

"I've got it," you called. After a while you came out of the bedroom. I asked if you'd turned the fan off in there. You said you had to go to D.C.

"Why?" I said. "What's up?"

"Marie," you said. "She was in a car wreck. She died this morning."

"*What?*" I said.

"Look, I have to pack. Would you please call and see what's the first shuttle I could get?"

"Jesus, no. Oh my God, Cindy. I can't believe—listen, I don't know if they even have the shuttle on weekends. Maybe we should just drive? By the time—"

"You're not coming."

"Say again?"

"Would you just call, please?"

"Cindy."

"Okay, fine. *I* will call." You hauled down the Yellow Pages.

"What the hell's going on?" I said. "Of *course* I'm coming with you."

"You see my family once a year," you said. "At Thanksgiving. That's a grand total of five times. And once at the wedding."

"This is completely batshit. I'm your *husband.*"

You rolled your eyes.

"Listen," I said, "if absolutely nothing else, it would freak your mother out if I wasn't with you."

"Helen knows everything is fucked," you said. "She's not expecting you. You're so concerned with the proprieties, write her a note. Truly. I'll hand-deliver it, how's that?" You went back into the bedroom and closed the door. I followed you in, wondering if at a time like this I should be asking what this everything-is-fucked business was about. Or were you entitled to slip stuff in and not be called on it because your sister was dead?

I ended up agreeing to everything: not to come, not to call, to let you deal with this in your own way, to let you breathe. Not to upset your mother by sending flowers. If I'd given you more of an argument, would you have broken down and confessed? Such a bizarre lie: you must have wanted me to bust you on it. So: one more time I failed you. On the other hand, you went to such lengths to make it convincing. So: one more time you arranged for me to fail you. While you packed, I wrote a draft of the note for your mother, then copied it cleanly on a sheet of your good notepaper. Quite a collector's item. What did you end up doing with it?

After helping you down with your stuff and finding you a reputable-looking livery cab I came back upstairs, made more coffee and decided to call in to work the next morning, take the week off and drive up to Joey's. I'd like to think I meant to spend some of the time thinking about Us. But really it was just a holiday: boozing, moping, bullshitting, listening to Miles Davis, wishing for women, drugs and money. Your sister had laid down her life (as I thought) so I could have a week off from you.

I got back from Joey's on Thursday night. You called on Friday, around noon: you were taking the shuttle, arriving seven o'clock.

"Want me to come get you?" I said.

"If you feel like it."

"Are you okay?" I said. "How's your mom holding up?"

"Look, I'll see you at seven," you said.

At ten after seven I watched stranger after stranger after stranger come down the carpeted passageway. You touched my arm.

"Hey," I said. "Where'd you come from?"

You shrugged. "I've been here a couple hours. I think."

"You're kidding," I said. "How come you didn't call?" Then I smelled your breath. "Well, I see you've used the time to advantage."

"The American Advantage," you said. "Now *I* have the advantage." You let your suitcase drop, and it fell on its side.

I picked it up and said, "Shall we?" You followed like a little girl who'd been bad. When we got to the escalator I turned around. "Have you eaten anything? Do you want to stop someplace?"

"Want to go home," you said, head down.

"So be it," I said. "I don't know what there is, but there's probably something."

"You don't *want* to talk to me," you said.

A Wronged Husband

It was the second-to-last of our silent car rides: me thinking of ways to open a conversation and imagining how you'd parry each one. I thought what a drag it was that you chose to get drunk. And then I thought how unfair it was to think that after you'd just lost your sister. (As I believed.) You were looking good, despite the shape you were in: your cheeks pale, your lips fat. It was the first sexual thing I'd felt for you since our confrontation over Kate, but I decided to stay angry. You showed better sense: when we got up the stairs and I put down your suitcase to unlock the door, you reached for my belt. To my credit, I was gracious.

The next afternoon, Saturday, you'd gone up to the Cloisters—you said—when the phone rang. "Hi, it's Marie," said the voice. "Is Cindy around? Listen, when are you guys ever going to come to Washington?"

"Who is this?" I said. "Goddamn it, who the fuck is this?"

When you came in, I said, "Your sister called."

"Oh," you said. "Well." You shook your head, sniffled. "Actually I'm surprised it took this long. But . . ." You shrugged. "It must've been weird for you. What did you end up saying?"

"*Why?*" I said. "Why would you be so stupid? I mean, *beyond* stupid."

"Sometimes you feel like being stupid, what can I say? Didn't you ever want to just be stupid? I have to blow my nose." You went into the bathroom and shut the door.

I shoved it open again. "So where were you?" I said. "Obviously you were with somebody. Who was the lucky guy?"

You tore toilet paper off the roll and wiped your nose. "Why do you assume it was only one?" You turned to face me, and struck a pose, palm out, the back of your hand to your fore-head. "Oh, Rick, I can't go on living a lie." You gazed ceiling-ward. "The truth is, it was all of your friends. Every last one. It was Stefan and Andrew and Alex—oh, and Gregory. Now, did I leave anybody out?"

"Okay, forget it," I said. "I mean, I'm through anyway. I truly am."

You buried your face in your hands. "Rick, I need your compassion at this terrible moment. The truth is, it was a woman. In fact, it was your dear friend and platonic coworker *Kate*. We just found that we had so much in common that we decided to have gay women's sex. Can you ever, ever forgive me?" You gripped my arms, then began to giggle.

"You're stoned," I said.

"Oh, yes, Rick, I *am* stoned. You're so perspicacious, always. And I'm just—shit under your feet." You dug your fingernails into my arms, then lifted your head and kissed my cheek so hard I felt teeth. Then you let go, stepped back and slapped me, and my glasses went flying. We looked at each other. You were red-faced, breathing hard. I was thinking:

She means to kill me.

I can't walk out with her in this kind of shape.

This will never end.

I will take her throat and rip it open.

I am observing all this from a great distance.

Then you began to sob, and I took you in my arms and pat-ted your back again and again, and smoothed and smoothed your hair, thinking: *Every minute of this is a minute out of my life.*

When you finally turned to the sink and began washing your face, I picked up my glasses and brought them into the living room. A Y-shaped crack in the left lens. I tried to figure out how to hide from you the evidence of what you yourself had done; all I could come up with was not putting them back on. The bathroom door closed. Now what? Were you using the toilet or swallowing handfuls of Bufferins and Sudafeds? Cutting your wrists? Not easy with a Good News razor. I could save your life by breaking down the door. But first I'd have to ask if you were all right in there, and that might enrage you—even *make* you suicidal. The thing to do was ask something else—*Hey, Cindy? I'm going to need to use the john pretty soon*—and see if you answered. But of course you'd see through it.

Finally you came out and sat on the sofa hugging yourself, your feet tucked under you. "I'm sorry," you said. "I am completely humiliated. And I need very much not to talk at this point."

"*You're* humiliated?"

"Don't," she said. "Listen, would you do something? This is crazy, but do you think you could pretend with me? Please? It would just be for a while, okay? Like until tomorrow? Can we just pretend we're all right? One more day?"

We managed it by drinking lots of wine. Or I did—I lost track of you. We called the good Chinese place for cold hacked chicken and cold sesame noodles, and I dug out my prescription sunglasses, and we lay on the bed in our underwear and watched an old Jackie Gleason variety show on cable. It seemed to be about a fat, unhappy man who dressed himself up on Saturday night to watch things happen around him. When he introduced the orchestra leader as Sammy Spear, I pounded the mattress. "God, it's too fucking perfect. It's like, the spear and the wound. Look at him—he's the open wound. He's the walking wounded."

"You're the walking drunk," you said. "You're so cute like that."

"I'm not walking," I said. "Lying right here. Check it out. Too goddamn smart to even think about walking."

Sunday morning, catnapping. I opened my eyes, looked at the clock, closed them, felt your thigh against mine, opened my eyes again, saw it was ten minutes later, closed them again. Wanted to keep on and on.

Then I woke up and saw you standing at the dresser, bareback, in underpants; I imagined a steely look on your face. I said good morning and you turned around. Your large, flat nipples. You came and took your watch off the night table and strapped it on. It was the look I'd imagined.

You said, "I'm going to pack some things, and then I'm going to go, okay?"

"Go where?" I said. "Would you tell me what's going on? I thought—"

"Please don't be stupid," you said. You took a T-shirt out of the drawer.

I closed my eyes before you pulled it over your head.

"Listen," you said, "you're going to come out of this just fine. If your platonic friend and coworker Kate won't take you back, you can always find another platonic friend and coworker. And if that one doesn't work out, then you go on to the next one. You know, until you find exactly the *right* one. So why don't you just go back to sleep, and when you wake up— presto: wifey's just an unpleasant memory."

"Where are you going?" I opened my eyes and you were pulling on a pair of jeans.

"To Unpleasant Memoryland. Poof." You raised a palm to your lips and blew.

"Cindy. Where?"

You zipped up and looked at me. "Boston," you said. "I should give you the address."

"Oh," I said.

You shrugged.

A Wronged Husband

"He's a lowlife," I said.

"He's not so bad," you said. "Fact is, he's a little like you. Anyhow, he's probably not forever."

"And then what?"

"Not your problem." You sat down on the bed to put on your running shoes. "Look, I promise you, this will be very easy. I don't want money, I don't want any of the stuff except for my grandfather's chair, which I'll come and get at some point. I guess I want the little rug that's in the other room. My books. I'll let you know when I'm coming down. And I'll call Marie tonight, to spare you any further embarrassment. Okay?" You picked up your purse and slung it over your shoulder, and said in your Robert DeNiro voice, "Don' worr'. I take care ev'ryt'ing."

"I can't believe this," I said.

"Look," you said, "I have to crank it, you know? If I'm going to make my plane."

"Can't I at least drive you to the airport?" I said. "And we could talk on the way? I really need to understand what's going on."

You sighed. "If that's your idea of a good time. But I don't know what you need to understand. Your bad wife is leaving you. For another man. You're a wronged husband. Now you can be happy."

Because Kate wasn't about to leave her husband and I wasn't about to leave you, she and I had agreed to be responsible. No hang-up calls, no leaving the office together, no being at each other's apartments even if it seemed perfectly safe, no overnighters anywhere, ever. But you and I had rules, too, though never codified: the gist was that neither of us was to go looking for what we didn't want to see. You were the one who violated that rule, by following me into the subway at lunch hour, riding to West Fourth Street in the next car, walking a block behind me to Kate's sister's building and watching from a bus shelter as I was buzzed in. I was the one who was trying to be protective.

Basically it was no different from the lie I told you about the Hav-a-Heart trap. We thought it was so ingenious, the way the trapdoor would fall away from under the mouse and tumble him into the box for deportation. But the day we baited it, I got home before you did, opened the thing to check, and *voilà:* a twitching, squealing mouse, hopelessly wedged into a corner between sharp edges of metal. He'd been trying to worm himself out through a place where the box didn't quite fit together. I watched awhile, then went looking for something. Nearest thing to hand was a screwdriver: I pressed the tip into his neck until I felt a snap. Then I hid him at the bottom of the trash, wrapped in the paper towel I'd used to wipe the inside of the box. When you came in, I told you the trap turned out to be useless.

"It's only been a *day*," you said.

"Right," I said. "But. One of them already managed to steal the bait and get away. We're either going to have to put up with mice or go to Plan B."

You shook your head. Sighed. "I don't know. I guess we can't really put up with mice, can we?"

One of our Great Conversations, in which nobody had to come right out and say it. And if I had a whole additional thing I wasn't telling, that was called being a good husband. Back then I loved to play the part.

I tug the shade back down, check the phone book and call the number for towaways. Busy. Eight million stories in the Naked City. I pull off paper towels, mop up the gin, pick up the pieces of broken glass—gingerly, remembering I'm in a stressful period. They go into a paper bag, which goes into an empty Tropicana carton, which goes into the trash so no one gets hurt.

A week ago today, at just about this time, I was driving you to LaGuardia. I asked you what that last weekend had been about, why you'd bothered to come back and put us both through it. You wouldn't talk. I insisted—it seemed wrong not to—but all the while I was thinking, *Why not just admit this is a relief?* So much traffic: people heading for the beaches. Sun glinting off windshields and bumpers. Good I had those sunglasses. We weren't moving fast enough to get a breeze going, and my shirt was soaked through. Shifting from low to second and back to low, temperature gauge getting close to the red. I remember passing a black van with an orange volcano painted on its side panel, then the van passing us. Its windows were up and the driver, a blond thug, was singing away unheard, beating time on the steering wheel as his girlfriend painted her nails. When we finally got to the terminal, you let me park and carry your suitcase as far as security. I put it on the moving belt, you set your purse next to it and turned to me before stepping into the frame.

" 'Bye," you said.

"This is really it?"

You smiled, beckoned with your forefinger and raised your chin. I cupped my hands around your shoulders and bent to kiss you—at least your forehead. You laid a palm on my cheek, pushed my head aside and whispered, "This is what you wanted."

Saturn

Somebody cuts the lights and Seth backs into the dining room pulling the wheelchair. He swings it around, then pushes it toward the table: Holly's birthday cake, a single candle flaring, sits on a board laid across the armrests. Her sister and her sister's new boyfriend are on their feet applauding. Holly gets up and starts clapping too, then feels stupid, stops and just stands there in the dark, her fingertips on the disagreeably coarse tablecloth. She's way too high. But if she doesn't dwell on any single thought too long, she can get through this. She hears Seth take a deep breath: he sings out the syllable *Haaaaa*, the others find his note and come in on *ppy-birthday*. She's deciding whether to sing along when they finish and start clapping again.

She stares at the candle flame as it strains in a current of air. It's so nakedly obvious that matter's changing to energy before her eyes that it seems strange people ever thought Einstein was strange. If anything is strange, it's her husband's refusing to get rid of his dead mother's wheelchair. Also strange that there's just the one candle. This is Holly's thirty-second birthday; so this lone candle must stand for celebration in the abstract. They're all looking at her. Right: this is a ceremony. She's in a ceremony inside a celebration.

She closes her eyes and makes a wish: for her and Seth to stop smoking weed, or at least for her to. Because she's been having these anxiety things (which is what this is) since around the time Seth started talking about leaving New York and buying a house here in Connecticut. Which just so happened to be right around the time she found herself beginning to ease into having a stupid affair; the only surprise is that she failed to see the connection when she first rested fingertips on Mitchell's forearm. Well, so now she's stopped having the affair, and maybe if she stops smoking weed too she'll eventually get back to normal. She opens her eyes and there's the candle. Okay, that's her wish. And it's possible that wishes actually work—like visualization, which *has* been shown to work. More clapping as she blows out the candle, then lights come on and the dining room springs back into place.

"So what did you wish for?" says Seth.

"She's not supposed to tell," Tenley says.

"*We* never had that. That's fucked up—you just wish to yourself?"

"Come on, *everybody* had that. I mean, I'm not making this *up*—God, *am* I? Whew. Speaking of fucked up, this stuff of yours, Jesus." It doesn't escape Holly that her husband and her sister have just said *fuck* to each other.

"That *is* amazing shit," says Tenley's new boyfriend.

"Actually, I have a wish that's *not* secret," Holly says. "I wish Seth would get rid of that wheelchair before his father gets here."

"Shazam," Seth says, and bows from the waist. "Or what's that thing? Not 'abracadabra.' Anyhow. Okay, tomorrow, boom, out she goes. Salvation Army. Hup, hup." He turns to Tenley. "So there goes your don't-ask-don't-tell policy."

The boyfriend takes a loud breath as if he's about to say something, then shakes his head.

"Um, why are we all standing up?" says Tenley.

"I think it's because we're stoned as pigs," Seth says. "What the *hell* does a genie say? This is driving me out of my mind."

"Well, I'm sitting down," says Tenley.

" 'Your wish is my command,' " says the boyfriend.

"Carl, what the fuck are you talking about?" says Tenley.

"Oh, right." She looks at Seth. "Is that the thing?"

Seth cocks his head. "Say again?"

Tenley shakes her head. "Too complicated. Why am I not sitting down?" She sits. Seth and the boyfriend sit. Holly sits, and somebody puts a knife in her hand. She can't help but picture slicing right across her wrist, but technically it isn't a thought about suicide: just a thought about something so extreme it would have the power to put a stop to this.

"So you going to cut the cake or what?" says Seth. "You look like you're ready to go postal over there." He opens his mouth in a silent scream, raises his fist with an invisible knife. "Okay, who am I? Famous movie."

"Oh-oh-oh," says the boyfriend, as if he's about to come. "*Texas Chainsaw.*"

Tenley looks at him. "You've just canceled yourself out." She turns back to Seth. "Listen, say hi to your dad for me. Not that I know him or anything. But he was great at the wedding. When he was dancing with Holly? *Amazing* dancer."

Holly slices down into the cake.

"Yeah. He's the last of a dying breed." Seth looks over at Holly. "Smaller piece. Okay, who says *that*? What movie?"

" 'Last of a dying breed'?" says Tenley.

"No, 'smaller piece.' "

"I *heard* you," Holly says.

"I'll give you a hint," says Seth. "The movie was both a sequel *and* a prequel, and the actor who—"

"Wait, so what was the *other* movie?" the boyfriend says.

"If I told you *that*, I'd be telling you—"

"No, he means the *other* movie, Seth," says Holly.

"Yeah, I know, but if—"

"Forget it," Holly says. "Does anybody want this?"

"I'm lost," says Tenley.

"Me too," Seth says. "God, I love the shit out of it."

After they get Tenley and her boyfriend settled in the guest room—*one* of the guest rooms—Seth talks her into having one more hit apiece; by now she's come down enough to think she might not freak out this time. Not only do they still have sex after moving to Connecticut, but it seems to her that Seth actually goes after her more, as if in compensation. She gets into bed; he lights a candle and puts the metal flask of massage oil from the Gap on the nightstand. But when he reaches over, she's right back in that *thing*. Shit. He brushes the back of his hand along her left breast, nails scraping the nipple. She can't get her mind to stop. How weird that she's been doing this with somebody else. But she's not anymore, so shouldn't this now be okay? Seth takes the nipple in his mouth. Holly begins to play with his balls, as she should, but they seem like some primitive carryover the human race could well do without. She senses the wheelchair's evil presence still down there in the darkened dining room. "You're going to get rid of the wheelchair, right?" she whispers. "Or put it somewhere?"

Seth stops; her nipple feels cold. "Put it somewhere? Mmm. Be glad to, ah, put it somewhere. Where might she have in mind?" One of Seth's endearments is speaking to her in the third person. She still hasn't figured that one out. Yes, she has.

"They can *hear* you."

"How?" he says, just as loud. "They're down the other end of the hall." True: she forgets how big this house is. "Anyhow, they might learn something."

"But you're going to get rid of it, right?"

"Aw. Old Man Wheelchair's bumming her out."

"I hate it."

"Somehow I don't think this is about the wheelchair," he says. "Could you keep doing that?" She resumes. "*Yes.* But listen, you're right, he doesn't need to see it. I'll bring it up and stick it in the hall closet."

"I thought you were taking it to the Salvation Army."

"Tomorrow's Sunday. I don't think they're open."

"But he's *coming* tomorrow."

"Right, which is why I'm putting it in the closet. You're not following what I'm saying." He takes her wrist and moves her hand to the place he likes her to go but won't ask for. "Listen, do you feel like, maybe, not putting your thing in tonight?"

She pulls her hand away. "I don't think that would be too smart."

"I think it might be *really* smart."

She rolls away from him onto her back, each hand gripping the opposite shoulder, elbows bent so she must resemble one of those big paperclips. She closes her eyes but has to open them when she starts seeing stuff like screen savers. "I'm too stoned to deal with this now," she says.

"Would you *ever* want to talk about it?"

"Not now," she says.

The wheelchair is called an Everest & Jennings. Holly understands the Everest part—*Towering above all other wheelchairs*—but why Jennings? It must just be a name. But since she can't seem to let anything be anymore, she's made up her mind that Jennings makes her think of journeying. So it would be *Forever rest from journeying*: her own little formulation. Except the whole idea of a wheelchair is to *keep* you journeying. As this one kept Seth's mother journeying her last years on earth. Her husband put her in it and wheeled her places.

Saturn

Even aboard an airplane, to move her to Florida—the state whose very name had once been a snobby joke with them—so he could wheel her out into warm ocean air every day of the year. He'd been a dean at Yale; she'd taught life drawing. After her stroke, he'd had to bathe her and help her when she went to the bathroom. *Help* meaning "wipe." Holly saw her only once: three years ago, at the wedding. Seth's father had wheeled her up the ramp into the church and all the way down front to the end of the first pew; when Holly did her walk down the aisle, she had to step around the wheelchair, and her big stiff skirt brushed against the woman's motionless arm. Seth's mother was like a big doll: couldn't walk, couldn't talk, couldn't feed herself. Well, could cry. A continuous whine punctuated by sobs and gasps: when the organ stopped, it filled the silence.

Four months ago they'd flown down for the funeral and seen her dead body—Holly's first. She'd always heard that they looked fake and waxy, but she found it oddly not-disturbing. Maybe it was good that her first one was somebody she truly hadn't known. Like practicing up for *her* mother. Who's only sixty-three, but nevertheless. Holly's father is sixty-six, living in Vancouver with his second family. (The younger boy's now twelve.) She has no plans to attend *that* funeral, however many years away it might be.

When they went through his mother's stuff, Seth told his father the same thing he's saying now, about taking the wheelchair to the Salvation Army. Instead, he'd shipped it up to New York, then made sure it was in the van for the move to South Norwalk. He wanted it as a guilty reminder of his father's selfless devotion, she assumed, which he was secretly afraid he himself wouldn't rise to, if and when. But now it's shaded into punk grotesque: Seth uses it as a footstool, a TV tray, and at the head of the table at dinners when they're short a chair.

Holly once said it made them seem like awful people. Seth said, "To whom?"

Seth's official reason for still smoking weed is that he doesn't want to, quote, go native, meaning end up one more suit on the train. (He in fact does wear a suit to work.) He wants them to, quote, live nicely, in a big house where family can come visit (kids, of course, in the back of his mind), but at the same time he doesn't want to get less crazy. So he'll smoke up before he goes for a run, and he's found a dentist in Danbury who still gives gas; last week he had a dope-and-classic-movie marathon: *The Godfather, Godfather II* and *Psycho*. While the magazine he edits and publishes is basically a trade journal, it's designed by a guy who used to be at *Spin*, and he commissions pieces from name writers. He's told T. Coraghessan Boyle's agent that he'd take fifteen hundred words on anything in any way related to marketing just to have Boyle's picture on the contributors' page—which Holly suspects is why he's never heard back. Before they left the city, Seth bought a secondhand Ford Explorer and put in furry speakers so big they take up most of the wayback; now he's got his eye on this particular sports car that Mazda makes, which looks completely European but costs like half. Holly, meanwhile, is trying to get *less* crazy. When he asked what kind of car she wanted—up here you really need two—she chose the top-rated Saturn. A dark green Saturn.

With all this company, she *can't* be crazy. Her sister, his father tomorrow, then, after he goes back to Florida, her mother comes in for Christmas. (Seth and Holly have agreed it would be just too weird to throw the two of them together.) And in between they've got his old college roommate coming up for a weekend with wife and kids. Seth even said something about maybe asking Holly's dad and stepmom sometime, but Holly cut *that* one off. He wants everybody, it seems, to admire

their new home. It's a white-clapboard, black-shuttered house—
"Classic Connecticut," the Coldwell Banker brochure called
it, "with today's amenities." Built in 1849, four upstairs bedrooms, new half-bath off the master bedroom, new kitchen
with slate countertops and a Jenn-Air range with six burners.
And since it was in South Norwalk rather than Westport, Seth
thought they could actually swing it, even though Holly's in-
come—she freelanced restoring rare books and documents—
could be unpredictable. There's a big old maple tree he thinks
they could save if somebody cut out the dead limbs and fertil-
ized, and a garden out back. Their first day there, after Seth
drove to the train, Holly put on work gloves and raked brown
vines into a pile beneath the eight-over-eight windows. In each
window, she could picture a black-suited old Yankee merchant
or minister, the long-dead owners of this fine, severe house,
looking down at her. She worked for half an hour, then took a
shower and drove in to Manhattan. To fuck her lover. Harsh as
that sounds.

All during the house-hunting, the mortgage application,
the closing, even the move, she'd managed to spend an afternoon or two a week with Mitchell, then go home to her husband. And for another few weeks, until she decided the
whole thing was too crazy, she'd drive into the city after morning rush hour, then back up to Connecticut before the afternoon rush began, to wait for her husband in their strange new
house. Holly was prettier than her lover was handsome—
Mitchell was getting bald and potsy, though in a cute way—so
he'd had to put up with her having a husband and everything
that involved: being kept on short notice, not being able to
phone, having to wear a condom in addition to her putting in
the diaphragm. When they played rough, she made him be
careful about scratches; but she was allowed to mark him because he had nobody to hide stuff from. (That she knew about.)

Finally, he'd had to put up with being told it was too crazy. What almost made them even was Holly's need to feel like shit.

For a lover, she'd chosen the curator who'd been giving her most of her restoration work for the past couple of years. So since the beginning of October, she's made less than a thousand dollars. Something else Seth doesn't know.

These last few days she's been trying to read *Madame Bovary*, a book she somehow missed in college. To drive home the where-adultery-ultimately-gets-you idea, though it's also part of her self-improvement scheme, along with learning about opera and getting serious about cooking. The beginning seems to be about the husband as a schoolboy, so it looks like it could take forever to get to the marriage and then the affair, but she means to stick with it. And now that she's going to stop smoking weed, that should help her concentration. She's figured one thing out: the reason she goes deeper into her this-is-not-me space with her husband than she did with her lover is that she didn't lie to her lover. Or didn't lie as much to her lover. But the lover, not the husband, had to wear the condom, so didn't that mean it was the lover who was more distant? And sure enough, she's given up the lover and stayed with the husband. So at least that part hangs together.

With her morning headache, Holly does a lousy job of fixing breakfast for everybody. She slices the grapefruits in half, but can't face getting in there with the knife and cutting the sections free. Nor does she use any of the six burners to cook them eggs, bacon, pancakes or even this great Irish oatmeal she bought. Her one big, bountiful effort is to fill the peacock-feather pitcher with milk and set out bowls and boxes of cereal: they've got their choice of Spoon Size Shredded Wheat or raspberry granola. When she goes to get coffee cups, Seth has come back from the store with the Sunday *Times* and he's taking down juice glasses. She huffs out a big breath at him: he's *in her way.* That was a shitty position he put her in last night.

She pours their coffee, then tries squeezing the ball of her thumb with the other thumb and forefinger, which is supposed to get rid of a headache. Without asking if anyone minds, she's sneaked the Jane Eaglen CD into the kitchen boom box; it's the first one, the Bellini-Wagner recital, which she likes better than the second one, the Mozart-Strauss, because it's more extreme, though maybe not the thing for a headache. Holly's still trying to come up with a formulation for Jane Eaglen. So far she's figured out that Leontyne Price is *steely and powerful*, that Victoria de los Angeles is *sweet-toned and smooth*, that Montserrat Caballé is *exquisitely controlled* and that Luisa Tetrazzini, with all that birdy-sounding stuff, is *virtually unlistenable.* In some other life she'd be able to set forth these opinions in conversation. Though so far Seth is putting up with her opera phase on principle: the principle that any and all music must be put up with, just as she put up with his dancehall-reggae phase. What is it with men and music? Mitchell's opera collection is so huge she'd wondered at first if he was straight. He was the one who'd put her onto Montserrat Caballé, calling her attention to Caballé's pianissimo, which suggested that he liked his women to be *exquisitely controlled.* And Holly became that for him, within the context of being a total outlaw. The word *adulteress* makes her think of wild tresses. A dress, ripped from bare shoulders. It also makes her think of the word *actress.*

As Jane Eaglen shrills out *"Hojotoho!"* Holly watches Seth mangling his grapefruit. What a bad, bad wife she is. But the granola's a hit: she's the only taker on the Shredded Wheat. On her first full day of being thirty-two, she doesn't want to start putting on weight.

After breakfast, Seth goes upstairs to do some work, and Holly drives Tenley and her friend to the station in the Explorer. It creeps her out to have anybody else in the Saturn after she's used it to go commit adultery. Her official excuse is that the car's a mess; she keeps it that way by chucking napkins, McDonald's bags and Diet Coke cans on the passenger-side floor. She's even tried to think of a plausible-sounding reason to trade in a two-month-old car. In which her husband just had a twelve-CD changer installed.

"I *still* feel like I'm buzzed," Tenley says. "You guys always get that wasted? I was so wrecked last night, I went to the bathroom and I couldn't, like, remember how to pee?"

"Wow, really?" says the boyfriend.

"It's sort of Seth's hobby," Holly says. "Like rock climbing."

"But what about you?"

"I just basically keep him company."

Tenley looks at her. "Yeah, I noticed." She sighs. "Oh, well. Anyhow, you've got a fabulous place." She pulls down the visor and lifts her chin to look in the mirror. "You know, the kitchen *alone*. God, I look like shit." She flips the visor back up. "Carl? You didn't hear that." Carl's in the backseat, drumming his fingers on Tenley's headrest.

"Thanks," says Holly. "It's not really my doing, but—you know, yeah. It's pretty great."

"So is he after you to have kids now? Carl, could you cut that out?"

"We talk about it."

"It just made me think, you know, choosing a house that big. And of course now that you're—anyway. So you never told me what he got you for your birthday."

"Oh. A CD thing for my car." He'd also gotten her the 1935 recording of Act I of *Die Walküre* with Lotte Lehmann, who he'd read was the all-time greatest Sieglinde.

"What kind?" Carl says.

Tenley looks over her right shoulder. "This is girl talk." She turns back to Holly. "Carl does have one *big thing* in his favor."

Saturn

Holly glances in her rearview mirror; Carl's just looking out the window. Tenley sighs. "God, I can't believe how *rich* you guys are—sorry, I know how that sounds, but I'm really sort of in awe." Tenley shares a two-bedroom in Park Slope.

"I guess I would be, too." Holly puts her left blinker on. The station's just up ahead, and that'll be that. "I don't know what I'm supposed to say. 'I'm still the same person'?"

"Oh, you *are*, totally. I mean, nobody would ever . . ." Tenley looks over at Holly, shrugs.

"Right," Holly says. "Say no more."

"I can say no more," Tenley says, in an Indian accent. When they were little, they must have seen *Help!* twenty times.

At two-thirty Seth and Holly start down for La Guardia in the Explorer, through a freezing rain. Can his father's plane even land? She wishes it would turn tail and take him back, which she suspects is the cover-wish for her real wish.

The plane's late because of the weather, but they've brought along a few sections of the *Times*, and she buys a cheap ballpoint to do the crossword puzzle. She's trying to figure out "Forsterian dictum (two words)" when the flight's finally announced and passengers start straggling in the gate. Seth and his father hug, then Van hugs Holly, mashing her breasts, his leather shoulder bag slapping against her pelvic bone. "Mmm," he says into her ear. "So *glad.*"

"We are, too," she says, and he releases her.

"Bumpy ride?" Seth says.

"Only along toward the last," Van says. "I was able to read until we started hitting turbulence around Washington. Then I figured discretion was the better part of valor and had 'em bring me a drink. Since I was too pusillanimous to haul out my own supply. Listen, I have a gift for you two." He pats the shoulder bag.

"A bottle of hooch," says Seth. "How did I guess."

"Oh, no, *that* I'm keeping. Like to have my little night-cap in my room. No, this is a one-of-a-kind—well, it is and it isn't. I'll have to give it to you when we get to your dacha. Couple things came loose, so I need to stop and get some rubber cement."

"Hmm. Mighty mysterious," Seth says. "Holly must have rubber cement in her workroom."

"Hell, of course she would. Losing my marbles here. Ah, which reminds me. Guy goes to his doctor, doctor says, 'I got some bad news. You have terminal cancer.' Guy says, 'Oh, *no*.' Doctor says, 'I got more bad news. You've also got Alzheimer's.' Guy says, 'Whew, thank God. I thought you were going to tell me I had cancer or something.' "

"Good one," says Seth.

"Except you've heard it."

"Still good."

Van stretches forth a hand and regards his palm as if holding what's-his-name's skull. "Age cannot wither nor custom stale. Speaking of which . . ." He gives Holly another quick hug. "You wouldn't happen to have an older sister? A much older sister?"

"I have a *younger* sister—well, you met her. At the wedding."

"I remember her well. Nearly as lovely as your lovely self. *Too* lovely, I'm afraid."

"But she does have low standards," Seth says.

"If she's got standards of any kind, that lets *her* out," says Van. "I remember when I used to have standards. It was back when Benjamin Harrison was president."

When they get back to the house, she starts a pot of coffee, which seems better than offering Van more to drink. Seth shows him around, carries his bags upstairs and comes back down to the kitchen alone.

"Mmm." He sniffs the air. "Good idea."

Holly says, "Why were you ragging on my sister?"

"Say what?"

"She has low standards?"

"*I* thought I was ragging on what's-his-name."

"That's not how it came across. You essentially told your father she was a slut."

Seth does that little take of his where he raises both palms and rolls his eyes upward.

"Why would you *do* that?" she says.

"Holly. I was talking about her sorry-ass boyfriend. Shit, I *like* your sister."

"Well, be more careful what you say, okay?"

"Okay. I'm sorry, babe." He smiles and holds his arms open. What can she do but go to him and put the side of her head against his chest? Though she didn't appreciate hearing that he likes her sister, either.

Van comes back down with his gift: a photo album filled with old pictures, captions typed on slips of white paper that he's rubber-cemented to the black pages. They sit on the couch, Holly between them holding it on her lap as Van points and narrates. The story of his marriage, basically, with what seem to Holly grudging glimpses of Seth: selected baby pictures and milestones in costume—Little League uniform, mortarboard, Abe Lincoln in a school play. In groom suit, gray jacket, striped pants, holding hands with Holly in her wedding gown. The last page has shots from the fortieth-anniversary party. Among displays of exploding tropical flowers, Seth's father, as tanned and smiley as an actor, works the room. Raises a champagne glass. Feeds a forkful of cake to Seth's mother, stonefaced in her wheelchair.

"This is great," Seth says. "I'm glad to have this." Holly's impressed: it's a good imitation of the normative reaction. Over to you, Holly.

"Thank you," she says. "This is going to be so wonderful to have." She rubs her index finger back and forth on the slip of paper that says OUR 40TH, SIESTA KEY, 1/8/95, and the smears ball up into springy grains of rubber. She's managed to imply that (a) his gift is not yet wonderful, and (b) it will be wonderful only when he, too, is dead. But Van puts an arm around her back, clamps her far shoulder and gives it a squeeze, apparently to express some feeling too powerful for words. He excuses himself and goes into the downstairs bathroom, and Holly turns back to that first page. A young man and woman in bathing suits, arms around each other's waists, water and mountains behind them: LILY AND VG, SARANAC, SUMMER 1957. In 1957, Seth's mother had looked like Winona Ryder, except that her thighs had that tubby look nobody minded back then. Van had looked like a younger, even handsomer Seth.

Holly bought lamb chops for dinner, but now that it's stopped sleeting, Van insists on taking them out for what he calls "our first night." Lately, he says, he's had a jones for Mexican food. A jones, yet. So Seth calls The El Coyote—which is what it's actually called, *The El*—while Holly goes upstairs to put on earrings and lipstick.

She's looking through her jewelry box when Seth comes in and closes the door behind him. He opens his top drawer, gets out his pipe and goes kitchy-koo.

"I don't think I should," she says.

"Oh, come on. I need my coconspirator. I can't do this straight."

"I thought you were *enjoying* it."

"Good," he says. "That means he probably thinks so, too."

After turning him down in bed last night, Holly can't totally punk out on this. But she only takes two hits to his four or five. That little bit she should be able to handle, or there really *is* something wrong with her.

. . .

The El Coyote is all welcome and abundance. Somebody's put wooden bowls of salsa and blue corn chips on their table before they even sit down; the menu calls this "Bottomless Chips and Salsa—Complimentary!" The tabletops are wooden factory spools polyurethaned to a gloss like honey.

Holly can't imagine how Seth got them here: he must be twice as wrecked as she is, if that's quantifiable. At one point they had to squeeze through a construction zone where the plastic mesh fencing whipped by just inches from her window and giant bulldozers, cranes and earthmovers loomed in pink light. And then all that confusion at the door when they had to stop and be looked up in a book—what seemed to Holly the kind of episode that could lead to getting arrested. She tries to recall how the Bible line goes: *Thou hast preparedest for me an table set before me in the presence of mine enemies.* But it would be good to stay away from thinking about enemies.

She hears the crunch of a corn chip all the way across the table. "Good salsa," Van says. "Salsa without cilantro is like a day without sunshine."

"Matthew Arnold?" Seth says.

"He will *never* cease to twit me about this," Van says to Holly. "One line—a very apposite line—in your wedding toast. From 'Dover Beach.' Apparently this was the ne plus ultra of fuddy-duddyism. See, years ago—this character was still in grade school—I used to teach nineteenth-century. Until I realized that my true gift was for glad-handing."

"You used to say it was for kissing ass."

"Ah, but there's a lady present."

"It's okay, she knows about these exotic practices." Seth crunches a corn chip. "Are you having a margarita?"

Silence. Holly looks up. He's looking at *her.*

"Oh." She tries to determine whether he'd implied that she should or she shouldn't, but the sound of his voice is back too far and getting farther. Would a margarita help bring her down or make it worse? She's pretty sure tequila comes from the same cactus as mescaline.

"Be working on your answer," Seth says.

"*My* arm is twistable," says Van.

"Maybe if I had a half?" Holly says. God, her mouth is dry.

"A small one?" What Seth means is *I'll help you through this, but you're being a drag.*

The waitress moves toward them, her healthy face appearing to glow from inside like a Halloween pumpkin, but there's a candle on the table to provide a reassuring explanation. All these little things will click back into place if Holly can just hang on. The waitress says her name is Andrea, and she recites the specials while looking them in the eyes. She has rings on every finger of both hands, even spoon rings on the thumbs; she's pretty and young and fetishy, and Holly feels the threat, which is insane given what *she's* been up to. In fact, Holly tried out fetishy things on Mitchell: an ankle bracelet, then a tiny silver stud piercing the web of skin between her big and second toes. Seth liked it, too.

When the waitress goes away, Seth's father turns to Holly. "So, are you nagging this character sufficiently about his health? He asks, having brought them to a restaurant specializing in fatty food."

This question has so much ironic spin that she gives up and says, "I don't know."

"Well, by my calculations, he's about to turn forty, and depending on whose genes he got the most of . . . You see what I'm saying. These last few years have put the fear of God into me. I go in every six months, religiously, get 'em to check my cholesterol, EKG, the works. Prostate exam—very important."

"Fingered for death," Seth says. "I have to say, one of my least favorite things."

Holly understands he has to say this in front of his father. In fact, isn't that why he said *I have to say*? Clever Seth! But she knows what she knows.

"Yes, well," says Van. "If you want to talk about least favorite things . . ."

"Yeah, you're right," says Seth. "I should be doing it."

"I've also got my living will witnessed and notarized. But if I'm in any shape to prevent *that* situation, believe you me . . ."

"Well." Seth looks over his shoulder, as if to see what's keeping their waitress. "Let's see how you feel if it ever gets to a point like that. I mean, how did Mom feel?"

Van shakes his head. "I wondered all the time. *All* the time. I used to look for any sign that—you know. Well, we don't need to pursue this. Holly, you look like you've been shot."

"I do?" She has no idea what else to say, though he clearly wants her to build on this and then they can all three be talking. She feels a leg against her knee and moves her knee away.

The waitress comes back and sets their drinks in front of them, baby drink for Baby Holly. She could swear the waitress smirked.

Van raises his glass. "As another fuddy-duddy writer once said: Only Connecticut."

"Hear, hear." Seth holds up his glass by the stem, prissy-pinkie. He means it ironically. He's doing all this stoned?

"To Connecticut," she says, trying to get in the same key. Seth and his father laugh, and she takes in an icy mouthful of salt, sour lime and poison alcohol. It scares her that this taste—which should be so familiar: a frozen margarita, no more, no less—is coming at her in components she can't recombine. She hasn't come down at all; in fact, she feels herself going to an even higher place. If she survives this, she will never smoke weed again.

The waitress comes back to take their dinner orders, and she and Van have quite the little flirtation. He says she looks exactly like someone he knew back when he was a graduate student. Somehow he makes it clear that he and this person slept together. "Of course this was many, many years ago."

"Not *that* many," the waitress says.

"It was a while back," he says. "She and I were studying oceanography with Matthew Arnold."

The waitress cocks her head. "Okay, you're kidding. Right?"

"Would I kid you?"

"You might." She narrows her eyes. "You've got that look." She walks away, her long Mexican skirt swishing.

"Whew," says Seth. "The air smolders."

Van picks up his glass. "I've got to get the hell out of Florida."

While they're undressing for bed, Holly tells Seth she can't smoke weed anymore. "I have to tell you," he says, "I don't think weed per se is the problem." He balls up his shirt and brandishes it one-handed above his head like a basketball, lightly touching his wrist with the other hand. He misses the hamper.

"It's the problem when it gets me too high to deal with anything."

"You get *yourself* too high to deal with anything."

"Okay." She doesn't follow. "But then wouldn't you say the solution is not to do it?" She turns her back and unhooks her bra.

"I'd say the solution is to look at what's really going on." He goes over, picks up the shirt and stuffs it into the hamper.

"Right. Well, what's really going *on* is, I get too high when I smoke."

He sighs. "Look, you know yourself best. I thought it was a fun thing for us. Sort of us against the world."

"I know *that*." She lets the "but" clause remain implied. Could he really have felt it was them against the world? Like, together?

He turns out the light and reaches over. No candle tonight.

"Listen," he says after a while. "Would it break the mood too much if I, you know?"

She was beginning to like what they'd been doing. "Won't it keep you up?" she says.

"Ah," he says. "She begins to get the idea." Holly sees his dark shape go over to the dresser. She hears the drawer slide open. "Shit, I need the light," he says. "Hide your eyes."

She closes her eyes, hard, and covers them with her fingers. Still, everything lights up red. What can it be but her own blood seen through her own eyelids?

She ought to be in bed, but instead she's out behind the house for some reason, in the dead garden; this can't be a dream because her bare feet are freezing. She wonders if Seth has noticed she's not there beside him, so she wills herself up into the air as high as their bedroom window. It works. Now, let's see if she can pass right *through* the window, as if it were a membrane. Yes! The glass stretches, gives way and reseals behind her, and she's back under the covers with no one the wiser. Her powers are beginning to scare her, but at the same time she understands that this could be a dream after all, so she tries waking herself up. And sure enough.

She gets out of bed, creeps down to the dark kitchen and feels around by the phone for the pencil and Post-It pad. She's got to preserve something of this; it's like no dream she's ever had. Primitive people thought you literally leave your body when you dream; this could be what just happened to her. She goes into the bathroom, closes the door and turns on the light. As she writes, she feels little prickly chills on her forehead.

Maybe she's got a fever and it was just a fever dream. She could be coming down with that bird flu; it started in Hong Kong, where people got it from chickens. It's like a pun: bird flew. And she was flying in the dream.

She takes two Advils, turns off the light and finds her way upstairs. Seth is still breathing away: sound asleep, unless he's as good a faker as she is.

Holly's aware of Seth getting dressed in the gray early morning; he always makes the 8:05 no matter what he was into the night before. When she wakes up for real, it's after ten. She finds the Post-It where she left it: stuck to the back of the nightstand where Seth wouldn't see. *Dream—I am out back (in garden) and find I can fly up and pass through bedroom window. Window is like a bubble.* The dream is pretty clearly about just slipping back into her marriage with no harm done. She props pillows behind her and tries to concentrate on *Madame Bovary* (maybe the translation's part of the problem), but she can feel Seth's father in the house, the way you know where the sun is on a cloudy day.

She gets up and showers. She's not the type of person who would ever have a bathroom off the master bedroom, but here she is. South Norwalk, Connecticut. She puts on the most unalluring stuff she can find: her loosest jeans, her hooded sweatshirt with the kangaroo pocket, running shoes with no socks. Down in the kitchen she finds half a pot of still-hot coffee, and a clean mug with a note under it: *Out for my constitutional. Back soon. Van.* She takes her coffee into the dining room and looks out at the garden. Whatever she was supposed to do with that pile of dead vines and leaves, she's never done it. She wants to put on Portishead, but it could make Seth's father feel unwelcome when he gets back. So she goes upstairs and brings her book down.

It's almost noon when he comes into the kitchen in sweat-
pants and windbreaker, carrying a *Times* and pulling a blue
sweatband off his head.

"I was wondering if you'd gotten lost," she says.

"Like an Alzheimer's patient."

"Exactly. Just what I was going to say," she says. "Is it
cold out?"

"My God, I can't remember." He drops his mouth open and
claps a hand to his forehead. "Actually, it's okay once you get
moving."

"How about some lunch?"

"I would *love* it." He sits down at the kitchen table, wet hair
pasted to his forehead.

"I could make you a ham sandwich—we have this great
country ham."

"Anything." Which in fact means anything *else*, right?
But she's not going to stand there neurotically naming off
possibilities.

"And a beer?" she says.

"That's a thought. Yes. Yes, please." He opens the *Times*.

She gets two slices of rye out of the breadbox, the ham and a
jar of mustard from the refrigerator. "Were you warm enough
last night?"

"It was fine. I like a room to be a little cool for sleeping."

"If you're cold tonight, there's extra blankets up in the hall
closet." She remembers the damn wheelchair. "Actually, why
don't I get a couple out for you and stick them in your room."

"If you think of it," he says.

She pours his beer into a pilsner glass she bought at Crate &
Barrel, holding the glass straight up so there'll be enough head
to leave an inch or so in the bottle. She glances over to make
sure he's not looking, then chugs it.

When she brings the beer and the sandwich over, he puts
the paper down. "This is splendid, thank you." He lifts the

glass. "Better days. And colder nights." He takes a taster's sip. "Beck's?"

"Sam Adams."

"Aha. So tell me something. Are you two getting along?"

"That's coming right to the point," she says. Did something happen last night? She can't begin to think back. "In answer to your question, yes. If we weren't getting along, why would I be here?"

"Ah. Miss Feist. *Mizz* Feist."

"Van, you're not trying to pick a fight, are you?"

"No. God, no. Just trying to get up to speed. I like you, believe it or not. The last few years have raised hell with my social graces."

"Since you bring that up," she says, "I've been meaning to tell you. Seth admires you so much for the care you took of her. I don't know if he's said that to you."

"Yes, well. Seth's a romantic. Small *r*. Can I tell you something? And you keep it to yourself?"

"Not tell Seth."

He turns a palm up.

She turns a palm up, too, and sits down across the table from him.

He closes his eyes, feels around for his beer, grasps it. "I hurt her," he says.

Holly thinks how to phrase the question, then says, "In what sense?"

Van shakes his head, eyes still closed. "You know, she was, one side of her, her whole left side, it was just dead. And this one day, she was taking a nap and I just—" Shakes his head again. "I stuck a pin into her arm. Right there." He jabs an imaginary pin into his left arm just below the shoulder. Winces.

"Accidentally, though."

"*Not* accidentally. Shit." Shakes his head. "Oh, boy. Okay, it's out now." Holly watches him wagging his face back and forth.

She wishes he'd open his eyes. "I did it to see, you know, if she'd feel it. Because I didn't know whether or not the nerves were still connected to the, you know, to the . . . Shit." He's still shaking his head.

"And did she feel it?"

"No. Not that I could tell. She didn't wake up."

"Well, then you *didn't* hurt her."

He opens his eyes and looks at her. "That's what you think?"

Holly shakes her head. "You were under so much stress. I can't even imagine—"

"No. Please don't bother. I didn't tell you this in order for you to come up with some little insight to get me off the hook." He looks down at her breasts; good she wore her sweatshirt. "By which I don't mean you're not smart." He's still looking.

"But Van, that doesn't negate all the, the whole—like taking care of her, taking her places, being with her . . ."

"Okay, you've said your piece. I've said my piece. Now what shall we talk about?"

"We could talk about where you're looking," she says. He goes red, looks down at his sandwich. "I'm sorry, I didn't mean to embarrass you. I guess I was getting back at you for brushing me off."

"Well, what the hell. You don't like me much anyhow."

"That's not so."

He holds up a hand to forestall further untruth. "No need. I apologize. This is one hell of a way to pay you back for the nice lunch."

"Which you haven't touched."

"Which I haven't touched." He finishes his beer and looks around the room. "What is *wrong* with me?"

"Do you want to talk?"

Shakes his head. "I am talking. This is what happens when I talk. I do apologize."

"It's all right. Would you like another beer?"

"Which I guess isn't the same as being sorry."

"It's all *right*," she says. "I just wish I could help."

"Not a thing you can do. I will take another one, thanks. Probably a bad idea, but what isn't. And then I'll get out of your hair. Go up and do some reading. I don't mean to sound—whatever the word is. Byronic."

Holly doesn't quite catch this. "Ironic?"

"Huh," he says. "Isn't it."

Holly sticks a load of clothes in the washer, then goes back to *Madame Bovary*. But lying on the sofa, under warm yellow lamplight, she can't keep her eyes open; behind her red eyelids there's an alternate story going, and she follows that for a while. She comes awake to a wet tickling on the sole of her foot. She jerks the foot away: Van's standing at the end of the sofa with something in his hand. With the brush from a jar of rubber cement.

"Are you insane?" she says. "What are you *doing*?"

"I couldn't resist. It's just a teensy little—here." He whisks a Kleenex from the box on the end table; as if in a magic trick, the same Kleenex now seems to be sticking up out of the box.

She grabs her foot with both hands and twists it around to look: an inch-long streak of cloudy goo across her instep. "Aren't you a little old to be acting like a first grader?"

"A *little* old? That's charitable. Here you go." He holds out the Kleenex; she ignores it and rubs at the goo with her fingertip. "I don't know why I did that. Maybe it *is* Alzheimer's. I actually came down to ask if I could borrow your car to run a quick errand."

"I have to go to Westport later," she says. "I'd be glad to pick something up for you." Has he been drinking in his room?

"Ah. I believe I'm hearing a no. After that little perfor-mance, I can't blame you for thinking—whatever you must think. I *am* sorry. It was . . ." He shakes his head. *Could* he have Alzheimer's?

"That's not—Van, it's perfectly fine if you want to take the car. I just thought I'd save you the trouble."

"This is getting baroque," he says.

"Really, it's fine. Take the car, by all means."

"I'm annoying you."

"You're not," she says. "I just—you know, you're welcome to take the *car*, okay? Do you know your way around?"

"What a question. Huh. You remember those old postcards? *Ve get too soon oldt und too late schmardt?* The dirty old man with the beard and the cane, all bent over, and this gal with a tight dress is walking—"

"I don't, actually."

"I'm dating myself," he says. "Just in case anybody should look at me and miss the point."

She sighs. "Van, you're not that old."

"Ah," he says. "Now, there's a woman who knows her lines."

Holly watches from the living room window as he backs out of the driveway, then goes into the laundry room to put the clothes in the dryer. She takes out the lamb chops. In *The Way to Cook* she finds a marinade with olive oil, dijon mustard, garlic and rosemary; she puts the chops in to soak. She straightens up the kitchen, sponges off the countertops, gets down dinner plates, salad plates and wineglasses—which is a little crazed with so many hours to go, but anything to put off *Madame Bovary.* She turns the radio on, listens for a few seconds, then re-alizes it's "Till Eulenspiegel's Merry Pranks," which they seem to play about forty times a week. She turns it off and goes back to the sofa. Charles's first wife spits blood and dies as the buzzer goes off on the dryer.

When Van's not back at four-thirty, she calls Seth at work. "What am *I* supposed to do?" he says. "Maybe he took a sentimental journey up to New Haven. The old goat's probably lurking around Machine City trying to pick up coeds."

"Coeds?"

"You've heard the expression? Look, if I'm going to get home by—"

"Okay, fine, thanks."

"Did you need the car?"

"I wanted to run up to Hay Day to get bread and salad stuff."

"So tell me what you need and I'll stop by."

"That's so out of your way. I'm sure he'll be back any minute. I probably worry too much."

"Speaking of worrying too much," he says, "how's your finances? I paid the mortgage today, so I was hoping you could take care of the bills. I've been putting them in my top drawer."

"Sure. No problem." She's got about six hundred left in her checking. After the bills, she'll have walking-around money for another couple of weeks. The bad heat bills won't start until next month. By which time she'd better think of something.

"I'm glad I married money," he says.

Her line here is *Me too.* "Okay, I'll see you soon," she says.

At quarter after five the Saturn pulls into the driveway. Van comes into the kitchen, gives her a courtly bow and sets a Barnes & Noble bag on the counter: Sue Grafton and her cute overbite. "Heigh-ho, heigh-ho," he says.

"So how was the mall?" This is to put him on notice that she's not without her own Sue Grafton detective skills.

"The mall," he says. "Yes. Very civilized. If you're expecting a philippic against malls, I'm going to have to disappoint you." She smells liquor breath.

"Where else did you go?"

"Oh?" he says. "Might I ask in what spirit you're asking?"

"Just a spirit of curiosity."

"Good. Good answer," he says. "Because not all sixty-seven-year-olds have Alzheimer's disease."

"What is this with you and Alzheimer's? Aren't people more likely to die in a car crash?"

"This is—this *may* be true. But you can have Alzheimer's and still die in a car crash. Or prostate cancer and die in a car crash. Or Alzheimer's and die of prostate cancer. How in God's name did we get onto *this*?"

"Can I see what you bought?" Holly nods at the Barnes & Noble bag.

"Very deft. Thank you. Yes, let's talk books. Books. All right: baroque as it may seem, I got a sudden hankering to reread Hazlitt. I found your *Portable Coleridge* upstairs and that made—"

"Not mine."

"Yours now, *n'est-ce pas?* At any rate, the reason I say civilized, I'm sitting up in your lovely guest room reading Coleridge on Shakespeare. This naturally makes me want to read Hazlitt instead, so I hop in your car, over to the mall, find the Barnes & Noble and *voilà*." He reaches in the bag and produces *Hazlitt: Selected Writings*. "Ten minutes from an idle wish to its fulfillment. Fifteen, tops. You can't tell me that's not a modern miracle."

"Can I see?" He hands her the book. William Hazlitt (1778–1830) seems to have been a great social and literary critic who said, "No one has come between me and my free-will." Like whoosie and her Calvins. It's not the world's zingiest quote.

"I haven't told your husband this," Van says, "but I've been thinking about maybe going back to teaching. Little adjunct position someplace. Help 'em screw some young guy out of a full-time job. Oh, brother. I better sit down." He pulls out a chair and sits, his palms flat on the table. "Better."

"Are you all right?"

"I'll put a narrow construction on that," he says. "Yes, I'm fine. You want to know what I've been thinking about all day? Of course you do. This is something that happened back when I was probably thirty-five, thirty-six—Jesus, *think* of it. It was the time when the students were discovering pot and all that. I'd contend with *them* all day long and then drive back home to Woodbridge. Spray the shrubs, whatever I did—well, you know." He waves an arm around, presumably to indicate the house and grounds. "Okay, okay, get to the *point*, Van. So this particular day, I'd suspended a student, to what purpose God only knows, and he came into my office—big, husky, blond boy, with one of those beards where it won't grow in on the sides? Just a little on the chin." Van rubs his jaw. "He was already on probation, and this was the next step. So I told him, 'You've got to start making better choices.' And he looks at me—surly little bastard—and he says, 'Like *what*?' And I said, 'Fucking?' Well. He goes bright red, the way blonds do? Because the whole time I'm thinking, Seth's Little League team's playing out of town this afternoon, so when I go home I'll get to be all alone with my wife. Boy, he was out of there like a shot. He either thought I was a pervert or just completely out of my mind. Isn't that a strange story?"

"Van, I have to tell you, it sort of bothers me that you drove my car after you'd been drinking."

He waves this away. "Oh, pooh. And pooh again. As in: *Pooh pooh*. A couple of vodka tonics in the afternoon does not a drinking make. Nor iron bars a cage." He stands up and walks to the refrigerator. "I guess you'd've had to see Lily to appreciate that story. But hell, you *did* see Lily. Once in the wheelchair, once in the box. And now you have the pictures." He shakes his head. "You know, the one thing that got to me. The day I took the handicap plates off the car. Not a day I'd care to live over. May I offer you one of your own beers?"

"No, thanks. May I have the keys, by the way?"

"Hmm. Then may I invite you back to T.G.I. Friday's? Which is the answer to your question. Where I was? I went in there thinking I'd just sit and have a drink and read Hazlitt. But, as it turns out, they have a big, you know, overhead TV, and they were showing a hockey game, and it was so—what's the word? *Restful.* They just skate around and around and around. It was like a fish tank. Am I painting an attractive enough picture? They also have a real fish tank, by the way."

"Keys?" Holly says.

"Of course." He digs in his pocket.

"I think it might be a better idea to go upstairs and lie down for a while."

"Now, *there's* an offer." He shakes his head. "Jesus, I *am* drunk." He dangles the keys, drops them in her palm. "Oh, yes. The old boy's definitely overdue for a nap."

Holly turns on the radio and opens the refrigerator; maybe there's enough stuff for salad in the vegetable drawer. *"I'm Daniel Zwerdling,"* she says, right along with Daniel Zwerdling after his *"Hello."* She knows all their voices. Was she to blame for that going-upstairs remark? She'd meant it to be free of any little edge of anything. And we all know what that's worth. On "All Things Considered" they're talking about Cuba's currently lively arts scene; she catches the phrase *this island nation.* She's got salad stuff galore, and they can do without fancy-schmancy bread. God knows if Seth's father will even be able to eat.

So. The lamb chops are marinating. Seth won't be home for at least an hour. And she's got no work to do—hasn't even turned her computer on for a week. Well, she could pay those bills. She goes up to their bedroom, quietly, so Van won't hear, and closes the door behind her. In Seth's top drawer she finds half a dozen envelopes with a rubber band around them, next to his stubby brass pipe and his old Edgeworth tobacco box. She opens the lid: it's full of sticky, piney-skunky-smelling buds, like tiny green shrimps, and she plucks out one and hides it in her kangaroo pocket. Thievery pure and simple. Then she closes the drawer, leaving the bills, having decided that—no, having *understood* that she's going to call Mitchell. She walks to the bed as if somebody were inside her body, controlling it the way a little man up in his little booth runs a giant construction crane.

"Well," Mitchell says. "What do you know. I was just thinking about you."

"Me, too," she says. "Then again, I'm always thinking about myself."

"You're a card," he says. "But."

She begins wrapping coils of phone cord around her index finger, whose nail she keeps short for her husband. "I'm not sure I *can* be dealt with," she says.

"Yeah, I always liked that about you. Though you don't sound too happy about it."

"I don't know, I didn't call to complain."

He clears his throat. "Which raises the question."

"I guess I wanted to hear a friendly voice."

"Oh? I was under the impression that you had all the friends you could use."

"Come on, please don't—you know." Suddenly feeling cold, she puts her free hand in her kangaroo pocket. She needs to get socks on, too.

"Holly, I'm not understanding this. Look, do you want me to meet you someplace?"

"*No.*" She fingers the sticky little bud.

"Okay."

The sound of him waiting for her to go on.

She takes her hand out of her pocket and sniffs her fingers: the resinous smell that she can never decide is pleasant or unpleasant. She must've had it in mind to meet him, get him high and seduce him. Re-seduce him. Seduce him doubly: Mitchell doesn't do drugs. "Oh, God," she says. "This was really a mistake."

"Yeah, sounds like."

"So I guess I should hang up."

"Whatever you think," he says. "I'm just taking this all in."

"I'm going to hang up now."

"What would you like me to say?"

"Okay, I'm hanging up." And she does. She hadn't thought she would.

She's halfway down the stairs when her pulse starts pounding in her throat. She lies down on the sofa, closes her eyes and instantly gets an image of a hospital corridor: a nurse enters left, looks at a clock on the wall, exits right. Holly's never been in such a hospital. Her eyes fly open: she's in the living room in South Norwalk. If she'd been traveling out of body, could she have got back this fast? Then it comes to her: this must be the rehab unit where Seth's mother died. She didn't *travel* there, that's insane; it was an image beamed to her by Seth's mother from wherever she is now. As a warning. A warning against getting old and paralyzed and dependent, with all your deeds past remedy.

Holly wakes up hearing Seth's key in the lock, and tries to sit up, but the tiny will inside her can't move the big body. Her hands can't make fists.

"You okay?" he says. He unwinds his scarf, then roughs up his hair and snow flies out.

"Is it snowing?"

"Yeah, it's beautiful. You should take a little walk. It's falling through the streetlights." He flutters his fingers down. She closes her eyes again and hears him open the hall closet. A jingling of coat hangers. "So where's the Emperor of Ice Cream?"

"Up taking a nap, I think. I'm going to nap a little more, too, okay?"

"Will you be able to sleep tonight?"

She doesn't answer. What conceivable business is it of his?

She hears him walk into the kitchen. A beer-top pops, the refrigerator door closes with a whump and she opens her eyes, needing to latch onto something real. The antique clock on the mantel says, as always, 8:25—according to Seth, the most esthetically pleasing time. The clock's one of his family treasures: a tall French-polished box with a glass door whose bottom panel is a painting of a pointy-roofed mill and water waterfalling over the mill wheel. Seth's father used to tell him it was the mill of God, grinding slow but exceeding fine. Seth laughs about it now, but Holly knows that in olden times they made everything mean something: a picture of a mill wheel on a clock could very well have been their code for, like, *Get to work because God's coming to grind you up.*

Seth comes out of the kitchen and starts up the stairs when somebody hollers, "Look out below!" He freezes, looks up, drops his beer can (which goes tumbling end over end, beer pulsing out) and jumps aside as the wheelchair, his father in the seat—gripping the armrests, eyes wild—comes bumping and leaping down the stairs, then flies off the last step and rolls to the front door.

Seth says, "Jesus fucking Christ."

His father gets out of the wheelchair, stately with drink. "Look what *I* found," he says. "Chariot of the Gods. I'll pay for banging up your stairwell, no need to worry about that aspect.

You cannot imagine"—he puts his hand on his chest—"what that was like."

"Are you all right?" Seth says.

Holly sits up and paws around on the floor for her running shoes.

"I shouldn't think so," says Van. "Good God, who in their right mind would do such a thing?"

"I'm going out," Holly says. "To whom it may concern."

"Say again?" says Seth.

"I'll call you."

"Wait, you're just—I don't get what's going on here."

"You can deal with this. That way you'll really have something to hold against me. I mean"—and she can't help laughing—"it's the least I can do."

The streets have a dusting of snow, tinted a sick pink by the streetlights, with black stripes from passing car wheels. But the snowfall has stopped: a beautiful sight she's missed out on. She sees that she's heading for 95, and understands that at the entrance she'll choose 95 South, bound for New York.

She stops at the drive-up cash machine and gets a hundred dollars; the receipt says she's now down to $537.33. Then she drives around behind the bank building, parks under the featureless back wall and feels in her kangaroo pocket. Still there: now how's she going to do this? She unzips her purse, finds a ballpoint pen and unscrews the two pieces, picks up a Diet Coke can from the floor and pushes in the cigarette lighter. She turns the can upside down (a last trickle wetting her knee) and lays the bud on the concave bottom. If a police cruiser comes back here to check out the suspicious car, she's fucked. The lighter pops out and she touches the orange end to the bud. When it starts smoldering she picks up the bottom part of the pen, puts the threaded end between her lips, poises the little hole over the bud and sucks, focusing the smoke into a narrow, tornado-like rope, twisting up the barrel and into her lungs. She coughs out a cloud of piney smoke, gets her breath, goes at it again.

On 95 she eases her way into the leftmost lane and makes the needle inch up a hair above 70, then a hair above that. She hits PLAY on the CD changer, a soprano starts up, she peels the Post-It with her list off the glove-compartment door and holds it up in her line of vision. Disc One? Okay, Joan Sutherland. Whom she has yet to figure out a thing for. Holly concentrates as the voice navigates its own upper reaches; essentially, Joan Sutherland sounds shrieky, though you don't want *that* to be your formulation. In fact, it's Holly who's about to shriek, in the midst of what's starting to feel like a major mistake: trucks all around, their wheels higher than her roof, their brutal chrome radiators higher still. Their rush and roar drowns the music, and everything feels motionless, as if she could open the door, step out and stroll around. She'd better try to take this seriously. There's a sign for a service area: two miles. Surely she can make it two more miles.

She parks next to a silver minivan that's taken a handicap spot, then follows footprints and a pair of bicycle tracks across the snow-dusted blacktop. What kind of parents would allow their kids to ride bikes in a service area on a snowy night? If she ever—but really, let's not even get into that. She wishes she could see falling snow.

Inside the doors it's suddenly so warm that she shivers reflexively. She's got bare ankles and a cotton sweatshirt. McDonald's to the right; rest rooms and phones to the left. She punches in Mitchell's number, then her credit card number. But it's Seth who says *"Yellow?"* How could he possibly have got there ahead of her? Wait, how could he even have found out? But of course she's called home by mistake.

"Holly?"

She cradles the receiver, then feels a rush and her heart thumping, as after a near fender-bender. What this little slip means is that Seth *is* her true love. Or (b) that she's even more self-destructive than she realized.

She prefers (b). And if nothing else, she can be stubborn. When her heart stops pounding she'll call Mitchell. No, first she'll go in and wash her face, which feels like it's coated with gray film.

Holly sticks her hands under the automated faucet for her little ration of water. How's this formulation? That late capitalism tries to make you feel at the same time degraded and magically powerful: water at my mental command! Lately she's been favoring that expression, "late capitalism," except how could anybody know it's late rather than still early? She pumps liquid soap into her palm and again holds her hands under the faucet in supplication, but the machine knows it's her asking for seconds, so she moves to the next sink, which duly mistakes her for someone else.

Back in the car, she fastens her seat belt and realizes she's forgotten to call Mitchell. She closes her eyes and she's in bed with Seth. He reaches over. She opens her eyes and sees snowflakes bouncing off the windshield. So her wish came true. She starts the engine for some heat, and Joan Sutherland gives an ungodly shriek. She punches the STOP button and something like silence is restored. It's nothing like silence.

Through the falling snow, an old man is pushing an old woman down the walk in a wheelchair, heading this way. He's wearing a plaid shirt and no hat—what does snow feel like on a bald head?—but she's bundled up in a puffy coat and an I ♥ NY baseball cap. She has a no-pleasure-ever-again stare; the man is smiling. Holly jams the car into reverse, refusing to witness what happens next. A crunching thud as she hits something behind her—the front bumper of a car trying to crawl past—and she stomps on the brakes. The man in the plaid shirt turns to look; the woman continues to stare; somebody's getting out of the car behind her. Holly decides to haul ass, but she can't back up, can't go forward. She puts her head down on the wheel. Couldn't this just stop right here?

The Mail Lady

I wake again in our bedroom, vouchsafed another day. May I use it to Thy greater glory. In the dimness, a throbbing line of sunlight along the bottom of the window shade stabs the eye. So the rain has stopped at last. (Memory spared. Reason spared, too, seemingly.) When I turn away, my sight is momentarily burned black, and I can't be certain whether I'm truly *seeing* Wylie's features in the photograph on the nightstand or simply remembering them. I close my eyes again, and in afterimage the fierce light reappears.

The radio's on downstairs and I hear that sweet song, now what on earth is that called? Sweet, sweet song. Our station comes all the way from Boston, and seems to be the one certain refuge anywhere on the dial. We still try the classical station from time to time—back in Woburn, we never deviated from WCRB—but lately we find it awfully heavy going. (I have it: "Edelweiss.") Now I hear a rustle of sheets. Alice is in here, making up her bed. And checking on me. I don't open my eyes. A pat to her pillow and she's gone.

In the first weeks after my shock, I slept fourteen, sixteen hours a day, they tell me. The brain, as they explain it, shutting down in order to repair itself. It's the queerest idea: one's body simply shoving one aside. These days I'm down to eight or nine hours (not including my nap in the afternoon), so I assume that much of what could be done has now been done. The key is to be thankful for what's come back. But try as I will, it frets me: I had been, for my age, an active man. Taking care that each season's duties be done. Trees and shrubs pruned in the spring, leaves raked and burned in the fall. I would sleep six hours a night, seldom more, and wake up—if not refreshed, at least ready for what might be required. Now, in effect, I'm a child again, put to bed early and hearing the grown-ups through a closed door. Like a child, too, with these sudden storms of weeping. I'm told they could still come under control.

Stroke: a stroke of the lash, for chastisement and correction. Yet something gentle in the word as well.

The next thing I hear is Alice down in the kitchen, so I must have dozed off again. Or, God help me, had a vastation. I can hear the stove making that snapping sound, like a dangerous thing. Then it goes silent again, or nearly so, when it lights. I say nearly so because I seem to hear the ceaseless exhale of gas and the rumble of blue flame burning. Just after my shock, my hearing became strangely acute (unless I was imagining it), as if in compensation for what I can only describe as the cubist way I was seeing things. Yet although my eyesight has returned to normal—thank You, Lord—that acute sense of hearing seems not to have been repossessed. So perhaps something else is being compensated for. I pray it's not some cognitive function that I'm too damaged to understand has been damaged.

Still, sharp as my hearing may be, it's impossible, isn't it, that I could hear a gas stove burning all the way down in the kitchen? Or—terrible thought—is what I'm hearing, or think I'm hearing, the hiss of unignited propane racing out of the ports spreading, expanding, filling the house? Well, and what then? Would I shout for Alice—who, being downstairs, may have been overcome already? Would I struggle up out of bed and try to make my way down the stairs after my new fashion, bad foot scraping along after good foot and cane? Or would I simply lie here and breathe?

Well, hardly a cheerful reflection with which to begin the day.

And good cheer—not mere resignation—is required of us. *To be unhappy is to be in sin:* I'm certain I've read that somewhere or other. Though perhaps it was the other way around. That would certainly be easier to swallow, but so trite that I don't see why it would have made an impression. Now, what was my point? Good cheer. I had wanted to say, it is available to us. Freely offered. We simply need to know where to look. And where not to. Back when Wylie was a little girl and Alice and I would have our troubles (I'd like to believe we never allowed them to darken her childhood), I used to say to myself, *But on the other hand, you have Wylie.* Though there were times when even that didn't mean what it ought to have meant, and at such times I would have to be stern with myself and say, *You must think of Wylie.* All this was before the Lord came into my life.

It's been many years, of course, since Wylie has lived at home. And many years, too, since Alice and I have had words. So things happen as they were meant to, and in the Lord's good time. Though I dread sometimes that I will pass on before I know, with my whole heart, that this is true. When in a more hopeful frame of mind, I think the Lord would never allow it, and that His plan for me includes revelations yet in store.

Certainly Alice hasn't presumed to question (in my hearing) the dispensation that now binds her to a piece of statuary in the likeness of her husband. (Now, that, I'm sorry to say, smacks of self-pity.) *In sickness and in health*, she must remind herself daily. She has never complained about being unable to leave me alone. Or about the friends who have stopped visiting. (We have seen the Petersons *once!*) Her strength shames me, much as I like to think that these past months have made

shame a luxury. (I have even been, God help me, incontinent.)
And from little things I overhear, I gather she's quietly making her plans for afterward. I'm afraid to ask about the details,
and ashamed that I'm afraid. Isn't this something she's owed:
a chance to talk with her husband about what must be on
her mind constantly? What may in fact have been on her mind
for years, since even before my illness (as she calls it) the actu-
arial tables were on her side. Although we've always taken
pride (I know it's blamable) in not being like the generality
of people.

It was my conversion, of course, that made me odd man out
for many of my working years. Research chemists tend to be
a skeptical lot anyway, and our company was particularly
forward-thinking. We were one of the first, you know, to have
moved out to Route 128. Eventually I decided it was best to
steer clear of certain discussions. *As much as lieth in you,* Paul
tells us, *live peaceably with all men.* Poor Alice, meanwhile, has
had to go from being the wife of a hot-tempered drinker to
being the wife of a religious nut, so-called. I remember one day,
shortly after my life had been transformed, I walked in on her
ironing one of Wylie's school skirts with the telephone wedged
between ear and shoulder. "I'll tell you, June," she was saying,
"I don't quite get it, but I'm not about to look a gift horse in
the mouth." Then she noticed me in the doorway and drew a
hissing in-breath as her arms shrank into her ribs and the receiver clunked to the floor.

Up here we've found our neighbors more congenial politi-
cally than the old crowd from work, if not so well informed.
The mail lady has told Alice that no one in town gets so many
magazines. The people we know, other retirees mostly, take
Modern Maturity and the *Reader's Digest.* The younger people, I
imagine, scarcely read a newspaper; Alice was dismayed to
learn that only two families in town get *Time.* But of course she

can make conversation with anybody, right down to the neighbor woman, that Mrs. Paquette, whose talk even in the summertime is mostly about how she can no longer stand New Hampshire winters. She was over again the other morning—or was it earlier this morning?—for coffee and chitchat. Which is what her life amounts to, as far as I can see, though what can my life seem in her eyes? I could hear them all the way downstairs.

"Well, if anything should happen to Lew," Alice was saying, "Florida's the *last* place I'd go. And I would certainly not go out and inflict myself on Wylie and Jeff."

I thought about the word *anything.*

I thought about the word *if.*

"I think I'd try and get myself one of those new little apartments over in Concord," she went on. "Have you been by there?"

I knew the place she meant. Brown brick and brown window glass. I'd had no idea that she'd even noticed it, let alone that it loomed so large.

I wake again when Alice comes in and sets my tray on the dresser. How long have I been asleep this time? I struggle up to a sitting position—now, that's something I couldn't have done a while ago!—then she wedges the triangular pillow behind me and I collapse back on it. She's taken to saying that I'm in the lap of luxury, getting my breakfast in bed. Can she think I don't understand (and don't understand that *she* understands) the truth of what's happened to me? To which good cheer is still the only adequate response—but true cheer, not this lap-of-luxury business. She hands me my eyeglasses, then walks over and tugs down on the string with the lace-covered ring at the end. Up goes the shade, and I sit there blinking like a nasty old owl, the white hairs on my knobby chest curling out between the lapels of my pajamas. How can she stand this, unless she looks with the eyes of love? Or unless she no longer truly looks. She places the tray across my thighs, the living and the dead. Orange juice, Postum, All-Bran and half a grapefruit. And this morning, a gaudy blossom from one of her gloxinias floating in a juice glass.

"Austerity breakfast," I say. Yesterday was a bacon-and-eggs day; I am not allowed two in a row.

"Posterity?" she says.

"Aus-ter-i-ty," I say, furious. I point to the food. "Austere," I say.

"Ah," she says, giving me a too-energetic nod. Can't tell if she's understood or not.

"On in the world," I say, a question.

"The world?" she says. "The news? Oh, they had the most awful thing this morning."

"Hear TV going," I say, meaning I *didn't.*

"The TV?" she says. "Yes, they were talking more about that airplane."

"Jet with a bomb," I say. We'd seen the report last night.

"Well, now they're saying that those people who were sucked out of that hole?" She makes parentheses with her hands to suggest a hole three feet across. "They're saying that they apparently were *not* killed when it went off. They found out they were alive all the way down."

"Out you're alive," I say. Meaning, *Well, that's one way to find out you're alive.* I was making a joke out of her *theys.* Which I suppose was heartless. Though what hurt, really, could it do? Who, for that matter, could even understand me? Alice cocks her head and squints, then just barges on. "And that poor woman was pregnant."

Enough and more than enough of the world-news roundup. I want her out of here now. Smear food all over my face in peace.

"I'm going to let you eat your breakfast before it gets cold," she says, though there's nothing to get cold but the Postum. "Do you need anything else, dear?"

The Mail Lady

I don't bother answering. But when I see her going through the door, away from me, I find that I'm weeping. It's one of the peculiarities: my body's heaving with sobs, the tears are rolling down my cheeks and off my jaw, yet really I feel not a thing. Or so it seems to me. I command the crying to stop: no use. Something undamaged in me is observing all this but can't get out of its own silent space to intervene. Quite a study in something, if you could get it across to anyone.

After the fit passes, I take my time eating. Obviously. (Now, there's a joke at *my* expense!) What I mean is, I'm dawdling to put off the process of dressing myself and getting myself downstairs. Dr. Ngo (you pronounce it like the fellow in James Bond) suggested to Alice that she convert the dining room into a bedroom, but I wouldn't hear of it, and Mrs. Midgely backed me right up. (These therapists call you by your first name, but as soon as I was able to make myself understood I let it be known that it was to be *Mr. Coley* and *Mrs. Midgely*.) "If he can do it once," Mrs. Midgely said, "he can do it every day." Going up and down stairs and dressing yourself are what they're keenest on your learning.

Most days, though, it hardly seems worth the struggle—a way I must fight against thinking. I'll sit in the living room and look at television, or read a magazine or work a crossword puzzle. A great mercy that my vision has straightened out again; at first I saw only parts of things, and letters and words refused to stay in their proper order. A mercy, too, to have been muddled enough in my thinking at the time that this didn't alarm me. Nowadays I'm able to read everything from the *National Review* to our local newspaper. I even read the Neighbors page, about people we don't know being visited by their grown children from out of state, and the notices of church suppers and bingo games we can no longer attend. Not that we ever did. To have ended up in a town where our next-door neighbors live in a trailer (it *is* kept up nicely) with a Virgin Mary sheltering in a half-buried bathtub—it's not what we had expected of life.

Now, stop right there and listen to yourself: when will you awaken to your abundant blessings? Which *continue* to be abundant. This, I have come to believe, is part of what the Lord means to tell me. My stroke is part of our long conversation.

I'm sitting on the bed trying to pull on my socks one-handed when I hear a car slow up. I grip the four-footed cane with my good hand, rock a little to get myself going, shudder up to a standing position and go *thump-scrape, thump-scrape* over to the window. When I finally get there, I see the mail lady pulling away from our mailbox in her high, big-tired pickup truck. Toolbox on it the size of a child's coffin. Sometime during the winter, I'm not clear just when, it was while I was still in the hospital, I remember Alice telling me about the mail lady towing that roughneck Bobby Paquette's car out of the snow on Lily Pond Road. (This is the neighbor woman's nephew.) Alice says her truck's equipped with a winch and I don't know what-all. A male lady indeed. Mrs. Laffond looks like a movie cowboy, sun-scorched and slitty-eyed. And that short hair doesn't help matters. Now, Wylie when she was growing up was something of a tomboy, too, but always looked feminine. An outdoor girl, perhaps it's better to say. Always enjoyed bicycling, played softball on the girls' team. If back then there'd been the agitation you see today over the Little League (and now even on into the high schools), Wylie would've been first in line, I'm sure. But for the sake of being modern, not mannish. Mrs. Laffond, though. It's nothing to see her in garage-man's getup: green gabardine shirt and trousers to match. There was a Mr. Laffond, but he left for parts unknown. (Small wonder, wouldn't you say?) Supposedly he drank. It would be entirely their own business, of course, if children hadn't been involved. Two little girls and a boy, Alice says. The one thing these people seem able to do is breed, if that's not an unchristian observation.

"The mail's here," Alice calls from down in the kitchen, over top of the music. "Are you done your tray?"

She'll find out whether or not I'm *done my tray*, as she puts it, when she comes back upstairs, not sooner. I won't have all this hollering in the house.

When I finally do get myself down to the living room, I find Alice working away with her plant mister.

"Don't *you* look spruce this morning," she says. I have on a pink oxford shirt and my gray wool slacks, neither spruce nor otherwise. "You know," she says, "I was thinking. You've been cooped up in here for days with the rain and all. Why don't we bundle you up warm and walk down together and get the mail? I think the fresh air would do you good."

"Sea a mud," I say. Just look at that driveway. They were supposed to have brought in a load of traprock last fall, but they didn't come and didn't come, which seems to be the way it goes up here. And then the ground froze, and then I had my shock.

"Such a beautiful morning," she says.

It's one of those early-spring days when you begin to smell the earth again. Painfully bright blue sky and the sun giving a false warmth. The branches of the bare trees seem silvery. Once I get down the steps, I stop and work open the buttons of my overcoat to let the air at my body, though what's wrong with me has nothing to do with the body. Halfway down the driveway I stop to rest, take Alice's arm to steady myself, and poke the muddy wheel rut with one of my cane's rubber-tipped spider legs.

"Get in out," I say, meaning *You'll never be able to.* "Moon vehicle need the moon vehicle."

"Moon vehicle?" Alice says. "Why are you saying a moon vehicle, dear?"

"Truck the truck," I say. What I'm trying to get across is the mail lady's pickup truck. I float my good hand up to show the tall tires. No use. Oh, I hate these times when Alice thinks I'm making no sense and I *am* making sense. But this is serious business, this situation with the driveway. To keep out of the mud, Alice has been driving along the edge of the grass, which is tearing up the lawn and now we'll have that on our hands, too, getting someone in to reseed it and roll it. On *her* hands, I suppose I mean.

The mail lady has brought a telephone bill, a letter from Wylie and the new *Smithsonian.* Good: there's this afternoon taken care of. Alice tucks the envelopes inside the *Smithsonian,* and we start back. It's become our custom to save the opening of the mail for when we get back to the house.

"Why, I think that's a robin," Alice says as we start back. "See? In that maple tree? No, over there—that's an oak tree."

Something or other flies off in the direction of the Paquettes'.

"I'm certain that was a robin," she says.

"So be it," I say. The way my mouth works now, I seem to be saying *Soviet.* This walk will have been enough and more than enough. I make her stop to rest three times on the way.

When we've finally gotten my things off—I manage the coat all right, but the overshoes prove too much—we go into the living room so we can sit comfortably over the mail. I open the telephone bill, and she opens Wylie's letter. Our old division of responsibilities: the human side for her. Though now my responsibilities are only ceremonial.

The telephone bill is sixty-eight dollars!

I study it and study it. Most of the calls are to Wylie. One to

Scottsdale, Arizona, which must be Alice's sister Celia. Framingham (her friend June Latham), Taunton (her brother Herb), Taunton again. Oh, I suppose it's correct. I've long given up trying to make sense of all those pages they send. I lay the thing down and look out the window.

"Wylie say?" I ask. It looks like such a long way down there to the mailbox. How had I managed it? The trees are dead motionless, even in their smallest branches, but beyond them, in the pure blue, a small cloud riddled with blue gaps is traveling steadily from left to right. Its shape slowly changes as it moves. On a high branch of our apple tree is perched a bird—a robin, if it pleases Alice to think so—that's lifting its throat and opening its beak. Singing, apparently. A tiny speck drops straight, swift and silent from below its tail. This simple process is not an occasion for shame. At least among those of His creatures who are not accountable.

Alice hasn't answered. I turn away from the window, and she's holding the letter out to me with an expression I don't know what to make of. Glad, but something else, too. It's the expression I caught when she first watched me, cheered on by Mrs. Midgely, lurching up a flight of steps. I take the letter with my good hand. Like all Wylie's letters, it's written in blue felt-tip on lined notebook paper. Since they never taught penmanship at that school of hers—I came close to pulling her out of there because of it—her handwriting, part script, part print, still looks like that of a child. Though by no means as bad as mine looks now. As for her style, so-called, we also have progressive education to thank.

Dear Mom & Dad,
I thought I would tell you this in a letter instead of on the phone because I thought you might like having this letter to keep. Not to keep you in suspense anymore, you are going to be grandparents! I am having a baby sometime the

beginning of December. We found out today and are so thrilled. I sort of wanted you to know right off by phone but thought this best. Please do phone though when you get this, but I decided you would like to have this to keep. Jeffrey sends his love.

Love you alot,
Wylie

Well, my first reaction is, why all this folderol about senti-mental keepsakes when the plain truth of it is, Wylie can no longer bear talking to me on the telephone. And of course such a piece of news might well have set me off, since I'm so—they have a wonderful expression for it—emotionally labile.

I tried to feel something more appropriate. I mean, good heavens, a grandchild.

"Oh, I'm so glad," says Alice. "I thought she didn't *want* children."

"Trend the trend now the trend," I say.

"The trend? I don't like to think of Wylie as part of any trend."

I wave my hand and say, "Shining individual," meaning *Fine, have it your way.* Alice cocks her head: more gabble she won't bother trying to decode. She looks at her wristwatch.

"Almost noon," she says. "So it's about nine o'clock." She picks up the phone.

It's so quiet in our house that I can hear the purr of the tele-phone ringing on the other end. Save this letter! Save it for *when*, for pity's sake? Things like this make you realize that Wylie still thinks of us as we were when she was a child. I recall the time, a couple of years ago, when she was still living in New York, we came down to visit and she walked Alice's legs off shopping. More to the point, look at her decision to move a continent away from us. The pace was slower out there, she said. The air was better. The air was better! I blame Jeffrey, in part. Of course this was before my shock; would she make the same choice today? I don't know. I don't suppose I want to know.

As Alice listens to the phone ring and ring, her smile becomes less and less a smile. Finally it's not a smile at all. She lays the receiver back down. Here we are.

It's a thing I try not to dwell on, but at times—talk to myself as I will, pray as I will for understanding—I can see no spiritual significance whatever in my ruin. And let's for heaven's sake not be mealy-mouthed about it: I am ruined, in this life. No appeal, no going back. Dragging a half-dead body from room to room, numb lips and steak-thick tongue refusing to move as I command. If I am of use at all anymore, it can only be as an example of patient endurance. Or, more likely, of the perils of cholesterol. Since I was neither a smoker nor (in recent years) a drinker, it keeps coming back to that, doesn't it? Apparently I've thrown away my birthright—the everyday miracle of a functioning human body—for the sake of two eggs, every morning for forty years, over easy. For the sake of two strips of bacon, wet with fat, laid parallel beside the eggs, and the whole thing set before me like the four and twenty blackbirds baked in a pie. Initially out of love and ignorance, then later, as the magazine articles began to appear, out of love alone.

"He's saying you can't teach an old dog new tricks," Alice said to Dr. Ngo, translating for me. "He hates the breakfasts."

"Ah," said Dr. Ngo. "Two time a week it not hurt him, you understand?"

I understood. This meant: why not pop off a little sooner with a few familiar comforts, since pop off I must?

"I am of more value than my pleasures," I said, or tried to say. What drunken smear of vowels came out I'm unwilling to remember. What I meant was that I mattered and must persist.

"Say that again, dear?" Alice said.

I shook my head no and swatted the air with my good hand: *Go away, go away.* What I had wanted to say bordered on blasphemy. Had I forgotten that I was to have life everlasting?

But since my purchase on *this* life (though no one will say so) seems none too certain, it has been decided that we must lose no time in wishing Wylie joy in person. Decided, I need hardly add, by Alice and Wylie. These days I'm doing well to get a *What do you think, dear?* And since Wylie is not to travel—in fact, must spend much of her time lying down—we are to come to them. So it's heigh-ho for Seattle. What do you think, dear?

What I think is, I'll do as I'm bid. If I can be wheeled aboard an airplane, I can certainly sit for six hours. What else do I do? These terrorists hold no terrors for me, not because I'm armed in faith particularly—I wish I could say I was—but because no place seems safer than any other anymore. When we left Woburn there was a bad element moving in. In Florida you have your drug lords, and people shooting at you from the overpasses on I-295. Our problem up here is the roughnecks who ride the back roads in loud cars. They listen to the metal music.

Alice keeps asking, *Aren't you looking forward to seeing Wylie?* Her aim is to keep me looking forward. What can I say but yes? Still, much as I love Wylie—and I *do* look forward—I must admit that she can be trying. She's become one of those people who put bumper stickers on their automobiles—at one point, I recall, she had replaced VISUALIZE PEACE with TEACH PEACE, which seemed to me at least a small step away from delusion—and who believe we can communicate with the plants and the dolphins. I blame Bard College. And I imagine Jeffrey encourages it. I used to tell her, *You'd best forget the dolphins and learn to talk to your Savior.* These days I've come to accept that these things sink in if and when He wills them to. Now, some Christians—our minister up here is one—will tell you that the whole what they call New Age is of the devil. We'll know someday: *Every man's work shall be made manifest.* But we can be sure today that it's a distraction and a time-waster, which is spiritual danger enough right there, it seems to me. *The night cometh when no man can work.* Wylie has told Alice that she's already begun talking to the baby inside her. I hope it takes what it's hearing with a good-sized grain of salt! I think Wylie imagines that this visit will have given her child at least this much acquaintance with its grandfather. Covering her bases, don't you see.

I'm ashamed to say I think about it, too. As if I were clutching at a moving train, crying, *At least remember me.* (Keep me mindful that another home is prepared for me and that I shall have a new body, incorruptible.) I can remember my own grandfather. Or at least I remember remembering him. He used to talk about the Civil War; he was twelve, I believe, when it ended. Now, *his* father had become an abolitionist—a Unitarian, he was—and when the news came that President Lincoln was dead, he had all the children dressed up in mourning. And my grandfather had a fistfight with a neighbor boy whose family hated the colored. The Coleys lived in Westerly in those days. And still lived there, in the old house, until my father died in '41, and we still went to the Unitarian church. You know the saying, how the Unitarians believe in one God at most. Supposed to be a joke. But it chills me now to remember that beautiful white church house from which the Holy Spirit was so resoundingly absent. Back then, of course, I liked the hymn-singing, and that was that.

I thought of my grandfather's story about President Lincoln the other night when we saw Aretha Franklin on the television, singing a song about the turnpike of love, I think it was, and lifting her fleshy arms above her head. A woman of her age and size ought not to be seen in a sleeveless dress. It seemed impossible that I could have lived so long as to have known someone who'd been alive when Abraham Lincoln freed the slaves. I don't know how we came to be watching such a thing; Alice and I used to enjoy Mahalia Jackson, but this one is too screechy. Sometimes we'll be watching a program and then find ourselves watching the next program and the program after without meaning to. Up here we still get all three networks, naturally. And PBS, if you can put up with their political slant. But those people on the local news programs! So young and so coarse-looking. And so poorly spoken, as if they had all just come out of two-year colleges. That's unchristian of me, I suppose. My own ruined speech is appropriate chastisement.

Just as my having had no son—I've often thought this—may have been chastisement for my pride in family. (There's only one family: the family of His saints.) Though perhaps it's another, more malignant form of pride to believe myself singled out for chastisement. But for whatever reason, I am the last of the Coleys. There are other people named Coley, of course, but of our Coleys I am the last. We have become a branch of the family tree of people named Gundersen. Alice and I are often asked—or were, back when we socialized—if Wylie is a family name. I'd always say, *Why, how'd you guess?* to make light of the unusualness. The Wylies are my mother's people. (Alice, of course, is a Stannard.) We knew the name might sound awkward with "Coley," so we gave her the middle name Jane as a sort of buffer. When I was a boy, I knew a Mary Carey who called herself Mary Jane—she hadn't been so christened—so we thought Wylie Jane Coley would sound all right. Naturally we couldn't have foreseen that the other children would call her Wylie Coyote and tease her by yelling "Beep beep" and running away from her. (It had to do with some show on the television.) I'm afraid it didn't mollify her when I told her that one of her Wylie forebears had been at the first Constitutional Convention! She called herself Jane from when she was eight or nine until she went away to college; then she apparently decided that "Wylie" would put her one up on the Wendys and Jennifers.

Though she hardly needed such help: even as a little girl she was always the prettiest in a group. Or so her father thought. She was almost plump in grade school. When I first went over to the Paquettes'—and if there's a silver lining to this whole business, it's that I'm always furnished with an excuse not to go over to the Paquettes'—I was reminded of her little belly by that wooden Buddha or whatever it is on top of their television set. (This in a supposedly Christian home! Of course, they're Roman Catholics.) When she was about twelve, though, she began to starve herself and hasn't stopped to this day. Now, I don't mean that she was ever in danger of going the way of that other singer, Karen . . . I've lost the name. (Alice and I watched that poor soul on the television along toward the last, and we could both see she wasn't well.) But even two summers ago, when Wylie came east, I noticed her ribs under her T-shirt when she bent to tie her shoes. (Carpenter, of course. You wouldn't think a Christian could forget *that*.) Alice, in fact, is concerned about the baby on this account. Another reason for our trip, though naturally she's not saying so to Wylie.

The story I always tell about Wylie—always told—is the time we went to Alice's brother's house down in Taunton for Christmas. Herb had married a Roman Catholic girl, and nothing would do but we had to go to their Christmas Eve mass. Well, when we got into the church, they had the biggest crucifix you ever saw hanging over the altar. The Christ wasn't quite life-sized, but it must have been a good three or four feet long, with skin the color of a Band-Aid and a white-painted loincloth. The eyes wide open on it. Believe you me, Wylie's eyes opened pretty wide, too: we, of course, had just the plain gold cross in our church. "Mommy?" she said, loud enough for everybody in the place to hear. "How come he's got diapers on?" To this day, Wylie hates to have that one told on her, though it's a perfectly harmless story.

These days I wear a diaper.

The story I never tell about Wylie is this. One afternoon I surprised her and the little neighbor girl behind the garage, both of them with their pants down. (This was at our house in Woburn.) I can still remember that little girl's name, Myra Meyers. Speaking of names somebody ought to have thought twice about. I sent her about her business, then grabbed Wylie by the arm and marched her right inside and whaled the living daylights out of her. These days, of course, they say you're not accountable: that you are what you are and not what you make up your mind to be. That it's all genetic—drinkers, too, like myself, or the mail lady's husband. That you're helpless to change yourself and certainly can't do anything for anybody else and never mind what God tells us in His word. Well, I believe I changed Wylie that day. Or at least helped her on toward the life she has now, with a husband (though not someone we might have chosen for her) and about to begin a family (however late). And away from—the old-fashioned word is *abominations*, but I'll say abnormalities. (My own theory is, that's what's wrong with the mail lady, children or no children.) I don't imagine Wylie realizes to this day—if she ever thinks of it— that each stroke burned with my love for her. But the day is coming when all that is hidden shall be revealed.

When I think back about the first great intervention in my life (I count my shock as the second), I'm ashamed to remember how long I tried to hold out. I first sought the conventional remedy for a man of my background and education. One takes one's child to see *Fantasia*, one dreams that night of the devil, one's terror does not abate the next morning, nor the next, nor the next. After two weeks of this, one scurries to a psychiatrist. To whom one is induced to complain about one's own childhood. One is talked around into trying to believe that one had such and such feelings about one's father and mother: the so-called family romance. (Oh, yes, I know the jargon.) It is pointed out that the word *abate* is in itself a not insignificant choice. The terror still does not abate.

Then one has a quote unquote chance encounter with a friend who quote unquote just happens to be a Christian.

This was a fellow named John Milliken, whom I'd known when we were both graduate students at Stanford. He actually took his Ph.D.; I'd had to leave and go back to New England when my father died. The little money Alice made at the library was barely enough for the two of us, and now there was Mother to think of. Eventually I was lucky enough to catch on with what was then a scrappy new company (a shoestring operation in those days, right after the war), willing to hire a young chemist without an advanced degree. Well, Milliken, to make a long story short, ended up working for an outfit we did business with and living just over in Arlington. So he and I would get together two or three times over the course of a year. We might have seen more of each other, but I was a new father and he was a bachelor. And Alice never warmed up to him, before *or* after.

One Saturday night, probably a month into my troubles, he and I sat late in the bar of the old Parker House and I opened up to him. Alice by this time had taken the baby and gone to stay with Herb and Evelyn in Taunton; we were not calling it a separation. Desperate as I was, I would hardly have told Milliken about it had I not been drinking. In fact, I was hoping he'd call it a night so I could slip over to Scollay Square, to a certain bar I had discovered and wanted to know more about. (The thought of which terrifies me to this day.) But Milliken kept sitting there, nursing his one Manhattan, nodding, putting in a word or two. More or less, I'm bound to say, in the manner of the doctor I'd been seeing. Though more kindly.

"Well, Lew," he said, when I told him about my dream and the terror that wasn't going away, "has it occurred to you to take this thing seriously?"

"What the Christ do you *think* I'm doing?" I said.

He shook his head. "Why don't I swing by your house tomorrow morning. I've got the hangover cure to end all hangover cures. Are you all right to drive, by the way?"

I was not. The room, in fact, looked tilted and seemed to be going silent. I was not all right to live.

"I think you'd best let me drop you," he said. "We can always pick up your car tomorrow. Unless you're afraid to be by yourself tonight. In which case, I've a fold-out sofa you're welcome to."

Years later, when I read C. S. Lewis—so often a help to me, and I wish I had the strength of mind to read him now—I was struck by what he said about his conversion. I believe I still have it by heart. *When we set out*—he was riding to the zoo in London in the sidecar of somebody's motorcycle—*I did not believe that Jesus Christ was the Son of God, and when we reached the zoo I did.* That's what it was like, riding to John Milliken's house. True, he did begin to pray aloud as we were passing over the Longfellow Bridge, with its stone towers like a castle keep. But around me it was quiet, and the faraway tune his voice was making seemed to blend in with something else that was happening. Out Main Street we flew and onto Massachusetts Avenue, and the people on the sidewalks seemed to pass each other in comradely fashion, like the angels in Jacob's dream—a thing I hadn't thought about since I was a boy in Sunday school—moving up and down the ladder that reached from earth to heaven. They began to be surrounded by a pulsing radiance, and I thought I saw some of them passing right through others. It didn't strike me as out of the ordinary. I looked over at John Milliken: his profile glowed along its edge from hairline to Adam's apple; light frosted his eyebrows. His lips were moving. I looked at his hands, gripping the wheel, his bulging knuckles imperfectly mirroring the wheel's knuckled underside, a patch of hair on the top of each finger. I closed my eyes, and sounds rushed back in: the rubbery, rapid-fire whapping of tire treads on pavement, John Milliken's voice saying *And in Jesus Christ's name we something something something*, a sweet-toned car horn off somewhere. When I opened my eyes again, there we were: just a couple of fellows in a car heading out Massachusetts Avenue.

But the whole point of Jacob's dream, as I now understand it, is that it's a *dream*. The door between this world and the spiritual world has closed, I have come to believe, and will remain so until heaven and earth shall be made new. This is where I part company not just with the Wylies of the world, but with the John Millikens. I soon shied away from the so-called spirit-filled church he brought me to that morning, where grown men and women stood blinking and babbling in no language, and he and I lost touch. He must be an old man now. I ended up with the Baptists—imagine what Great Grandfather Coley would say to that!—and have mostly felt at home there. With the doctrine if not always with the people.

Of course, there are Baptists and there are Baptists. The fellow up here, for instance, turned out to be—not a modernizer, exactly, but more missionary than pastor. Collecting cans of food is all well and good, but need we congratulate ourselves by stacking the cartons right there in the sanctuary? And where, meanwhile, was the spiritual food? Alice and I hardly need sermons against the metal music. I told him straight out, I said I'd sooner sit home and read God's word. His answer to that was that it was a changing world. "Well, there you go," I said. "Isn't that all the more reason?" Like talking to a wall. He's a young man, with the same haircut as the television people and a suit that's too tight on him; he shaves so close his jowls gleam. He was probably glad to see the back of me. He probably said to himself, *Like talking to a wall.*

So that was more or less the end of our churchgoing, except for Easter Sunday, when you still stand a fighting chance of hearing a sermon instead of a public-service message. Easter falls early this year; we'll still be in Seattle. (God willing.) I wonder if Wylie couldn't be talked into going to services with us. How she used to plead, when she was a teenager, to be left at home: what if her friends saw her! I sometimes fought down a mean impulse to tell her it was like going to a bar where sailors met businessmen: anybody who saw you there had a guilty secret, too.

But that secret was mine, to live with as best I could. They'll never convince me I was wrong not to have burdened Alice with details of the danger I'd been in. *Bring it to the Lord in prayer,* the song says. It doesn't say, *Bring it to your wife in guilt.* Very much out of fashion, I know, the idea that certain things are between you and the Lord, period. And yes: that morning, in Everett, Massachusetts, in that shabby wainscoted church— the church smell comes back to me, the smell of varnish, the smell of musty hymnals—I made confession. But before a crowd of strangers, whose care was for a soul that could have been anybody's.

It's Wednesday morning, and we're about ready to be on our way. Alice has locked the cellar door and the toolshed, carried her gloxinias to the bathtub, plugged the reading lamp into the timer, set the thermostats (except in the bathroom) down to fifty. And I've spent the morning trying to compose a letter. It may be the last piece of business I'll do, formally handing down to my daughter what remains, and I chose to do this last thing without Alice's help. It may also be foolishness—our plane will probably not go down, I will probably live on until the cost of my care eats up all our money—but I felt the need.

Dearest Wylie,

Airplanes I think are not so dangers but I am put in this today what you need to know and send by itself. Our lawyer Mr. Plankey who can explain. He is our will and his card you put away when you need it.

A day goes by with you and my prayers. When you look after your own child you remember He died and still looks after.

Loving father,
Lewis Coley

Oh, this is all wrong, preaching away as I've sworn a hundred times not to do. But too late now; let it stand. I seal the envelope—even pulling an envelope across the tongue, and at the same time moving my head in the opposite direction, takes analytic thinking—and put it with the bills to be left in the mailbox.

In our forty years of marriage, Alice has always done our packing, but never before has she handled the bags. I sit at the kitchen table and watch her out the window, struggling, dragging her right leg along in tandem with the avocado green Samsonite suitcase braced against her calf, head bowed to avoid the branches of the little cherry tree. Which I ought to have pruned last year. I must have assumed there would be time.

And, again, I find that I'm weeping. It's the sight of her walking away from me. I hear the car trunk slam; I must stop this before she comes back in to get me, though I don't know *how* to stop. A lovely beginning for our trip.

She pulls the car up onto the grass by the back door, but lets me do the steps by myself. There are more steps here than at the front door, but these are easier; a couple of years ago, I had a fellow come around and put up a railing. Nothing fancy, just pressure-treated two-by-fours. Back when breaking a hip in icy weather was my worst imagining. Gripping the rail with my good hand and hanging the cane from the crook of my arm like some antique gentleman, I make it down the steps all right. But by the time I've gotten myself into the car and the door closed, I'm done in. Enough and more than enough. And now there's the ride all the way down to Logan yet to do, and after that whatever's involved in getting a crippled man through a busy terminal, and after that the hours in the air and after that the journey's unimaginable other end.

We start down the driveway, Alice keeping one wheel up on the strip of grass between the muddy wheel ruts and the other wheel on the lawn.

"Forget the mailbox," I say, meaning *Don't*. I'm making a joke on myself, the joke being that I'm an old fussbudget.

Alice just fetches a sigh. So I sigh too and look out the window, tapping the fingers of my good hand on my good knee, for all the world like a stroke patient. Though deep down I can't believe it, I remind myself that this may be the last time I'll see this lawn, such as it is, with its untrimmed shrubs and the rocks I used to hit with the lawnmower. I try to give it the looking-at it deserves. And fall short, as always. This was what we had worked toward, and we came here too late to love it.

"Why don't I pull over close to the mailbox," Alice says, "and you just put down your window and pop the things in."

"Get stuck," I say.

"Good heavens," she says, "Mrs. Laffond goes in and out of here every day."

The Mail Lady

She gets the car over so that my mirror almost scrapes the mailbox, and I feel my whole side of the car go down. Oh, brother. I roll down my window as if nothing were wrong (trying to work magic, in spite of all I know and believe), pull open the mailbox, stick the envelopes in, push the thing shut and flip up the flag. As I roll the window back up, I look over at Alice, who looks at her watch and then at the dashboard clock. Her mouth is twitching. She steps on the gas: the wheels just whine and spin. She cuts the steering hard to the left, guns the motor and we sink deeper.

"No no no no," I say. Doesn't the woman know you want to keep your wheels straight?

She jams it into reverse, guns it again, and the back tires just spin deeper.

"Cut your wheels!" I cry, meaning *Don't*. So of course she does, except she can't because we're in so deep. "Rock have to rock." Damn it, she has to rock the damn car, if it'll even rock.

"I don't know what you're saying," she says.

"You car rocking!" I holler. She slams it back into drive, the wheels spin and she glares over at me.

I say, "Damn fuck."

"Well, why don't *you* try it then," she says. Then she says, "I'm sorry, Lew, I didn't mean that." But the harm is done: I'm bawling like a big angry baby.

"Lew," she says, "I'm so sorry. It's truly my fault." I entertain the thought that I'm weeping to punish her. Which may be so, but I can't stop it now.

"Lew," she says. "Now, listen to me a minute. Try and listen. Will you be all right to sit here while I go back up to the house?"

"Do what?" I say.

"I can't understand you, dear."

I try harder. "You what to you do?"

"I guess I'm going to try to raise somebody on the phone," she says. "Maybe one of the boys from the Shell station would come up."

I've got the blubbering stopped now. "Plane make the plane," I say, meaning *We'll never.*

"Well, Lew, I don't know what else to do," she says. "I'll leave the motor running so you can have the heater."

I don't turn to watch her walking up the driveway for fear it'll set me off again. I put the radio on, just in time to catch the end of some bouncy tune from way, way back. Can it have been "The Dipsy Doodle"? But then the announcer comes on to say the time is 10:08, and I turn it off. The last thing I need is to be hearing the time every two minutes. The dashboard clock says 10:07. I take a glove out of my pocket and drape it over the dashboard so that it blocks my view of the clock. I stare out the windshield at the road we should be on and listen to the motor humming away. We've been very satisfied with the Lumina.

An idling engine consumes a gallon of gasoline an hour. Or used to years ago. (It said so in the owner's manual of some car we had, and it always stuck in my mind for some reason.) An hour. It would be a good hour before anybody got here, if they ran true to form. Oh, brother. Well, there's not a thing you can do about it. I go back to the hum of the motor.

But wait now. Sunk in mud, motor running: couldn't this clog the tailpipe, making carbon monoxide seep inside? Isn't this what they do, trapped and Godless men going out to the garage with the hose from the vacuum? In fact, it's beginning to seem to me that I'm starting to feel sleepy, that something's woozy with my thoughts. You better reach over, turn the ignition key.

I let it run.

Before shutting my eyes I decide I'll take a last look around at things. And when I turn my head I see somebody pulling up

The Mail Lady

in front of the Paquettes'. I see them sit there a second, then pull out again, coming right at me. If it's a car full of roughnecks I'm helpless out here. I spot Alice, but she's far away, she's on the doorstep, opening the door. They're still coming. I stretch over with my good hand and blow the horn. But she's already in the house. They're halfway here, coming fast now. And now I see it's something too high up off the ground to be a car. Oh, I'd rather the roughnecks than what's going to happen now. It's the mail lady in her moon vehicle. And we are saved.

A NOTE ON THE TYPE

This book was set in Bodoni Classic Roman, a typeface named after Giambattista Bodoni (1740–1813), the celebrated printer and type designer of Parma. The Bodoni types of today were designed not as faithful reproductions of any one of the Bodoni fonts but rather as a composite, modern version of the Bodoni manner. Bodoni's innovations in type style included a greater degree of contrast in the thick and thin elements of the letters and a sharper and more angular finish of details.

Composed by Stratford Publishing Services, Brattleboro, Vermont

Printed and bound by R.R. Donnelley & Sons, Harrisonburg, Virginia

Designed by Robert C. Olsson